SPONTANEOUS
HUMAN
COMBUSTION

SPONTANEOUS HUMAN COMBUSTION

JENNY RANDLES

& PETER HOUGH

BARNES & NOBLE BOOKS

NEW YORK

1993 Barnes & Noble Books

ISBN 1-5661-9173-4

Printed and bound in the United States of America

04 05 06 07 08 09 M 9 8 7 6 5 4 3

Contents

REFERENCES

List of Illustrations

Picture Credits

Tony McMunn: 1, 6, 7, 8. *Halifax Evening Courier:* 2, 3
Birmingham Fire Brigade: 4. St Petersburg Police
Department: 5. *That's Incredible*, CBS Television: 9.
Jenny Randles: 10, 11. Peter Hough, 12, 13.

List of Figures

Prologue

Maeve was as quiet as possible when preparing the coffee and setting out two mugs – banging crockery around was too obvious a way of expressing resentment – and while the water was coming to the boil she stood at the window and breathed deeply, forcing herself to relax. The news from Doctor Pitman about her father's X-ray tests had been unexpectedly good, suggesting that his abdominal pains resulted from nothing more than some vague colic. His medication was bound to conquer the problem in a day or two, then she would be able to get back to her job and resume a normal life.

While she was waiting for the coffee to finish percolating she became aware of a sweetly heavy smell of burning drifting into the kitchen. She guessed that her father was, as occasionally happened, experimenting with an exotic new brand of tobacco. She poured the coffee, set the two mugs on a tray and carried it towards the front room. The sweetish odour grew overpowering as she moved along the hall and now she could actually see a light-blue haze in the air – a first intimation that something out of the ordinary might be taking place.

'Dad?' Maeve opened the door to the sitting-room and gasped with shock as she saw that it was filled with blue smoke. Dropping the tray, she ran into the room, fully expecting to see an armchair on fire. She had heard how quickly some modern furniture could burn and also knew how vital it was to get people clear of the fumes without delay.

There was no sign of a blaze, nor could she see her father anywhere.

It was difficult to make out anything through the billowings of the curious light-blue smoke, but it seemed to Maeve that there was a blackened area of flooring near the television set. She went towards it, gagging on the sickening sweet stench in the air, and her hands fluttered nervously to her mouth as she saw that what she had taken to be a black patch was actually a large hole burned clear through the vinyl and underlying boards. Several floor joists were exposed, their upper surfaces charred into curvatures, but – strangely – there was no active flame. In the floor cavity, supported by the ceiling of the utilities room below, was a mound of fine grey ash.

'Dad?' Maeve looked about her uncertainly, fearfully, and her voice was barely audible. 'Dad, what have you been ...?'

At that instant her slippered foot touched a slightly yielding object on the floor. She glanced downwards – still an innocent, with thresholds of terror still to cross – and when she saw what was lying there she began to scream.

The object, easily recognizable by its signet-ring, was her father's left hand.

Introduction

When we decided to research a book on the controversial topic of spontaneous human combustion, neither of us realized the extraordinary problems we were getting ourselves into. As investigators of unexplained occurrences, we had been intrigued by the possibility of SHC for a number of years. When a teenage girl tragically burst into flames before her horrified friends in 1985, some media sources quickly dubbed it 'spontaneous human combustion'. This gave us the opportunity to do some first-hand research and ask questions that had not been asked before.

A 17-year-old girl whom we shall just call Jacqueline had taken part in a cookery exam, but had waited for several minutes by the classroom door before leaving. About three minutes later, on the stairs between floors, her back erupted into flame. She died fifteen days later in hospital. At the inquest, the Home Office chemist thought she must have been leaning against a lighted cooker which had started her catering jacket smouldering, later to burst into flame because of the draughts in the corridor. However, not one witness saw smouldering, or smelt anything. There was nothing up until the moment that the tragedy occurred.

Under cross-examination, his theory proved to be no more than speculative. In fact we felt that the entire official investigation left a lot to be desired. A joint report by the fire brigade and Shirley Institute, which conflicted with the Home Office conclusions, without endorsing SHC, was denied as evidence at the inquest.

The results of our investigation were not published for some time out of consideration for the teenager's family. We refused to participate in a media circus which toyed with real people's lives. Yet eventually we had no choice but to recount what we had uncovered.

A much-cited article in the journal *Fortean Times* and a chapter in our book, *Death by Supernatural Causes?* was the result. The book was the culmination of our research into several mysterious deaths and injuries attributed to a variety of paranormal phenomena, only one section of which referred to SHC. However,

11

the incredible idea that people really were, quite literally, combusting for no apparent reason was so mystifying and little-explored that it cried out for deeper study.

Indeed such a detailed look at the phenomenon of SHC was something *we* had badly needed as we struggled to unravel the mystery of the 17-year-old's death. We could not find one, so in the end became driven to write it ourselves.

Although circumstances dictated that we could not start work in earnest on the project until two and a half years later, we began scratching the surface almost immediately. We were astounded to discover that apart from Michael Harrison's somewhat contentious book, *Fire From Heaven*, first published in 1976, there were no other books devoted entirely to the subject. We came across a number of general books on the paranormal which featured a chapter on SHC, and read many newspaper and magazine articles, but all these did were recycle the same dozen or so cases, most of which were many years old. They did this time and again without any fresh perspective or insight. It was obvious we were going to have to work hard and dig deep.

In writing *Spontaneous Human Combustion*, we decided to adopt the position of objectivity we have endeavoured to attain for our previous works. We realized that the subject would gain nothing from a sensational or trivialized book slanted towards the position of the 'believer'. Neither would it benefit from the equally myopic position of the 'sceptic' or his even more short-sighted cousin the 'debunker'. We decided to gather the facts – and if they were found wanting, to say so. Mixed in with this would be the results of our own investigations into various cases, and interviews with the people that count: witnesses, fire-officers, cremation experts, police officers, biologists, forensic scientists and physicists.

We wanted to leave no stone unturned in our search for answers, from those who said that the phenomenon could be entirely explained away in mundane terms, through to particle physics and the Kundalini experience associated with yoga.

To encourage all these people to come forward, we sent letters to various specialist magazines requesting information and informed opinion on the matter. They were published in popular magazines and scientific journals, eliciting case material and professional comment from many countries, including Britain, America and Australia. We were to discover that there was a veritable ground swell of information and opinion existing in pockets, but little of it was banded together in any cohesive form.

We had our book! Actually that sounds like the Monty Python recipe for rat pie: *Get a rat and put it in a pie.* Of course what lay ahead was months of hard effort, travelling to interview people as far afield as Australia, endless letters and telephone calls, weeks spent following up dead-ends, migraine-inducing days poring over microfilm records, battling unexpected fears and secrecy, organizing the material, then finally writing it all up ...

Composing a book which deals with bizarre deaths is like walking a tight-rope. There is a genuine scientific mystery here which deserves a thorough airing, but human nature being what it is, there is a certain degree of entertainment associated with an exploration of 'the unknown'. We appreciate this, but believe that the entertainment factor is associated with the *mystery* and not with the death itself. We realize that in some of the recent cases described, relatives will not want the strange details of their loved one's demise raked up for public consumption.

We do not know what to do about that, but it is a problem we have fully taken into consideration and not simply ignored. What we have done is adopt pseudonyms for victims where their identities have not previously been made public, and also in some other cases where we feel they have received minimal exposure. We have marked these with an asterisk, thus *; although we have the real names on file. We have also tried to reassure some relatives of our sincere purposes. If, by laying bare the facts of how someone met their death it can help forge a better understanding for the future, then not only is it justified to do so, but it may even give that death some meaning.

To this end we spoke briefly with Jacqueline's mother. She was resigned to the speculation about her daughter's death, but thought there was a normal rational explanation.

'It was a freak accident,' she said, sadly. 'The fact Jacqueline had just left a cookery lesson was too much of a coincidence.'

We wanted to illustrate in a dramatic way the classic components of alleged spontaneous human combustion, to demonstrate vividly to the casual reader the extent of the mystery. Yet we realized it would be in bad taste to dramatize an actual case. What we have done then, with kind permission of the author and his publisher, is reproduce part of the prologue from Bob Shaw's excellent novel, *Fire Pattern*. This will be found at the front of this book.

There remains little else to say, except read on, weigh up all the facts (or, you may conclude, the lack of facts), listen to the expert witnesses, assess the various theories, then make up your own mind on this burning question ...

PART ONE
The Evidence

1   A History of Incineration

The perceived phenomenon of spontaneous human combustion is not a modern mystery. Accounts stretch back many centuries, so it is safe to assume that inexplicable incinerations have always occurred. It is not the purpose of this chapter to list every known instance. The repetition might become tedious, and besides, certain cases will be used later to illustrate relevant points. However, it is necessary to recount a historical sample of the phenomenon to give the reader a fair idea of its spread, and its effect on literature and society in general.

Incidents are recorded as far back as 1613 and may well be found in even earlier form if systematic studies were conducted, but the first case reported in depth occurred in Italy. In *Philosophical Transactions*, 1745, appears an article headed: 'An Extract, by Mr Paul Rolli, F.R.S. of an Italien Treatise, written by the Rev. Joseph Bianchini, a Prebend in the City of Verona; on the Death of the Countess Cornelia Zangári and Bandi, of Ceséna'.

It recounts how the Countess Cornelia Bandi seemed in normal good health until suppertime on the evening of her death. At the meal she felt 'dull and heavy' and she retired immediately afterwards. Once in bed she talked with her maid for three hours or more, finally falling asleep, the maid closing the bedroom door behind her.

The following morning, when the 62-year-old countess did not rise at her usual hour, the maid entered the bedchamber and called her name. Not receiving a reply, and fearing that illness or an accident had affected her mistress, the maid opened a window and observed the following:

> Four feet distance from the bed there was a heap of ashes, two legs untouched, from the foot to the knee, with their stockings on: between them was the lady's head: whose brains, half of the back part of the skull, and the whole chin, were burn't to ashes; among which was found three fingers blackened. All the rest was ashes, which had this perular quality, that they left in the hand, when taken up, a greasy and stinking moisture.

The air in the room was also observed cumbered with soot floating in it: a small oil lamp on the floor was covered with ashes, but no oil in it. Two candles in candlesticks on the table stood upright; the cotton was left in both, but the tallow was gone and vanished. Somewhat of moisture was about the feet of the candlesticks. The bed received no damage; the blankets and sheets were only raised on one side, as when a person rises up from it, or goes in; the whole furniture, as well as the bed, was spread over with moist and ash coloured soot, which had penetrated into the chest of drawers, even to foul the linens; nay the soot was also gone into a neighbouring kitchen, and hung on the walls, moveables, and utensils of it. From the pantry a piece of bread covered with that soot, and brown black, was given to several dogs, which refused to eat it. In the room above it was noticed, that the lower part of the windows trickled down a greasy, loathesome, yellowish liquor; and thereabout they smelt a stink, without knowing of what, and saw the soot fly around.

It was remarkable, that the floor of the chamber was so thickly smeared with a gluish moisture, that it could not be taken off; and the stench spread more and more through the other chambers.

The case was also attested to by one Scipio Maffei, 'a learned contemporary of Bianchini'. This case, more than most, resembles many of the later cases where incineration has taken place indoors. Of particular note is a fire that has the capacity to destroy a human being, yet leaves combustible materials nearby relatively untouched. This latter component has also been noted in draftier locations, and indeed also – but less often – out in the open air.

A Dr Booth reported the following incident in the *British Medical Journal* of 1888:

On the morning of Sunday, February 19, I was sent for to examine the remains of a man, 65, a pensioner of notoriously intemperate habits. I found the charred remains of the man reclining against the stone wall of the hay loft. The main effects of combustion were limited to the corpse, and only a small piece of the adjacent flooring and the woodwork immediately above the man's head had suffered. The body was almost a cinder, yet retained the form of the face and figure so well that those who had known him in life could readily recognize him.

Both hands and the right foot had been burnt off, and had fallen through the floor into the stable below, among the ashes; and the charred and calcined ends of the right radius and ulna, the left humerus, and the right tibia and fibula, were exposed to view. The hair and scalp were burnt off the forehead, exposing the bare and calcined skull. The tissues of the face were represented by a greasy cinder, retaining the cast of the features, and the incinerated moustache still gave the wonted military expression to the old soldier. The soft tissues were almost entirely consumed.

On my return from other work, later on, I found that the whole had been removed. The bearers told me that the whole body had collapsed when they had tried to move it *en masse*. From the comfortable recumbent attitude of the body, it was evident that there had been no death struggle, and that, stupified with the whisky within and the smoke without, the man had expired without suffering, the body burning away quietly all the time.

Apparently, highly inflammable hay, both loose and bundled, was not even scorched.

As illustrative of an outdoor instance of suspicious incineration, here is an account by a Dr B.H. Hartwell, of Ayer, Massachusetts, originally published in the *Boston Medical and Surgical Journal*. On 12 May 1890, while making a professional call on the outskirts of the town, Dr Hartwell was summoned into a nearby wood by a girl stating that her mother was 'burned alive'.

Hastily driving to the place indicated a human body was found in the actual state of conflagration. The body was face downwards; the face, arms, upper part of the chest, and left knee only touching the ground; the rest of the body was raised and held from the ground by the rigidity of the muscles of the parts. It was burning at the shoulder, both sides of the abdomen, and both legs. The flames reached from twelve to fifteen inches above the level of the body. The clothing was nearly all consumed.

As I reached the spot the bones of the right leg broke with an audible snap, allowing the foot to hang by the tendons and muscles of one side, those of the other side having burned completely off. Sending my driver for water and assistance, I could only watch the curious and abhorrent spectacle, till a common spading fork was found with which the fire was put out by throwing earth upon it, the flesh was burned from the right shoulder, exposing the joint from the abdomen, allowing the intestines to protrude, and more or less from both legs. The leg bones were partially calcined. The clothing unburned consisted of parts of a calico dress, cotton vest, woollen skirt, and thick, red, woollen undergarment.

The subject of the accident was a woman, forty-nine years of age, about five feet five inches in height, and weighing not far from one hundred and forty pounds of active habits and nervous temperament. A wife and mother she was a strictly temperate person, accustomed through life to hard work, one who, in addition to her household duties, went washing and cleaning, besides doing a good share of the work in a large garden.

On the fatal afternoon she had – as the place showed – been clearing a lot of stumps and roots, and had set fire to a pile of roots, from which it had communicated to her clothing or it had spread into the woodland and had set fire to the clothing during her endeavors to stop it. The body lay about two rods from the burning pile. As proof that the flesh burned of itself and nothing but the clothing set it afire, it may be stated that the accident occurred after a rain; that the fire merely skimmed over the surface of the ground, not burning through the leaves; that there was nothing but charred leaves under the body; that her straw hat which lay several feet distant was simply scorched; that the wooden handle of the spade was only blackened.

The above case is interesting in several particulars. It is the first recorded case in which a human body has been found burning (that is, supporting combustion) by the medical attendant. It differs from nearly all of the recorded cases, in that it occurred in a person in middle life, not very fat, and not addicted to the use of alcohol. It is interesting in a medico-legal sense. It proves that under certain conditions – conditions that exist in the body itself – the human body will burn. We have abundant proof in the many recorded cases of so-called spontaneous combustion (seventy-three are chronicled in medical literature) that the body has been more or less completely destroyed by fire under circumstances that show that it will support combustion, and that this has given rise to the belief in the spontaneous origin of the fire.

Dr Hartwell makes some interesting observations towards the end of his paper, particularly his remarks concerning alcohol. As we shall see, that substance was central to a Victorian explanation for inexplicable human combustion. Note also, that although a source of ignition was close by, the flames seemed to have 'skimmed' over an area of damp leaves, and other combustible materials – a straw hat and spade – were hardly touched. Recently, fire experts have formulated an explanation of how this can happen *indoors*, but their theory could not possibly apply in these cases.

A typical supposed alcohol-centred conflagration is the classic case of Grace Pett. What is interesting in relating the story here, is the additional information which surfaced just a few years ago through the diligent researches of Peter Christie. It seems there were certain aspects of the case that subsequent reporters chose to suppress! The story as commonly told is this:

Grace Pett was the pipe-smoking wife of an Ipswich fisherman, who met her death on the night of 9 April 1744, aged sixty. An idiosyncrasy of the lady was to come downstairs during the night and sit by the fire smoking her pipe. On that particular night, her daughter, who slept in the same bed with her, did not perceive her rise, and was not aware she had gone until the following morning.

After dressing, the daughter went downstairs and found the remains of her mother in the kitchen.

The woman was stretched out on her right side, head nearest the grate, body extended across the hearth, legs beyond on the wooden floor. Apparently the remains had the appearance of a wooden log, baked rather than ravaged with flame, and still glowing. The trunk was incinerated, resembling a heap of coals covered in white ash, and the head and limbs were burned too.

There was no fire in the grate, and a candle, close by, had burned down entirely in its candlestick. Although fat from the body had so penetrated the hearth that 'it could not be scoured out', the floor was not even discoloured. Near to the consumed body were some children's clothes and a paper screen. These had suffered no injury. It is interesting, considering that smoke inhalation is the prime cause of death in fires, that the daughter had not been aware of a conflagration until she actually had sight of her mother. There are indications too that there were other people staying in the house that night, none of whom had been aware of a fire.

The body was still incinerating. When the daughter threw water over the remains, a fetid odour filled the air, which almost suffocated her and several neighbours, who by this time had arrived to assist the girl. Once again, in later reports, much was made over the 'fact' that Mrs Pett had consumed 'a large quantity of spirituous liquor' that night to celebrate the return of another daughter from Gibraltar.

Peter Christie, reading an account of the case in Michael Harrison's book *Fire From Heaven*, thought he would track down its source. One of Harrison's sources was Sir David Brewster's *Letters on Natural Magic addressed to Sir Walter Scott*, dated 1832. Peter, having an 1842 fifth edition copy of this book, found that the details agreed with contemporary accounts of the affair. However, he was determined to track back as far as he could and discover where Brewster had found the report to begin with.

In a branch of the Suffolk Record Office, he looked through back copies of the *Ipswich Journal* for the relevant date, and found the following item: 'On Tuesday Morning (April 10) a Woman in St Clement's Parish was found burnt to Death in her own House. This unhappy Affair was attended with several extraordinary circumstances, but they are so variously related, that we cannot at present give our Readers any particular Account of them.'

Strangely, Peter Christie could find no follow-up story in subsequent editions of the newspaper. He did however check parish records and found that the Pett family was labelled as 'Poor'. Then, through a nineteenth-century local history book, he learned of a short-lived publication called the *Ipswich Magazine*. It contained two references to the case. The first of these was a letter to the editor by one 'J.S.', with additional comments by someone signing themselves 'B'. After giving the story as recounted by Brewster, J.S. then continued with a narrative every bit as strange.

According to J.S., Grace Pett had a reputation of being a witch, 'among some of her ignorant neighbours'. A local farmer called Garnham was convinced some of his sheep, taken ill, were bewitched. He was advised by a 'white magician' called Mr Winter to burn one of them, presumably to break the spell. The farmer thought the whole idea was a nonsense, but his wife decided to try the experiment.

Mrs Garnham made one of her employees bring a diseased sheep into the backhouse. There its four legs were bound and it was laid in the hearth. Still alive, it was set on fire. J.S. then recounts how the bandages tying the poor beast's legs burned through in the flames, at which the animal tried to escape but was forced with a pitchfork in its side to remain in the fire until dead.

According to these accounts, the sheep was burned on the same night that Mrs Pett, allegedly responsible for its illness, met her fiery death.

Subsequent commentators ignored this aspect of the case, no doubt of the belief that spontaneous combustion was enough to swallow at one sitting, without adding witchcraft and sympathetic magic! But does this detract from the SHC aspect of the case, or simply add to its bewilderment? Superstitious nonsense, or does it demonstrate, as some believe, a supernatural component to spontaneous fires?

In its day, the witchcraft dimension was well established. Peter was able to procure a book published around 1875, entitled *Grace Pett. A tale of witchcraft* by Elizabeth Cotton. The narrative included a series of verses recounting the tale from beginning to end. According to these, after Grace Pett died 'on the Unscorched ground', the disease afflicting Garnham's sheep abruptly ceased.

Peter Christie dug deeper, and discovered more letters, published even earlier. One of the letter writers, a Mr Gibbons, had actually interviewed Grace Pett's daughter, and two other people who had been in the house at the time of the incident, one of whom was named as 'Boyden'. Peter was pleased to receive a copy, from the Royal Society of Great Britain, of a letter by a Mr R. Love – apparently the earliest documentation on the case, dated 28 June 1744. Details of this letter are given in the aforementioned *Philosophical Transactions* which we had the good fortune to track down.

Mr Love attended the inquest and learnt that the women retired at about 10 p.m. and the body was found at 6 a.m. The letter stated there was no fire in the grate, and, contrary to some subsequent reports, Mrs Pett 'was not in liquor nor addicted to drink Gin'. It confirmed that the extremities and parts of the head were not burned, neither was the wooden floor even scorched. The bones were calcined so completely that the remains were easily shovelled into a coffin.

Despite all of these anomalies, the jury brought about a verdict of accidental death.

A study of eighteenth- and nineteenth-century documents illustrates that rare abnormal fire deaths and injuries were as prevalent then as they are now. The phenomenon also attracted the serious attention of individuals in the medical sciences. Not believing in the supernatural, they sought a logical explanation, and looked for a common denominator. The common denominator seemed to be *drink*.

This was an explanation that was acceptable at the time. The Victorian era was one when drink was considered an evil in many Christian homes and the temperance movement was growing in strength. The portrayal of burning victims as suffering divine retribution because of their consumption to excess was a powerful weapon when established within rumour-soaked society. The warning to drunkards was clear. You could pay with your life!

It was soon 'demonstrated' that all victims of mysterious incineration were 'drunkards', including those who were not! Grace Pett is a good example of a victim reported at the inquest as not addicted to alcohol, and who was not drinking on the night of her death, but who in later legend was conveniently said to have consumed 'a large quantity of spirituous liquor'.

Most people have a drink occasionally. One of us (we are not saying which) ferments large quantities of wine and beer for the consumption of family and friends. He (or she) upon spontaneously bursting into flames, would be a prime target for the alcohol-related theories of the nineteenth-century medical experts!

In an undated reference, issue 184 of the Victorian journal *Notes and Queries*, appears a table of nineteen cases compiled by a Dr Lindsley from, we are told, the *Dictionnaire de Médecine*. They range from 1692 to 1829. Under the heading 'Habit of Life', it is stated variously about the fire victims; 'abuse of spirits for three years' ... 'indulged in frequent fomentations of camphorated spirits' ... 'took a pint of rum daily' ... 'habitually drunken' ... 'she drank brandy as her only drink' ... 'a drunkard' ... 'drank brandy only for many years' ... 'abuse of wine and Eau de Cologne' ...

The reasoning was that alcohol, being highly flammable, could through long abuse be absorbed through the body to the outer layers of skin, rendering a person highly combustible. An accidental brush with a candle flame, or a hot coal spitting out of a fire contacting the body, was all that was needed to turn a person into a blazing inferno. What was considered incombustible because of its sixty per cent water content was rendered combustible by its retention of alcohol fuel. Scientists had to accept that people were being mysteriously burned – the evidence was plain, yet they had to find a logical explanation. These incinerations, that often left surroundings untouched, were contrary to what was normally required to incinerate a body.

The Mirror of Literature, Art and Amusement, pointed out in 1838 that the Romans were well practised in reducing the dead to ashes, so are modern Hindus. Indeed, so much fuel was required that cremation was too expensive an affair for the poor in Roman times. What was – what *is* – required are about 'two cart loads', according to 'the most eminent British medical jurist', Dr Christison, quoted in the article. Two cartloads of faggots and several hours were required to bring about the total combustion of the last man in Europe to be burnt at the stake.

In the article, the author made the following observation surrounding the difficulties of incinerating a body in the average home – a difficulty that contemporary sceptics claim does not exist.

> The murderer of Mrs King occupied several days in burning the body, in a common chamber-grate; and though the murderer, Cook, five or six years ago, got rid of a great part of his victim's body in two days, by cutting it in small pieces before putting it on ʼhe fire, much seems to have been buried, without having been on the fire at all. Indeed, the bones cannot be calcined without the heat of a furnace.

Faced with these difficulties, is it surprising that when medical men sought to make sense of the phenomenon, even though they were loathe to embrace the 'supernatural' concept of SHC, they were forced to look for a milder, yet equally revolutionary concept. What was discussed amongst medical men was 'preternatural combustion' – a hypothesized condition where the human body can attain an unusual condition of high combustability and may burn if subject to an external heat source. The consumption of vast amounts of alcohol seemed for many to provide the answer to this proneness to combustion.

The main difference between SHC and PC is that the former originates *inside* the body and requires no independent source of ignition. The aforementioned Dr Christison looked upon preternatural combustion 'as a well ascertained fact' but was less certain about SHC because 'generally speaking, some ignited body (such as a candle or pipe) has been discovered near the remains of a body'. This point of view was also shared by American writer Dr Beck 'whose work on Legal Medicine' [said Dr Christison] is still the text book most resorted to, even by English students'.

In 1806, a pamphlet was produced in Paris by Pierre Lair, entitled *Essay on the Combustion of Humans; products of the Abuse of Spirituous Liquors*. At around that time, a Dr Swediour announced that cases of spontaneous combustion were not as rare as had been previously thought. He said that during his travels 'persons experience the effects of this combustion'. It was recommended that the abundant drinking of milk would prevent combustion!

Victims did not have to be drunkards for alcohol to be blamed for their grisly deaths. When it was discovered that the Countess Bandi of Ceséna had a habit of massaging into her body the camphorated spirits of wine, that was good enough. But was it right; did the alcohol of an habitual drinker render that person more combustible than his teetotal neighbour? Not all medical men in the nineteenth century thought so.

Baron J. von Liebig, famous for isolating titanium, discovering chloral and his work on meat extracts, made an analysis of fifty recorded cases of preternatural combustion in 1851. He concluded that flesh which has been saturated in alcohol, as in the case of anatomical preparations, is *not* combustible. When ignited, the alcohol merely burns off, scarcely charring the flesh. The *corpses* of 'drunkards', he pointed out, have never been found to be combustible, so why should the living? Further tests, which included injecting alcohol into the bodies of rats over a period of time, then setting them alight, showed that alcohol could not be retained in the fabric of the body, rendering it highly combustible.

However, the alcohol/SHC-related debate suited the arguments of Bible-bashing evangelists perfectly. This was a time when drunkenness was endemic, so despite the evidence, Christian moralists continued to profess that the demon alcohol was literally a one-way ticket to the fires of hell.

But it was the high visibility given to the phenomenon by novelists which attracted the attention of the public, especially that accorded it by Charles Dickens.

However, the earliest literary account was given in a novel entitled *Wieland*, by the American gothic novelist Charles Brockden Brown, published in 1796. A German pietist, 'Wieland' of the title, is practising his religious rites in a shack which serves as his chapel, when the fire strikes. While the man is found partially incinerated, true to form, the chapel is unharmed. It is reasonable to assume that Brown based his fiction on the real life case of Don Gio Maria Bertholi, an Italian priest, who, like Wieland, survived for several days. The incident was reported by a Dr Battaglia, the surgeon who attended the injured man, in a journal dated October 1776.

The priest was staying at his brother-in-law's and was shown up to his room where he requested the use of a handkerchief, to be placed between his shoulder and shirt. Devout priests wore shirts made of horsehair for penance, and the handkerchief would be used to relieve discomfort during devotions.

A few minutes after he had been left alone, the agonized screams of the priest could be heard throughout the house. The other occupants entered the room and found Bertholi prostrate, surrounded by a light flame which receded as they entered and finally vanished. It was the following morning before Dr Battaglia examined the patient.

He found the skin of the right arm almost entirely detached and hanging from the bone, and from the shoulders to thighs, the skin equally injured. The right hand was the most severely burned part, and here, putrification had already begun.

The wretched man complained of a burning thirst and convulsed horribly. This was accompanied by fever and delirium, his excrement contained 'putrid and bilious matter', and he was exhausted from continuous vomiting.

Bertholi had told the doctor that all he remembered was a blow like a cudgel to his right hand, then a lambent flame which attached itself to his shirt, immediately reducing it to ashes, while leaving the cuffs untouched. His trousers and the hankerchief he had borrowed minutes before were also untouched, and while his hair was not even singed, his cap was totally consumed.

Although there had been no fire in the grate of the room, there had been a lamp, which, it was claimed, had been full of oil. Now it was empty and the wick burned down to nothing.

The patient died four days later in a state of unconsciousness. Dr Battaglia could find no explanation for either the injuries or the priest's rapid decline. Even before he died, the smell of rotting flesh had become insufferable. Dr Battaglia claimed to have seen worms crawling from the still-living body, and nails falling from the fingers. Altogether a more horrifying account than the fiction.

Captain Frederick Marryat, best known for his Civil War classic novel, *Children of the New Forest*, used SHC to dispatch one of his characters in another book called *Jacob Faithful*, published in 1834. In the scene, Jacob enters the cabin of a barge looking for his mother:

> The lamp fixed against the after bulkhead, with a glass before it, was still alight, and I could see plainly to every corner of the cabin. Nothing was burning – not even the curtains to my mother's bed appeared to be singed ... there appeared to be a black mass in the middle of the bed. I put my hand fearfully upon it – it was a sort of unctuous pitchy cinder. I screamed with horror ... I staggered from the cabin, and fell down on the deck in a state amounting to almost insanity ... She perished from what is called *spontaneous combustion*, and inflammation of the gases generated from the spirits absorbed into the system.

There were several other well-known writers who used spontaneous human combustion in a factual way to bring about the end of a fictional character. Many of them used the device to illustrate a just reward of over-drinking.

Nikolai Gogol, in 1842, wrote *Dead Souls*, in which a blacksmith catches fire 'inside' through 'too much drink'. In his 1849 novel, *Redburn*, Herman Melville describes how 'greenish fire, like a forked tongue' issued from between the lips of a drunken sailor as it consumed him. But author Thomas de Quincey used SHC to warn of another social evil growing at that time, the evil of opium-taking. The phenomenon was also used by Mark Twain and by Emile Zola in his 1893 classic, *Le Docteur Pascal*. But the book that really brought SHC and its alcohol connotations to the attention of the Victorian public was Charles Dickens' *Bleak House*. Dickens chose to inflict the phenomenon on wicked drunken Krook, discovered by two characters, Mr Guppy and Tony Weevle. At this point they are leaning against the window-sill of Krook's room.

'What in the Devil's name,' [he says,] 'is this! Look at my fingers!'

> A thick, yellow liquor defiles them, which is offensive to the touch and sight and more offensive to the smell. A stagnant, sickening oil, with some natural repulsion in it which makes them both shudder ... When he brings the candle, here, from the corner of the window-sill, it slowly drips, and creeps away down the bricks; here, lies in a little thick nauseous pool.

Now they go in search of Krook, and Tony Weevle is the first to look into his room.

> 'I couldn't make him hear, and I softly opened the door and looked in. And the burning smell is there – and the soot is there, and the oil is there – and he is not there!' – Tony ends this with a groan.

Mr Guppy and Tony Weevle enter the room together, confronted by Krook's cat.

> The cat ... stands snarling – not at them; at something on the ground, before the fire. There is a very little fire left in the grate, but there is a smouldering suffocating vapour in the room, and a dark greasy coating on the walls and ceiling. On one chair back, hang the old man's hairy cap and coat ...
> They advanced slowly, looking at all these things. The cat remains where they found her, still snarling at the something on the ground, before the fire and between the two chairs. What is it? Hold up the light.
> Here is a small burnt patch of flooring; here is the tinder from a little bundle of burnt paper ... and here is – is it the cinder of a small charred and broken log of wood sprinkled with white ashes, or is it coal? O Horror, he *is* here! and this from which we run away ... overturning one another into the street, is all that represents him.

This scene, abridged here, was to cause a public debate between Dickens and a Mr Lewes. Lewes, an affirmed sceptic of the phenomenon, thought it was wrong for Dickens to treat spontaneous human combustion as a factual device in his book. Dickens was at pains to point out that he had studied thirty cases of SHC in preparation for the scene. More than that, as has been demonstrated here, Dickens used SHC at a time of great public and medical debate on the subject, with medical, and non-medical men, lining up on both sides of the divide.

The subject of spontaneous and preternatural combustion in human beings was a lively topic for debate in the eighteenth and nineteenth centuries. Many of the explanations for the alleged phenomenon which are under discussion today had their genesis in these times. Intestinal gases, alcohol and the newfangled fad of electricity were all thought to be probable causes, along, of course, with a body of opinion which stated that the phenomenon did not exist in the first place, but could be explained away in rational terms. Out of all these, only the question of alcohol, in terms of enhancing combustibility, was proven to be scientific nonsense.

Even so, the idea survives today. Some sceptics see a link between alcohol abuse and incineration, but in a very different way from that ever intended by the Victorian moralists. They argue that an intoxicated person is more liable to stumble or be in less than full possession of their faculties. As a result they may well be prone to accidents with fire.

That is all very well, but some cases, we have discovered, seem to defy any sort of rational explanation.

2   The Burnings at Sowerby Bridge

Those searching for a paranormal, or supernatural answer to spontaneous human combustion could do worse than examine the following story. It dates back to the turn of the century, and the facts are so remarkable that if we had not substantiated it ourselves, we would have suspected it of being one of those tall tales told to a friend of a friend.

It was a distant relative of the deceased who alerted us to the case. An article had appeared in the *Halifax Evening Courier* of Saturday 13 April 1985. When Mr Hellowell read the piece, he was doubly amazed. The story was astounding enough, but even more so when he realized the two young victims were related to him. He questioned an elderly family member who confessed she knew all about the tragic incidents. Apparently it had been a closely-guarded secret during the ninety-two years since its occurrence.

Despite the story appearing in the newspaper, it was not picked up by anyone else, so we present it here for the first time. We contacted the editor, Edward Riley, who confirmed he had written the article. It was based on original *Courier* accounts published in 1899, drawing on the evidence presented at the inquest.

Mrs Sara Ann Kirby, Mr John Henry Kirby and their daughters, Alice Ann Kirby aged five, and Amy Kirby aged four, lived in Sowerby Bridge, now in West Yorkshire. The family resided in Hargreaves Terrace on London Road, until the parents fell out and separated. When this happened, although the two little girls were still officially listed at their mother's address, Alice Kirby went to live with her father and grandmother at no. 45 Wakefield Road.

Wakefield Road and London Road run parallel to one another, exactly a mile apart on opposite sides of the Calder Valley. The roads are linked by Fall Lane which crosses a canal and the River Calder.

On Thursday 5 January 1899, Mrs Sara Kirby went outside Hargreave Terrace to get some water from the well, twenty yards away. It was 11 a.m. Because it was raining heavily, the task took no more than two minutes. As she re-entered the house, she heard screams and found Amy ablaze. Mrs Kirby told the inquest: 'If she had had paraffin oil thrown over her she would not have burned faster.'

Another witness claimed that flames a yard high were coming from the child's head. It was stated that Amy was afraid of fire. Indeed there was no evidence of matches or charred paper. After it was all over, Mrs Kirby, in great distress, started down Fall Lane to communicate the tragedy to her husband. But the distress was compounded, when, halfway across the valley, she was met by a messenger from her mother-in-law. The messenger was bringing terrible news. Sara's *other* daughter, Alice, had been discovered ablaze. The pair were reduced to hysterical tears as they each related an identical story.

Grandmother Susan Kirby had left young Alice in bed while she visited a neighbour. When she returned, she found the child 'enveloped in flames and almost burned to death'. There were no spent matches or burned paper, and the fire in the grate had not been disturbed. *The time was exactly 11 a.m.*

Both girls were taken away in the same horse-drawn ambulance to the Royal Halifax Infirmary. Alice died at 3 p.m. that day, and Amy just before midnight. In another of those strange name-related 'coincidences' seemingly endemic in SHC matters, the doctor who attended them both was called Dr Wellburn. You will see that such synchronicities of name appear to be part of the alleged phenomenon.

Oddly, considering the climate at that time, spontaneous human combustion was never mentioned at the inquest. Despite the lack of evidence, the coroner concluded that both deaths were an accident, and the jury agreed. But one juror admitted: 'We have no evidence to show how the fire occurred in either case.'

The coroner referred to the circumstances as 'strange' and 'remarkable' that the children should be burned at the same time, yet was prepared to dismiss them as yet another 'shocking coincidence'.

There is a lot we do not know about this case. There was no reference, for instance, of any fire damage to furnishings. Some will argue that had the expertise of modern forensic science been available, a rational explanation for the fires might have been forthcoming. But in all fairness, just what are the chances of two sisters, living apart but separated by just a mile across a valley and whose homes were in sight of one another, catching fire at exactly the same time and with the same lack of evidence of a rational cause?

It is a sad and distressing case not reduced by our academic interest. The girls' mother carried the tragedy with her for fifty years, dying in 1949, aged seventy-seven.

3 Heated Exchanges

KISSING COUPLE BURST INTO FLAMES ... PREACHER EXPLODES INTO
FLAMES IN THE PULPIT ... DEMONS BURNED MY HUBBY TO A CRISP ...
TEASED FATTY EXPLODES IN FLAMES ... MAN EATING CHILLI BURSTS
INTO FLAMES AND DIES ...

Believe it or not these are real newspaper shout-lines we came
across in our research. They represent the public image of SHC –
what look like tall tales told in even taller headlines often featuring
gory artwork. They suggest SHC is a subject found only in the
sensational press and never given serious consideration by the more
respectable media sources.

We are not suggesting that these particular accounts have no
substance in truth. We did check out some of the many examples in
our files and usually (but not always) hit a brick wall in our
enquiries. However, we were simply less inclined to treat
sensational presentations with unqualified respect and preferred to
focus on cases that we pursued personally, or had been offered by
bona fide sources such as fire-officers.

Yet it is important to make clear that the truth or fallacy of
spontaneous human combustion is independent of how some
newspapers choose to report it. Screaming headlines and graphic
images may make money and tantalize those who seem to have a
morbid fascination with such a gruesome phenomenon, but overall
what stands out is the incredibility of these happenings. They are
puzzles in need of solutions and are better served by sober reflection
and responsible treatment. After all, we are dealing with cases
where very often human beings have lost their lives in a terrible
manner. Frequently there are living relatives whose grief and
suffering needs to be remembered. Even where someone survives an
SHC incident the physical and emotional scars can remain for a
very long time.

Of course, establishing the truth about SHC can only occur if the
issues are openly and rationally discussed. There has to be a balance
on the one hand between care and concern for those who are the
victims and the responsibility we have on the other to try to

understand what is happening. This is one reason why we often use pseudonyms or use no names at all in detailing incidents.

Having said all of this we find it hard to understand the actions of some media sources when dealing with SHC. For example, one American newspaper spoke of a case only six weeks after a student's death and long before the inquest. They reported speculation about SHC as fact, and aside from other minor matters, such as getting her name wrong and saying she lived in the *town* of Cheshire, it even falsely insisted she was a schoolgirl.

But most distressing of all was an artist's reconstruction. So soon after her death it presents a garish picture of a young girl, seemingly standing in the open, wearing school uniform and surrounded by flames as two other schoolgirls gaze immobile at the scene. Not only does this misrepresent the facts in almost every respect, but even if it was accurate, the morality of inflicting such an image on friends and relatives whilst the girl's death was still painfully fresh in their minds must, in our opinion, be open to a great deal of doubt.

A case worth discussing illustrates some of the problems that have to be confronted in the light of these remarks.

On 21 July 1988 the north-east England newspaper, the *Hartlepool Mail*, published a front-page story headed 'Woman in blaze mystery'. It told how police in Durham were baffled by a case where an elderly lady had been seriously burnt in a mysterious fire. The report alleged that police had 'not ruled out the possibility' that this incident was caused by SHC.

Thanks to Cleveland journalist Paul Screeton we have established the basic facts as these. At 10.30 a.m. on the morning of 20 July 1988 neighbours saw a 71-year-old woman and her husband in trouble in their garden at Wheatley Hill, a town east of Durham City. Emergency services were immediately alerted. It seems that the woman's clothing was on fire and her husband was frantically beating out the flames. Although these were eventually put out he burnt his hands in the process. The man was allowed home after a few hours hospital treatment but his wife was seriously burnt on the face, head, chest and back and remained in hospital for some weeks. Her extremities were apparently not affected by the flames and there was no obvious source of the mysterious blaze itself. Both fire services and police were said to be puzzled as to how it had started.

Subsequent press reports up to two weeks later indicated that the woman's injuries 'still stumped police' but that the SHC cause mentioned in all previous stories was now 'not considered likely'. The woman had talked briefly to the police and her husband had aided them, allowing enquiries to completely rule out 'any suspicious circumstances'. A CID officer commented that they retained an open mind but this did not include 'keeping the possibility of spontaneous combustion uppermost....' None the less they were still baffled as to what had triggered the fire.

As no death resulted and suspicious circumstances were ruled out police follow-up was inevitably limited and the matter seems to have drifted to a non-conclusion. We did approach the Durham police but they were apparently unwilling to offer us any help on the matter.

In addition the couple who were involved did not respond to our requests for an interview, although we were forewarned by the newspaper that this was likely to be the case. They had repeatedly refused to speak with the press at the time. Their privacy must be respected, which is why we do not identify them by name here.

Why then did these two elderly people react with such antipathy? It seems that they were very upset about the way in which this incident was linked with SHC from the very start of the affair.

Indeed, the day after the *Hartlepool Mail* first broke the story they followed it up with a full-page feature article on the mysteries of SHC. It was a reasonably well-constructed piece that jumped to no conclusions. It referred to the Wheatley Hill case as having 'prompted all kinds of speculation about a very bizarre phenomena' (sic) before offering a few case histories from ancient times and a brief discussion of a more recent incident. The article also featured a report that American sceptics Nickell and Fisher (sic) had proposed the 'candle effect' as a cause for the phenomenon.

It also reported on the American debunking group, CSICOP – the Committee for the Scientific Investigation of Claims Of the Paranormal – who as recently as 1987 were alleging a link between SHC and drunkenness. As we have seen, this is a very old argument, largely discredited. It also featured an interview with a Newcastle medical physicist, John Haggith.

Haggith had argued that SHC was in the same league, scientifically speaking, as levitation and he could think of no physical reason for it to occur. However, he believed that the solutions were to be found in more mundane areas – such as matches in the pockets of a victim accidentally igniting, or static electricity building up in clothing. As balance, more positive remarks about the subject were offered by a local fire-officer who seemed to think it could sometimes occur.

When he first alerted us to the Wheatley Hill case in 1988, Paul Screeton, who works for the newspaper in question, pointed out to us that as far as he knew no official source had actually mentioned

SHC. It featured in the news item simply because a journalist had 'liked the idea'.

When compiling this book we asked Paul Screeton for more information and he was quite happy to allow us to quote his opinions. He felt that the case 'was blown out of all proportion' via 'investigator involvement'. The resulting stories had caused the family to get upset and led to them refusing to cooperate further. Consequently the whole episode fizzled out and the public never got to know what really happened – if that could ever have been established under the circumstances.

As Screeton said: 'Personally I think it was just some gardening mistake – but who knows? I don't think SHC was involved, but there again it is tantalizing to speculate.'

We do not suggest that anybody behaved badly here. But the incident does demonstrate just how difficult it can be to talk about and investigate mysterious fires when the possibility of SHC looms. The reactions of victims, their families, the press, police, fire services, doctors – in fact many groups within society – all have a role in moulding public opinion on what has taken place. A very difficult juggling act is required to balance all these things in deciding whether SHC played a part in any particular case.

This incident might suggest that it is best to be cautious until other options fail completely. Bringing SHC into the equation so rapidly can have a negative rather than positive effect, although the journalist concerned may well argue that if a thorough exploration of the matter was to be undertaken someone had to mention SHC up front. Most officials probably would never do so or may not even be aware that such a phenomenon might exist outside the supermarket tabloids and supernatural mythologies.

The fire-officer that the *Hartlepool Mail* briefly mentioned turned out to be William Cooney OBE. In 1991 he was the county fire officer for the whole of Cleveland. We requested an interview and he was kind enough to grant one to us. His views on some of the dilemmas discussed above were felt to be of great value.

In fact, Cooney had presented a paper in May 1986 to a fire-officers seminar on the question of spontaneous combustion. The seminar was really investigating how chemicals in bulk storage can generate heat and provoke a spontaneous fire, but in his paper the county officer did add a section on SHC. He argued that in the few cases which could not be rationally explained, SHC appeared to start within the body and comprised some source of ignition of inflammable gases which were internally generated.

Cooney was refreshingly hard-headed about which cases should be termed SHC and which should not. He found it difficult to regard either the Jacqueline or the Jack Angel cases as examples, because neither fitted the stereotype he believed exemplified the phenomenon. (Jack Angel will be discussed in great detail in a later chapter.)

> The fire starts from within the body, but the extremities are what survive. I do not believe that you can suffer SHC if the hand, for example, is the primary source. At least this is what the evidence seems to suggest. Take the analogy of a bonfire. If we light one of these then the bits of wood at the edges are what get left – not the pieces in the middle. These are consumed. The fire in SHC always starts from the middle. This is one of the indications you would look for in a fire death situation to suggest the possibility of SHC.
>
> Human bodies can be consumed by a fire. Bones can turn to ash in certain fire situations.

A lot of firemen and cremation experts have disagreed with the above statement.

> In experiments where fat wrapped in cloth has been set alight to demonstrate that the human body could burn like a candle, an external source of heat was applied to get them going. They do not suddenly ignite by themselves, do they? That is what makes the reports of SHC so remarkable, because apparently, ignition is 'spontaneous'!
>
> Many cases of alleged SHC involve someone found by a fireplace. These are not actual SHC because here you have an ignition source. If an elderly person comes into contact with a fire, windows and doors are shut and we end up with a fire situation then that is not SHC. In real examples of spontaneous combustion the only possible heat source is from within. We have to be very careful about how we distinguish what is and what is not spontaneous human combustion. If there is an external source of heat available, then in my view it should not be termed SHC.

As a consequence of all this, William Cooney thinks there are relatively few candidates for SHC each year.

> I suggest it is a very, very small percentage of cases. The bulk of fire services just accept a situation as a fire death – not a fire generated from within the human body. They may look at it and conclude that its cause is 'unknown'. However, even if the cause was SHC then sometimes this may have created a secondary fire which has destroyed the evidence. So it would never be easy to deduce any case as SHC. In fact, I do not believe that any official report for the fire services could ever conclude this explanation for an incident because of these problems.

We deal with tens of fire deaths a year throughout the UK. The average fire-officer goes in and finds a body or the remains of a body and he deals with it. The chances are high that the fire itself has destroyed the evidence for whatever has caused the conflagration. You would really have to look very hard for signs of possible SHC and I cannot instruct my officers to spend the time to do this. They cannot spend their time sifting through the debris for human body parts that might have survived.

Another factor is fear of the unknown. This affects many people. But I am prepared to go out in public and say that there is something happening. We have to investigate this situation.

The county officer has thirty years' experience to his credit and feels there is a clue to the phenomenon in the reports of blue flames sometimes seen at incidents:

The bluish flame suggests that the body has erupted. The amount of gases produced within the human body is potentially explosive. In effect we are a great blob of hydrocarbons – a melting pot of dangerous substances. Perhaps in some circumstances we can just "go off".

William Cooney was mindful of the difficulties regarding the public discussion of SHC. He believes that only by thinking rationally about the problem and not leaping to conclusions might we reach an appreciation of what could be happening.

Look, I am a simple fire-officer. All I can say to such people is let them prove to me that there is evidence for any particular explanation for this thing. But what annoys me is that the experts and professors say that SHC just is not true. Fine, but as a fire-officer I have to pick up the pieces. So if it is not true and does not happen we need to sit down and work out what exactly does occur. Because at the end of the day my fire-officers say that SHC does happen and that's what counts, isn't it?

4 Q.E.D.

On 22 April 1989, the BBC1 science programme *Q.E.D.* turned its attention to the subject of SHC. Entitled *A Case Of Spontaneous Human Combustion?*, the programme-makers sought to demonstrate that the phenomenon did not exist, in that it presented nothing new to science.

We were approached some months previously by BBC researchers keen to solicit material from us for inclusion in the programme. They had read a book of ours, *Death By Supernatural Causes?* which included a section on the subject. This had intrigued them. The title of our chapter, *A Case Of Spontaneous Human Confusion*, has some resemblance to that adopted by the *Q.E.D.* programme, then in the planning stage. At that time we had started collating material for the present book, and for various reasons were not happy about taking part and declined to input into the project.

Apparently we had upset someone on the production team by this decision, which we had carefully and fairly tried to explain. When one of us later arranged with the *Radio Times* to write a feature to tie in with the programme, the offer was mysteriously rescinded. We were told that someone from the series had advised the *Radio Times against* including our work and they felt they had to agree as the magazine relied upon *Q.E.D.*'s cooperation.

Teresa Hunt, the programme's producer, was later commissioned to write a book on SHC, but her publishers told us they abandoned the project when she was 'unable to complete the manuscript'.

Ironically, like the case which had started the whole thing off for us, one of the incidents used in the documentary also featured a suspicious gas cooker.

Detective Sergeant Nigel Cruttenden of Kent police described how he had been called to a baker's shop in Folkestone town centre to investigate the death of a man found in the kitchen. The corpse was very badly incinerated.

The remarkable thing was that he was so badly burned, but the rest of the kitchen was hardly touched by fire. For instance, there was a dustpan and brush made of polythene only inches away from the body, and there was a small air vent made of plastic which had a small amount of charring. The ceiling, made of polystyrene tiles – these weren't touched at all!

Nigel Cruttenden's first thought was that the victim had been murdered, then moved and burnt elsewhere. But there was no evidence of murder. Suicide was considered next, but there was no petrol or matches in the kitchen.

This seems like a genuine mystery, but the detective and his colleagues tried to rationalize it and came up with an explanation. 'Having ruled out murder, suicide and SHC, the only thing then left for the death of Barry Soudain was that he had a heart attack, caught himself on fire by the lighted gas stove, fell to the floor then burnt like a candle from above and downwards.'

This is fine as a supposition, a *possible* explanation for the fire, although it cannot be proven. A number of questions spring to mind. Apparently, SHC was ruled out, but how did the detective decide what SHC was, and how then did he rule it out? Did the victim have a history of heart complaints? Of course there is always a first time, but if the man was known to have a malfunctioning heart it would strengthen D.S. Cruttenden's argument. Thirdly, was the stove actually switched on when the remains were discovered?

We wrote to D.S. Cruttenden for answers to these questions, but received no reply. However, we did receive information from the coroner in charge of the inquest, Mr Brian Smith. Apparently, 44-year-old Barry Soudain lived alone in a flat over the Folkestone bakery, and was employed as a general cleaner and handyman.

Despite D.S. Cruttenden's conclusions voiced on *Q.E.D.*, the verdict at the inquest was quite a different matter. The medical cause of death was unascertainable due to the destruction of the body, and an open verdict was brought about. As far as a fatal heart attack was concerned, the victim was not known to have suffered from heart disease. That organ and others were destroyed in the fire. Further to this, evidence was presented at the inquest of 'inhalation of fire products' in the victim's lungs. For a time at least, Mr Soudain was still alive and breathing while his body incinerated.

He may not have suffered a fatal heart attack, but Barry Soudain had been, and probably still was at the time, an alcoholic. His blood alcohol level was 268 mg in 100 mg of blood. In short, Mr Soudain should have been in an advanced drunken state at the time of death, although the condition of drunkenness often depends on an individual's regular, or irregular, use of alcohol. Alcoholics become hardened to the actual sensory effects of drink.

There was speculation that the incident had occurred up to fifteen hours earlier, as the deceased had last been seen alive at 7.30 p.m. the previous night. Certainly he did not seem drunk at that time, according to Mr and Mrs Gower, owners of the premises. They bumped into him in nearby Sidney Street and had a short chat. The couple last saw their lodger heading towards his flat. It was Mr Gower, using a key to enter the premises at 10.30 a.m. the following morning, who discovered the charred remains.

As we shall see, in order to fit in with the theory espoused on the programme to explain SHC, it was necessary to place the incident as far back in time from the discovery of the remains as possible. But, what viewers were not told, and which we have discovered since, was that when Mr Gower had got over the initial shock of entering the kitchen, he became aware that there was a kettle placed half over a blazing gas-ring. *This ring was not switched off until the police arrived. The kettle was still half-full of boiling water at this time.*

Did Soudain *fill* the kettle, then when it boiled, lift it half off the ring maintaining contact with the flame to keep it on the boil? Was it at this point that he caught fire, or is the lighted gas-ring a red herring? If the ring was the source of ignition, this still does not explain a number of things, not least of which is how the body was so thoroughly destroyed. More importantly, how long would it have taken a kettle just half-full of water to have boiled away? Certainly not fifteen hours, or anything like it. *Surely the incident must have occurred that morning, perhaps only an hour before discovery* – a very important factor as we shall see shortly.

The coroner did not think there was an easy explanation. 'I have an open mind about the possibility of spontaneous human combustion,' he told us. 'Just how *did* Barry Soudain die?'

We also spoke to the coroner's officer, P.C. Coombs, who added his comments. 'At the end of the day there were a lot of questions which just could not be answered.'

One can find a 'rational' explanation for anything if one tries hard enough, but does this necessarily equate with the truth?

The programme itself *did* present some food for thought, but was blighted by an apparent need to demolish the entire mystery in one all-embracing theory. The rather superior tone of the narrative, read by an actress, only served to convince knowledgeable viewers that much of the programme was a whitewash. Even so, *A Case Of Spontaneous Human Combustion?* was a rare contribution to the SHC controversy, and it is worth studying in detail.

It started – and ended – with the case of Alfred Ashton, an elderly gentleman who lived alone in a terraced house in Southampton. Apparently a neighbour visited him at 6 p.m. on the evening of 8 January 1988, to make a cup of tea. At around 10 p.m. neighbours smelt burning. Some time in-between Mr Ashton became incinerated. In his opening statement, Roger Penney, investigating fire-officer of the Hampshire Fire Brigade, had this to say: 'I've been to many fateful fires over the years, but I've never seen anything quite like this. The only way I can explain it is to consider SHC.'

The inquest concluded that the means of Mr Ashton's death was 'cause unknown', and an open verdict was arrived at. Here is the fire-officer's graphic account of the discovery, since repeated to us personally.

The first thing I was aware of was the extreme heat and smoke in the room. As I stepped into the room I noticed the floor was very slippery. On looking around, I noticed that the windows were blackened by smoke, but they were not broken. As the smoke began to clear, I realized there was a hole in the floor, and across the hole was a body. What I found amazing about this fire was the complete devastation of the body. There was virtually nothing left.

Alongside the hole was an electric fire, although Penney stated 'it wasn't switched on at the time'. On the other side, close to the body, was an anorak hanging on the back of a chair, showing just a little heat damage at the bottom. On a chair alongside that was a pile of newspapers, which although brown with smoke, were not damaged by fire. The plastic casing of a television set on a worktop was completely melted. 'Looking at the body again, I noticed that the trousers, shoes and socks were not damaged at all. The cut-off point where the body had smouldered was a clean cut.'

In fact all that remained of Alfred Ashton was his legs and feet. Everything else was completely incinerated.

The programme then cut to former Gwent CID, scene of crime officer, John Heymer, who recounted his feelings upon being confronted by a similar fire death in a house at Blackwood, Ebbw Vale. We discuss this case in full in a later chapter. 'I had never experienced SHC until I entered that room. Everyone; Police Officers, Superintendents, standing around, were absolutely dumbstruck. They knew that what they were seeing was impossible.'

Heymer said it was like stepping into another world.

After having introduced several examples, *Q.E.D.* then set about to demonstrate that spontaneous human combustion did not exist, and that 'even in the most bizarre cases there's no need to resort to the supernatural. Science can provide a perfectly rational explanation for all of these deaths'.

David Halliday, a forensic science expert for the Metropolitan Police Force, stated that in every case of this type he had examined, there was always a good ignition source nearby. After examining photographs of the Southampton and the Folkestone cases, he pointed out the electric fire and the gas stove as ignition sources. We have already discussed the difficulties with the stove, and a similar difficulty arises with the electric fire.

Fire-officer Roger Penney, clearly stated that on arrival he found the fire switched off. At the start of the programme, viewers heard Mr Penney favouring SHC as an explanation for the death. However, at the end Penney appeared to contradict himself. 'All we could assume is that the gentleman fell on the fire, or close to the fire, and gradually the radiated heat ignited the body and slowly smouldered, burning through the floor and indeed the cable.'

In order to clarify these points, we decided to contact Mr Penney, but discovered he had retired. Initially we were put onto a Mr Frank Bowen. Frank is now a divisional officer in the area concerned with Press and Public Relations, but at the time of the discovery of Alfred Ashton's remains, he was a Brigade Specialist Fire Investigation Officer, and had talked to Roger Penney about the case. 'When we first came across the scene, that was our reaction. There didn't seem to be a rational explanation, so we thought it must by SHC. However, when we investigated further we decided there was a rational explanation for Mr Ashton's death.'

According to Frank Bowen the electric fire did not have a switch on it, so it was switched off in the sense that power to it had been stopped by the burning body. It was the mains cable from the socket, passing beneath the floorboards which had been charred, not the cable from the fire to the socket. Had the victim fallen against the device? 'There was insufficient remains to conclusively prove what exactly had happened, but we did learn that Mr Ashton had a medical history of fainting attacks.'

More than that, Alfred Ashton was a regular drinker who went to the local pub and took nightcaps at home.

Despite Frank Bowen's certainty, the coroner at the inquest had found a rational explanation wanting, and had ruled an open verdict instead of misadventure. Why was this? 'You'd better ask the coroner,' was Mr Bowen's reply.

We presume that the 'we' referred to by Frank Bowen meant the Hampshire Fire Brigade, and *not* himself and Roger Penney. We have since spoken to Mr Penney, and according to him, Frank Bowen had nothing to do directly with the investigation of Alfred Ashton's death. Roger clarified his comment made in the programme concerning the fire being switched off, and added a new twist.

> Frank Bowen is right; there was no switch on the electric fire, but there was a switch on the *wall* socket. When I examined it the following day, it was in the '*off*' position. Now, someone involved in the investigation could have done that, it's difficult to say, I didn't think of looking when we first came across the remains.

Frank appreciates that the position of that switch at the time of the incident is of paramount importance, but added, 'I wasn't happy. There were so many strange things. If the fire was the source of ignition, I cannot understand why the body was incinerated, yet a hand which was right by it survived untouched.'

What were Roger Penney's thoughts about the *Q.E.D.* programme? '*Q.E.D.* was a disappointment. They cut out a lot.'

In most rooms of a modern house there are various sources of possible ignition – electric, gas and coal fires, wall heaters, cookers, cigarette-lighters, matches ... But is it scientific to assume that any of these could have begun a fire when there is no hard evidence? Is just 'being there' sufficient reason? In truth such 'evidence' is circumstantial not evidential.

Reading through press reports of mysterious fire deaths, one of the most common explanations is ignition by smouldering cigarette. Often this is arrived at as a last resort, when all other possible ignition sources have been ruled out. But in reality, how easy is it for a cigarette to start a fire? Michael Harrison, in his controversial book, *Fire From Heaven*, makes the following observations of his own friends and relatives.

> One let a cigarette burn its way down through the arm of a well-stuffed chair; one fell fast asleep in another well-stuffed chair, with the remains of a cigarette attached to his limp fingertips, where it had burnt itself out on a new Axminster carpet: two others had managed to make a lighted cigarette burn its way through a pillow and some inches through blanket, sheet and mattress; while a fifth, who had laid down to rest on a bed in his dressing gown, had let the cigarette burn its way through the thick double collar of the gown.

Apart from having very careless friends, Michael Harrison does make a very important point. None of these incidents resulted in a fire! Ironically, backing for this was received from Philip Jones,

Home Office forensics expert at the Jacqueline inquest. When asked by the coroner whether a lighted cigarette could have caused the student's jacket to burst into flame, he replied that contrary to popular belief, it is very difficult for a cigarette to cause a fire.

After 'establishing' a source of ignition, *Q.E.D.* then went on to expound their main hypothesis; that the end results of the crematorium could happen by chance in the average home. Dr Dougal Drysdale based at Edinburgh University was introduced to help demonstrate this. Det. Sgt. Cruttenden had already theorized that the victim had 'burnt like a candle from above and downwards'. Dr Drysdale produced a sausage-shaped piece of animal fat wrapped in some cloth which was lit at one end. On the programme, and later, in an interview with us, he explained the theory.

> The idea that the body can burn like a candle isn't so far fetched at all. In a way, a body is like a candle – inside out. With a candle the wick is on the inside, and the fat on the outside. As the wick burns the candle becomes molten and the liquid is drawn onto the wick and burns. With a body, which consists of a large amount of fat, the fat melts and is drawn onto the clothing which acts as a wick, and then continues to burn.

Indeed, Dr Drysdale's sausage did just that. But what about the bones? In most SHC cases even bones are reduced to ash. The wick-effect experiment had already been demonstrated on television in an item on SHC on *Newsnight*, BBC2, January 1986. Then it had been carried out by Professor Gee, Emeritus Professor of Forensic Medicine at Leeds University. Bones were not included then, either, although the professor glibly assured the interviewer that if there had been, he was sure they would have reduced to ash – a claim that no one has been able to demonstrate. Professor Gee has since retired due to ill health, so was unable to help in our enquiries. What did Dr Drysdale have to tell us?

> In a crematorium you need high temperatures – around 1,300°C, or even higher – to reduce the body to ash in a relatively short period of time. But it's a misconception to think you need those temperatures within a living room to reduce a body in this way. You can produce local, high temperatures, by means of the wick effect and a combination of smouldering and flaming to *reduce even bones to ash*. At relatively low temperatures of 500°C – and if given enough time – the bone will transform into something approaching a powder in composition.

To demonstrate this, Dr Drysdale introduced viewers to a 'muffle furnace' – a computer-controlled oven about the size of a domestic microwave. He intended placing an animal bone on a tray within the furnace for *six* hours at 500°C. The camera then cut to the end of the process, and we heard Dr Drysdale state that *eight* hours had now elapsed, and he would now remove the bone which he claimed earlier would be reduced to '*something approaching powder*'.

The tray was removed and still contained a recognizable bone. Only when the scientist chipped at it with a sharp implement did it begin to break up. Dr Drysdale speculated that if the bone had been left in the furnace for *twelve* hours it would definitely have reduced to powder ...

We tracked down people involved in these interviews. When we spoke to John Heymer, he was very scathing about the TV programme.

> *Q.E.D.* was a farce! They came to me and I didn't want to do the programme, but they assured me they were doing a serious documentary. So I gave them access to all my records, full details of several cases. I also gave them a filmed interview which lasted over half an hour. When the programme was aired, they had completely changed their approach and seemed to be going all out to disprove the phenomenon. I was very annoyed. In fact I tried to phone the producer but was told she was on holiday abroad. In my opinion the programme did not represent what this phenomenon truly is.

Heymer was equally critical about the experiments used in the film as evidence against SHC. Of Drysdale's experiment with animal fat wrapped in cloth, he made a remarkable assertion. He claimed that Drysdale had told him afterwards that the film-makers had brought him a piece of 'fat that stunk to high heaven'. The scientist could *not* get this to burn, so midway through the filming he switched it for one that did.

We approached Dougal Drysdale, who is based at Edinburgh's Unit of Fire Safety Engineering. Surprisingly, he was also not over-generous in his praise of *A Case of Spontaneous Human Combustion?* 'I became involved against my better judgement,' he commented. 'I was approached because I have had one or two slanging matches in the press with uninformed persons.'

Did he believe that his experiments had disproved SHC, as the *Q.E.D.* programme hinted?

> I have no experimental data to prove that it can or can't happen. There are overwhelming scientific arguments against it, and there is no mechanism by which it could occur. Personally, I believe that the

'wick effect' can account for the total body destruction. Ignition is *not* spontaneous but is external.

Nevertheless, Dr Drysdale confirmed that, while the theory has been tested in the laboratory, 'no one has been able to convert the bones to ash under these conditions.'

Did this not argue strongly against the wick theory as an explanation for SHC? The reduction of bones to ash is perhaps the most difficult factor to explain. Dr Drysdale considered otherwise. 'I think this failure to reduce bone to ash is simply because no one has seriously tried to reproduce the effect. It would require significant research effort – and there are more important things to worry about!'

Dr Drysdale was kind enough to suggest that a book such as this one was needed. He also directed us to a letter he had published in the house journal *Fire*, dated 14 March 1986. Co-written with A.N. Beard, also of the Unit of Fire Safety Engineering, they tackled the essence of SHC, in what is a very perceptive and well-argued piece. Effectively they suggest that there is a three-stage process through which one must go; establishing that SHC exists, then that it is either 'natural' or 'preternatural', and finally, how it might be accounted for in terms of today's scientific world view.

They demonstrated that sometimes cases of fire can be baffling without being SHC. An example is cited from their own files of a man who lit a cigarette as he left his workplace and became engulfed in flames. Only after enquiry was it discovered that the man normally hosed down his clothing with an air line before setting off for home. On this occasion, in tragic error, he had used an adjacent oxygen line instead. His clothes were full of oxygen molecules when he lit his cigarette, and these were ignited, turning him into an inferno.

As the authors rightly contend; 'To say that a phenomenon is unexplained is not to say it is inexplicable'. They feel that even if SHC is established 'there would seem to be no good reason to assume that it could not be accounted for on the basis of existing theory'. But they conclude: 'The possibility of the existence of SHC should not be dismissed out of hand, but much more needs to be known about the combustion properties of the human body in different conditions'.

But *did* Dr Drysdale switch the sausage during the *Q.E.D.* experiment as was reported? We put John Heymer's allegations directly to him, and he responded willingly. 'The BBC supplied a piece of meat which was not very good. It stunk! I have carried out the experiment many times in my laboratory and never had any trouble getting it to work. But it proved very difficult with the sample they brought.'

But was the piece substituted mid-experiment?

> You mean was the experiment rigged? No – not really. I did have to change to a different piece of meat to get the wick effect to operate, but it was from the same batch the BBC supplied. They did edit out some minutes while we were trying to get the thing going. It took a long time in this instance. It may well take a long time in such tests, but in the end it *will* go. Of course it depends upon the amount of fat in the sample. The type of cloth used also seems to be important. Some types are better than others.

Did he think this meant that corpulent people would be more likely victims of the wick effect? 'That is the implication – yes. And many are. But not all victims are fat. There are instances where the victims are lean.'

Roger Penney had some thoughts on the animal fat experiment too.

> Whenever this effect is demonstrated, the smouldering tends to taper off, in that the fat might stop burning, but the material it is wrapped in continues for a little while. In Alfred Ashton's case, the burning had stopped *suddenly*. There was no tapering off; the trousers, the flesh and the bone had all stopped burning at the same moment. These were clean cuts.

Q.E.D. addressed another problem illustrated by the three deaths they were examining. If the body was reduced to ash, how was it that the furnishing and other items in the room were largely untouched by fire? They turned to Stan Ames, Head of Reaction to Fire Section, of the Fire Research Station in Borehamwood, Hertfordshire.

He explained that fire was not a haphazard process, but included a number of well-established stages, each one involving well-known physical and chemical processes. In an outdoor fire, he continued, fire growth is by flame contact. The first item is ignited and the flames ignite the next item and so on. But for fires inside a building, the process is different.

> The heat and smoke from the first item rises into the upper part of the room and forms a layer under the ceiling. As that layer thickens it gets hotter and deeper, until it descends, touching other items in the room such as a television set. The oxygen level will go down. When it reaches 16% *it suppresses burning, and becomes a smouldering fire.*

Ames's theory was that at 16% the already burning body would continue to smoulder, but that other combustible items in the rooms would not now light due to insufficient oxygen. However, the heat generated by the smouldering body would cause things like the plastic casing of a television set, or a polythene dustpan and brush, to melt. In this way a body would burn to ash without destroying the building and its contents. This included, we presume, the anorak found hanging over the back of a chair, only inches away from the remains of Alfred Ashton.

To test this hypothesis, a chair, substituting for a body, was placed inside a sealed chamber and set alight, then left for six hours. The process was filmed for *Q.E.D.* While this was happening, the solemn voice of the narrator confidently informed us: 'The most important feature of this experiment was to demonstrate that the smouldering process could sustain itself long enough to reduce a body to ash – or in this case an armchair to its springs.'

Once again, what was promised did not materialize. The seat and the back of the chair, although badly burned, were still remarkably intact. Certainly, it was not reduced 'to its springs'. Worse still, according to what both Heymer and Penney told us, there were many false starts, as it took all morning to get the chair to light.

We question the scientific validity of an experiment which substitutes an object composed of highly inflammable material for organic tissue consisting of at least 60% water. We talked to Stan Ames and asked him several questions. For instance we wanted to know how long the magic figure of 16% would be maintained before the oxygen content would drop even lower, and whether less oxygen would mean that even smouldering could not be supported? We also asked if the experiment had been carried out using an animal carcass, suitably wrapped in a sheet, which we felt would scientifically test the smouldering theory and the wick effect.

The comments provided for the *Q.E.D.* programme were not based on specific research into this phenomenon [SHC], they were provided from a general understanding of fire science. The question concerning the time scale of the smouldering behaviour is difficult to answer. Each room would have its own air leakage rate and this would tend to control the level of oxygen in a smouldering fire. Our experience has shown that deep seated smouldering can take place and this is an indication that high levels of oxygen are not essential for the reaction. However I know of no work where the minimum oxygen concentration for smouldering has been established.

Neither am I aware of any work carried out on smouldering animal tissue other than that done by Dr Drysdale at Edinburgh University for the *Q.E.D.* programme. I was involved in the burning of a pig for the Metropolitan Police many years ago, and, using a fire grate filled with smokeless fuel we were able to reduce the pig to ashes (with the exception of the teeth, intestines and its contents) in thirteen hours.

Tom Tullett's book of the forensic murder investigations of Professor J.M. Cameron, *Clues To Murder*, has a chapter entitled 'The Teddy Bear Murders'. This details how, in the 1970s, two men disposed of the bodies of five murder victims, including a 10-year-old boy, through burning.

Originally arrested for armed robbery, it emerged that John Childs and Henry Mackenny cut their victims up in Childs' flat, and burned the pieces in an eighteen-inch-wide grate in the living-room. Professor Cameron visited the flat where it was necessary to prove that a body could be disposed of in this way.

An experiment was carried out there in secret. The floor was covered in polythene, and a dead pig, weighing eleven stone, was cut up into log-like pieces by a pathologist. For thirteen hours the pieces were fed into the fire, at the end of which, according to Tullett; 'the pig was totally destroyed and there left just a pile of ash'.

Were the bones destroyed too? The murderers could not do it with their human victims. After several days of burning, charred bones still remained which had to be hammered into dust. Mr Ames told us that in the case of the pig, they were able to reduce even its bones to ash. We asked him if this could be due to the greater ratio of fat to bone structure in the pig? He could not answer that question, but provided other reasons.

> You must appreciate that our experiment was carried out under controlled, scientific, conditions. By using smokeless fuel we were using intense radiated heat which I monitored carefully using a thermal sensor. It was the sort of temperature a blacksmith would use to heat metal to a deforming condition – cherry to white heat. I also controlled when, and in what quantity, flesh was to be placed in the fire. About half way through, too much tissue was added and it reduced ventilation. We placed a board over the opening to create a draught.

Finally, *Q.E.D.* tried to convince viewers they had solved the mystery: 'So even in the most bizarre of these cases, there is no need to resort to the supernatural. Science can provide a perfectly rational explanation for all of these deaths'.

But Stan Ames was not so sure. 'I must admit I've not got a clear picture in my mind of how a body can be incinerated through smouldering. My comments in the programme were directed towards one particular case. I don't think any of us expected *Q.E.D.* to end on an entirely conclusive note.'

In fact there seem to have been a lot of problems with *A Case Of Spontaneous Human Combustion?* Many more emerged during our own researches. For our evaluation of the phenomenon we decided to do something which *Q.E.D.* could have done but chose not to do. We put their explanations to cremation specialists.

Mrs Valerie Bennett is a local government officer and a qualified superintendent of Overdale Crematorium in Bolton, Lancashire. She is responsible for cremation and burial in an area which stretches as far north as Preston. Mrs Bennett oversees four thousand cremations *annually.*

She admitted from the outset that she knew very little about spontaneous human combustion. But she and her husband – an embalmer of twenty-six years – plus other specialists, had seen the programme. At this point they were also shown some pictures of SHC victims. They were shocked by the pictures. Not emotionally, but *professionally.*

They could not believe the utter devastation of the bodies, the lack of even skeletal remains. Mrs Bennett shook her head as she handled the photographs. 'We are cremating bodies between temperatures of 600-950°C for on average 1½ hours, and bones, not ash, *always* remain.'

But what if the cremation process was continued for several hours, we asked, would that reduce the bones to powder? 'All that does is burn the bones further and turn them black. You would still end up with bones – not dust. The larger bones are still recognizable such as the pelvis and thigh bones.'

We were escorted around to the back of the crematorium by Mrs Bennett and her senior cremator of eleven years, Peter Thornley, to see first-hand what she had described in words. The gas-fuelled furnaces are also termed 'cremators'. There are five of them at Overdale working full-time. Peter took us over to one of the cremators which was at the end of its cycle. He switched off the gas and opened the hatch door.

The walls glowed red hot and there was a whiff of something stale. But we saw exactly what had been described. The corpse had been subjected to terrific heat at over 600°C for 1½ hours. It was an energy that had *vapourized* an entire wooden coffin, skin, muscles, sinew and internal organs – yet – what remained, what could not be destroyed by the inferno, was a recognizable skeleton … 'What the heat does do, is make the bones brittle,' Peter explained. 'Once cooled the bones are raked from the cremator, and this action breaks most of them up into smaller pieces.'

Peter showed us a tray containing bones which had been raked earlier from another cremator. They were on average several inches in length. 'But as you can see, what we are left with are *bones*, not powder or ash.'

There is a final process which does reduce the bones to dust so they can be placed inside an urn and presented to relatives. The remains are put into a 'cremulator'. Peter took us over to the machine and explained how it worked.

In many ways it looks and works like a heavy-duty spin-dryer. The bones are placed inside a drum along with eight heavy iron balls, each weighing several pounds. When the machine is switched on the drum revolves and the bones are pounded into dust.

Back in more comfortable surroundings, Mrs Bennett voiced all our thoughts.

> I cannot see that a fire in an ordinary room can achieve what we cannot under intense heat and controlled conditions. We've had cases where someone has fallen on a fire and died. Their clothes have caught alight, but no one has ever burned right through. There is always flesh and a skeleton left. Actually, women burn hotter and quicker than men, because proportionally, women carry more fat.

We found this last piece of information particularly ironic. If *Q.E.D.*'s hypothesis was correct, then there should be a higher number of female SHC victims than male. Instead, all three victims cited in the programme were men.

Mr Bennett added:

> There was an horrific accident on the M6 a few years ago. A whole family were incinerated when the van they were travelling in rolled over and the petrol tank ignited. My company was called out to retrieve the remains. I attended the accident. The unfortunate victims had been subjected to very intense heat and flames, yet skeletons remained intact and there was quite a lot of flesh left, including internal organs.

Peter Thornley added: 'Even in the cremation process, the skull is incredibly hard to destroy, yet in many of these [SHC] incidents, even the skull is gone!'

There were further surprises, too. *Q.E.D.* needed oxygen starvation to account for the other unburned items in the room. It was claimed that the body would slowly incinerate in these circumstances. Yet the cremation process occurs under exactly opposite conditions to these. During cremation, the cremator is continuously fed copious quantities of fresh air under pressure by the use of fans. If this was not done, then what would be the result, we asked Mrs Bennett. 'The body would be hardly burned,' she replied. 'I just cannot see how a human body could generate sufficient heat to turn a room into a cremator!'

Peter added: 'If we turned the oxygen off, the body would just go black. It wouldn't continue to burn.'

Overdale also carries out the cremation of foetuses aged eighteen to twenty weeks old. Mrs Enid Giles, Assistant Superintendent, gave us this remarkable piece of information.

> The foetuses go into the cremators at the end of the day when the gas and air is switched off. They are left overnight, during which the cremator is gradually cooling, although it would be impossible to touch the bricks even the following day. In the morning you can make out ribs, skull and even legs. If you blew on them they would go away, but the point is, they are *there* – and they are not even fully formed bones. The scientific explanations in the programme did not convince me that bones can disappear like that in a living room.

There was one fatal flaw with *A Case Of Spontaneous Human Combustion?* which unfortunately most viewers would have had no chance to be aware of. SHC does not only occur inside airtight rooms, in such a way as might conceivably fit the scenario *Q.E.D.* painstakingly endorsed. It also happens in well-ventilated buildings and cases have even been recorded in the open air. Perhaps most significantly of all, there are survivors, people who have spontaneously caught fire but have been luckily rescued before the flames brought death. Unless these people are all lying – a suggestion for which we can see no justification – some of them *know with certainty that they did not catch light through a smouldering cigarette, or fall against an open fire.*

We will leave the last word on the documentary with fireman Tony McMunn. Tony was instrumental in the making of the earlier BBC2 Newsnight feature, and subsequently advised behind the scenes of *Q.E.D.*

> I spent time with Teresa Hunt putting the programme together. She wanted me to appear on it, but I didn't want to. At that stage I'd had enough. I went through the subject in great detail with her. She was putting it together disjointedly. The programme was clinical but it wasn't very interesting. At the end of the day they didn't solve anything much.

5   The Truth About Mary Reeser

Of all the cases alleging spontaneous human combustion, the most published is that of Mary Reeser. Since the incident, in 1951, the story of the 'cinder woman' has appeared worldwide in hundreds of magazines and books.

For example, a glossy advertising brochure for the *Time-Life Library of Curious and Unusual Facts* was circulated to millions of households during 1991. Beneath a picture of Mrs Reeser's remains were words that began; 'No one has ever explained it ... not even the many investigators who witnessed the grisly scene the next morning'.

Here, for the first time, we present an enquiry into the full facts of the case, including fire reports, FBI laboratory analysis and St Petersburg police files containing statements from the many players involved in this strange death.

Mary Hardy Reeser was a woman of habits. She lived in an apartment situated at 1200 Cherry Street, St Petersburg, Florida. The 67-year-old lady believed in eating well, and at five foot seven was plump, weighing more than twelve stone (170 lb).

Her life revolved around her son, Dr Richard Reeser. A typical day began before 6 a.m., when she would listen to the radio and do some washing. Between 7 and 8 a.m. she ate a hearty breakfast and waited until her son arrived for morning coffee around 10 a.m. Later, she would go into town to do her son's banking and return at 4 p.m. for a rest before having dinner at Dr Reeser's house. Mary would return home about 8 p.m. and lie down with the lights out listening to the radio until she was ready to retire. Often she would take sedatives before going to sleep.

But on Sunday 1 July there was a disruption to the orderly life of this doctor's widow that was to lead to her death.

Mary Reeser was not a happy woman. Her home was originally in Pennsylvania, where she was one of the most visible citizens in the small town of Columbia. Her husband was the town's leading doctor, and Mary was a socialite who enjoyed gourmet cooking and playing bridge. Most of all she loved her only child; Richard junior. Richard followed in the footsteps of his father, graduating from Cornell Medical School, and was assigned to troops stationed in Florida during World War II. After the war he decided to set up home permanently in St Petersburg, with his wife Ernestine, and three daughters.

In 1947 Richard's father died, and three years later, five weeks before her death, his mother decided to move to St Petersburg to be near her son. It is a decision that many aged parents make when they are left on their own. But Mary was not aware until she had moved how much she was sacrificing. When she did, it was too late.

In Columbia, Mary Reeser had a large house filled with antique furniture. She left this, along with her friends, for an apartment near her son. As Dr Reeser, now eighty-one, recently told reporter Jacquin Sanders:

> She missed her old life, her friends, her position back home. She hated the hot months here and had tried to get back and rent an apartment for the summer. But there had been a little business boom in Columbia, and her friends couldn't find her an apartment. For that reason she was depressed in the last days of her life.

On that final, hot day, Mrs Reeser came to her son's house for dinner, then offered to baby-sit the youngest child while the rest of the family went to the beach. But Richard and Ernestine had noticed her depressed state of mind, and returned after only an hour. Richard found his mother sitting in a chair, crying. It transpired that the reason for this concerned a friend from Columbia who was supposed to have come for Mary to take her back there to look for an apartment. Unfortunately the friend had broken her leg and the trip was abandoned. Mary asked her son to take her home, but Richard decided he needed a shower first.

After showering, he discovered that his mother had begun to walk home alone. He asked his wife if she would go and try to find her, and give the elderly woman a lift the rest of the way. It seems Ernestine Reeser did not find her mother-in-law until she reached the apartment. By now it was around 5 p.m. Ernestine stayed a short while then left. Strangely, she was to tell questioning police officers that she could shed no light on the reason her mother-in-law came home early.

The depression must have played on Richard Reeser's mind because at about 8 p.m. he turned up at the apartment with one of his daughters. Mary Reeser was sitting in her easy-chair wearing a nightie. She had not eaten and had taken two Seconal sleeping-pills, and was smoking a cigarette. Dr Reeser noted something else too, something which may have had a direct bearing on the almost total incineration of his mother.

After all the fuss and tears, the old lady now seemed relaxed and content. She told him she planned to take two more pills before retiring. Richard Reeser kissed his mother good-night, and walked away, never to see her again.

But Dr Reeser and daughter Nancy may not have been the last people to see the woman alive. Neighbour and owner of Allamanda Apartments, Mrs Pansy Carpenter, saw the old lady either just before Dr Reeser's arrival, or just after his departure. She too said Mary was wearing a rayon nightie, with the addition of black satin slippers. Mrs Carpenter said her tenant seemed upset, but was led to believe this was due to a family quarrel, although Mary did admit she was a little disappointed about not being able to make the trip to Columbia.

After speaking to her, Mrs Carpenter left the apartment, and at about 8.50 p.m. went to buy the old lady some ice-cream from a nearby drug-store. But as she passed the apartment, she noticed the lights were out and the radio turned off. Presuming Mary had retired, the landlady decided not to disturb her.

At 5 a.m., Monday 2 July, Pansy Carpenter was woken up by a dull thud, similar to the slamming of a door. She went outside to investigate, and finding nothing, started back towards the building. As she did so, Mrs Carpenter thought she could smell burning, similar to an over-heating electric motor, and went and turned off a water-pump in the garage. Then she returned to her bed. An hour later she got up and brought in the morning's newspaper. This had been delivered at around 6.30 a.m., and delivery boy, Bill Connor, was to tell police that he smelled no smoke nor did he see anything suspicious.

At this time Mrs Carpenter thought it was odd that Mrs Reeser was not up. The habitual radio programme could not be heard, and the smell of burning experienced earlier had now gone.

At 8 a.m., a Western Union telegram boy, Richard Bruce, arrived, asking for Mrs Reeser's apartment. Pansy Carpenter took the message, and decided to deliver it personally together with the newspaper which she had read. It was at this point that the grisly discovery was made.

Allamanda Apartments is a single-storey block split into four dwellings. A screen door allows access to a hallway off which are two of the apartments, including Mrs Reeser's. Her unit consisted of three rooms.

When Mrs Carpenter arrived at the screen door, she found it unlocked, and hot to the touch. She called to the telegram boy that something was wrong, but he carried on walking at first, so she shouted to some painters working across the street that there had been an 'explosion'. Bruce returned to the building, together with two workmen. The inner apartment door was unlocked too, and ajar. One of the men, called Clements, looked inside, backed away, and advised Mrs Carpenter to call the fire department. She did so and also telephoned Dr Reeser.

Richard Bruce stated that there was quite a lot of smoke, but not much fire. All three agreed that the 'heat' was not 'intense heat'. These observations received a professional qualification from Assistant Fire Chief Griffith. What fire remained – on a wooden joist beam over a partition – was easily put out with a hand-pump. The interior of the apartment was filled with smoke, however, and Chief Griffith opened windows to allow it to dissipate. It was not until he was on his way out of the room that he realized there was a fatality. He saw a foot sticking out of some ashes.

Many of the above details are gleaned from a special police report written by investigating officers Lee and Boyd of which we have been able to obtain a copy. Here are the officers' observations (emphasis added).

Upon entering the screen door to a hallway, a left turn is made to get to the door of the apartment in question. This door was partly open on our arrival, and we were informed by Mrs Carpenter that that was the way the door was when she first discovered the fire. The hall between the apartment of Mrs Reeser, and the other apartment in the wing was well smoked up from a distance of about three feet from floor to ceiling. The ceiling was heavily smoked and the face plate to the switch in the hall was melted out of shape. This is approximately eight feet from the door to the Reeser apartment.

The entire apartment ceiling was blackened by smoke. Drapes in the dining area were blackened around the top but were not scorched. Screen window in the dining area was clogged with soot. Folding doors between the dining area and the kitchen were also blackened but not scorched. *Face plates on light switches in the apartment were not damaged at all.* Folding doors from living area to dressing room were scorched around the top. The heater in the living room appeared in good shape and was turned off. The bathroom was heavily smoked, although there was no damage to light fixtures. Two plastic bathing caps hanging behind the bathroom door were not damaged. There was a heavy burning in the partition between the living area and the kitchen, although papers on the table top water heater which was against the wall, were not scorched.

The kitchen equipment, which is all Frigidaire, consisting of a refrigerator, three burner stove and table top water heater, are in good shape, and show no sign of an electric short. None of the furniture left in the apartments shows any fire damage. The sheets on the one day bed which have been made up are not scorched and have their original life. Two candles which were on [a table] in the dining area were melted. A plastic curtain in the dressing room was in no way damaged by fire.

The furniture in the apartment is as follows: Two day beds of which one was made up. A corner table between the two beds on which stood a fan, electric clock which had stopped at 4.20 a.m. [but which worked normally when plugged into another socket], and a table model radio. One straight backed chair, four dining room chairs and table. One buffet [table] on which was an electric fan and the two candle sticks. Kitchen equipment as described above. In the dressing room was one chair and a chest of drawers. A mirror over the chest was broken.

Not present in the house, but which was reported as having been present at the time of the fire, was an over stuffed easy chair, end table and lamp. The chair was destroyed by the fire with the exception of the springs. The end table was destroyed *with the exception of two small pieces of the legs.* The legs are the bottom portions of the table and are hardly scorched. The lamp was of a wooden standard which was burned off. The lamp shade was destroyed, but the bulb would still burn and the hard rubber switch was not damaged.

The investigation which followed showed that the authorities were approaching the case from a *criminal* angle. This possibly explains the involvement of the FBI, which some writers have considered to be significant. This level of follow-up is not unusual in SHC cases where it would seem that the only way a body could be consumed so thoroughly is through deliberate outside aid. The obliteration of evidence through fire is often the method used by a criminal – particularly in cases of murder, as we have already seen.

Police were interested in life insurance policies and the provisions made in Mary Reeser's will. Mrs Carpenter had told police that although Mrs Reeser was in the habit of leaving her apartment door open, the screen door was always kept locked. On this occasion the apartment door was ajar, and the screen door *unlocked.* As no mention is made of the other apartment being occupied, one wonders why the screen door was not secured. Was it a simple oversight? Could an opportunist thief have entered the apartment, killed Mrs Reeser, then set her ablaze? Or had Mrs Reeser unlocked the door later that night to let in someone who was known to her?

If criminality was to be a viable scenario, then evidence of fire accelerants would be needed. These would have to be used to ensure the body would burn, destroying evidence of a knife wound or blow to the head. After investigation, the FBI reported: 'An examination showed the presence of no oxidizing chemicals, petroleum hydrocarbons or other volatile fluids, or any chemical substances used to initiate or accelerate combustion.'

A greasy substance was found 'saturating' an unburned section of rug and Mrs Reeser's slipper. This turned out to be human fat. The police report continued:

> The absence of any traces of volatile inflammable fluids does not preclude the possibility that such fluids were used in destroying the body of the deceased. Because of their nature, gasoline, ether, and similar inflammable fluids are consumed ordinarily in the early stages of a fire. Where there has been almost complete combustion, as in this case, it would be most unlikely to find such fluids even though they had been present at the beginning of the fire.

So incinerated was Mrs Reeser that only a few teeth, a (reputedly) 'shrunken skull', a charred liver attached to a piece of backbone, a large bone which appeared to be a hipbone and a left foot in a black satin slipper – completely intact from just above the ankle – remained. In fact, identification of the 'body' by Dr Reeser and Mrs Carpenter was made by the only recognizable remaining part of Mary Reeser; her foot.

Those confronted with the destructive power of a fire which could destroy a living being composed largely of water, yet leave an apartment containing highly inflammable substances relatively untouched, were dumfounded. Of course Mrs Reeser was also well-endowed with fat, and so a good potential candidate for the wick effect. An FBI laboratory report on the case, dated 31 July 1951, said as much, justifying its conclusions as follows. 'Once the body starts to burn there is enough fat and other inflammable substances to permit varying amounts of destruction to take place. Sometimes this destruction by burning will proceed to a degree which results in almost complete combustion of the body.'

The FBI knew 'almost complete combustion' was possible because of other cases they had on their files, 'formerly believed' to be 'spontaneous combustion or attributed to preternatural causes'. The report also had an explanation for the lack of incineration of the apartment generally.

> The absence of any scorching or damage to furniture in the room can only be explained by the fact that heat liberated by the burning body had a tendency to rise and formed a layer of hot air which never came in contact with the furnishings on a lower level. This situation

would have occurred particularly if the fire had smouldered rather than burned freely.

Not everyone was convinced that the explanation was that simple. Dr Wilton Krogman of the University of Pennsylvania, anthropologist and expert on the effects of fire on the human body, was brought in to add his opinion. Dr Krogman's opinions have been used over the decades to bolster the spontaneous, or preternatural combustion scenario. Krogman cited that temperatures of almost 3,000°F would be necessary to destroy a body as completely as Mrs Reeser's. He reportedly said about the Reeser case: 'I regard it as the most amazing thing I have ever seen. As I review it, the short hairs on the back of my neck bristle with vague fear. Were I living in the Middle Ages, I'd mutter something about black magic.'

Various writers have taken Dr Krogman's comments to mean that he was a supporter of SHC as an explanation for this case. Not so, according to senior fireman Tony McMunn. Tony spoke to Krogman during his own researches, and learned that the anthropologist was not a supporter of the hypothesis. His estimate of the temperature required to consume Mrs Reeser's body is also somewhat dependent upon the length of time involved in the incineration. This cannot be known except to within a range of several hours and so the figure quoted by the scientist is open to some dispute.

In addition, it is almost never reported that according to a letter in the November 1985 issue of *Fate* Krogman never personally saw the remains of Mary Reeser. His opinions were based on second-hand observations and presumably photographs but his enquiries only began after she was buried. This letter was from two independent and seemingly excellent research workers Joe Nickell, a former private detective, and John Fischer, an analyst at a Florida crime laboratory. If true it is a point that must temper Krogman's often-quoted comments about the strangeness of Mrs Reeser's allegedly shrunken skull.

This skull was mentioned in an article published in the *St Petersburg Times* on 9 August 1951. The author, Jerry Blizen, referred to 'a skull, shrunken to the size of a cup', without giving the source. This unsubstantiated claim has been repeated uncritically by numerous writers down the decades. A quote from Krogman was used in the May 1964 edition of *True* magazine, where he states: 'Never have I seen a skull so shrunken.'

In the FBI laboratory report, dated 31 July, of the fourteen specimens listed for examination, there is no mention of a skull at all, never mind a shrunken skull. There is listed, however, 'particles of bones found in ashes'.

Nickell and Fischer blame Krogman. He, they claim, 'merely referred to second-hand news accounts and spoke of "a roundish object identified as the head" '. They sought the advice of a forensic anthropologist, David Wolf, who theorized that Mrs Reeser's skull probably burst in the heat. He thought the 'roundish object' could have been a globular lump that can result from the musculature of the neck where it attaches to the base of the skull. This seems feasible as Dr Reeser told us that the 'skull plate' was recovered from the ashes.

At what time had the conflagration occurred? The electric bedside clock had stopped at 4.20 a.m. But why had it stopped? Was this the time when the fire burnt out the electric wiring in that part of the room? Would it have stopped anyway through some other, unrelated malfunction? Possibly not, as it worked fine afterwards, according to Nickell and Fischer. But even this presents a mystery.

When Mrs Carpenter sensed danger just after 5 a.m., she thought there was a smell like an over-heating electric motor. Electricians George Lowe and Harry Garnett examined the electrical system in the apartment to determine if an electrical fault was the cause of the fire.

There was no sign of voltage or amperage overload. Although the switch face plates were melted, the switches themselves were not damaged. There was just one burned-out fuse, and that was to the hot water heater. This was explained by the fact that the conduit to the heater passed directly over the burned spot on the partition, and it was conjectured that the heat had melted the insulation and the cable had shorted out, blowing the fuse.

George Lowe speculated that it would have been possible to have started an electrical fire without blowing fuses by attaching electrified wires to the chair springs. The metal springs would heat up as the current passes through them, forming an electric current, such as found in a kettle. This theory was not taken seriously by the investigating officers. Lowe admitted it would require some experimentation by a knowledgeable person, and insufficient heat would be generated to consume a human being.

Was this vindication of the controversial wick effect? The FBI thought so at the time, and so did Dr Richard Reeser.

July 1991 was the fortieth anniversary of the tragedy. To commemorate the incident, the *St Petersburg Times* published an indepth article. In it, Dr Reeser bemoaned the fact that not one writer, FBI agent or scientific expert, including Dr Krogman, ever asked his opinion on the cause of his mother's incineration. We wanted to set this error to right, and invited Dr Reeser's comments. This is what he said.

> The facts were that my mother was an overweight woman of five foot five, accustomed to taking a night time sedative, in this case, Seconal, and was a cigarette smoker.
>
> After visiting her around 9 p.m., she was dressed in her nightie sitting in a large overstuffed chair with two fans blowing (floor fans). Her turned down bed was about three feet away. She had taken two Seconal capsules and was smoking.
>
> In my opinion (my wife concurs), she fell asleep in this chair, the cigarette fell into the corner of the chair and began smouldering. The draft created by the fans produced a steady and consuming furnace-like fire that ultimately consumed everything. A few chair springs were found besides the skull plate and heel bone of my mother. That's it. That's the way it was. Of course an unusual, to say the least, and spectacular death with an astonishing end.

This factor regarding the floor fans is very interesting. It only emerged a few years ago, and was not previously discussed, as far as we know. Fans are necessary in crematoriums to provide air under pressure to aid incineration. In this comparison, the chair, like the coffin, would provide the added fuel necessary to start the process. The comparison falls short in that cremators are small enclosed chambers with a controlled temperature and air flow – and the first cremation on a cold chamber requires the ignition of gas jets. A smouldering cigarette would seem somewhat inadequate.

There are several things reported by a variety of writers over the years which are inaccurate, or uncertain. For instance, we have already heard that Mrs Carpenter was awoken by a sound similar to the slamming of a door, yet it is often reported that the smell of smoke woke her up. Nickell and Fischer state in an article in *The Fire And Arson Investigator* that the windows in Mary Reeser's apartment were open all night. Yet Assistant Fire Chief Griffith told police officers that when he first entered the apartment he opened windows to allow the smoke to dissipate. How could Griffith have opened windows which were already open, or did he mean he opened *extra* windows?

Nickell and Fischer were repeating what journalist Jerry Blizen wrote in his article published in the *St Petersburg Times* of 9 August 1951. In it, Blizen stated that telegram boy Richard Bruce 'didn't notice any smoke, despite the fact the windows were open'. Where did Blizen obtain this information, particularly as much of the rest of his article was based on a statement issued by Police Chief J.R. Reichert which was derived from the same sources we have had access to? However, Reichert himself, in a private letter to Chief Inspector John Kelly of Philadelphia Police Department, wrote that 'the fire was discovered by the landlady when she observed a large quantity of smoke pouring out the windows of the apartment'. This apparently was not so.

In the 1991 *Time-Life* brochure it is emphatically stated that on the night in question 'there was no lighting'. This was meant to scotch one lead police obtained from an anonymous and badly written postcard (addressed to the 'Cheif of Detectiffs' – sic). This stated simply of Mrs Reeser's demise that 'A ball of fire came through the window and hit her. I seen it happen'. Michael Harrison, in his book *Fire From Heaven*, asserts there *was* lightning in the sky that night. Thunderstorms are in fact a very common phenomenon on the evenings of hot summer days in this part of Florida. More than one in three such days develop them by late afternoon.

There is one fairly obvious likely reason for *Time-Life*'s seemingly inaccurate claim that there was no lightning on the night Mrs Reeser died. This reason is that they give the date of the tragedy as twenty-four hours earlier than it actually was! Their brochure's statement 'on the night of 30 June/1 July there was no lightning ...' may well be true but is hardly relevant to the case and rather misleading.

Mrs Reeser did not like the hot Florida summers. The intense heat was compounded for her by the fact she was overweight. Apart from the floor fans, there were other fans in the apartment. It would make sense for her to leave some windows open for ventilation, except that she was on the ground floor, and they might constitute a security risk. Was this why the apartment door was open? Did she think the screen door was locked?

Ironically, if the windows were open, as Nickell and Fischer believe, this would discredit Stan Ames's theory on the lack of fire damage to surroundings in other human incineration incidents. As we have already seen, Ames's hypothesis needs a sealed room for it to work. However, Nickell and Fischer suppose that the concrete floor of the apartment was instrumental in containing the fire.

There was another item missing in the apartment apart from the armchair, nightie and greater part of Mrs Reeser herself. That was a black rayon house-coat or dressing-gown. In articles published in *The Fire And Arson Investigator*, June 1984, and *The Skeptical Inquirer*, summer 1987, Nickell and Fischer state that Mrs Reeser was wearing her house-coat when she incinerated. This 'fact' has been repeated by previous writers, and seems to stem – again – from the Blizen article. According to the testimonies of Dr Reeser and Pansy Carpenter – the last two people to see her alive – Mrs Reeser was only wearing her nightie.

This seems to make sense. A woman suffering from heat to an extent that floor fans were operated to cool her, would hardly be likely to add to the discomfort by wearing a dressing-gown. What happened to the garment? Perhaps it was worn by Mrs Reeser after all, *but not at the time the witnesses saw her, the time when it has been speculated by most sceptical theorists that she fell asleep and dropped her lighted cigarette onto the chair.*

This is crucial, because the wick theory is only tenable if the body is allowed *hours* of time to smoulder away.

The special police report of Lee and Boyd refer to 'two day beds of which one was made up for a bed'. A 'day bed' is what in Britain we would call a 'bed settee' or sofa-bed. It seems that in Mrs Reeser's apartment one was used as a settee, and the other utilized permanently as a bed. The two painters, in their statements to police, made a very important observation. Clements, who did not enter the apartment, but looked through the open door, said that the bed had the appearance of having been slept in. The other man, Albert Delnet, the first person to explore inside the room, noticed that the bedclothes were turned down, appearing as if someone had slept there.

It is out contention that Mary Reeser did not remain in the chair and fall asleep. Mrs Carpenter passed by outside at just before nine. She noticed that the lights and radio were turned off. Obviously, this suggested to her as it suggests to us that Mrs Reeser had gone to bed.

Can we suppose that she might have risen at some time during the night, donned her house-coat and then gone out into the hallway, unlocked the screen door and stood there a while getting some air? Had she then returned to the apartment, forgetting to re-lock the outside door, and collapsed into the chair where the conflagration – by whatever means – had overtaken her?

Nickell and Fischer state that 'almost twelve hours had elapsed' from the time Mrs Reeser was last seen smoking in her chair, to the moment her ashes were discovered. They cite this to show there was time for the wick effect to take place. But if we accept that the old lady went to bed, and arose 'later', the smouldering theory becomes pure speculation and more difficult to justify. At what time did Mrs Reeser arise? How long would it take for four sleeping tablets to wear off – closer to 4.20 a.m. – when the electric clock apparently stopped working?

In the debris were discovered melted glass and metal fragments. The FBI laboratory report stated that temperatures in the vicinity of 1,000-1,100°F were required to soften the glass. This temperature corresponds to bright red heat.

Was the rest of the room – indeed the building – saved because, as Tony McMunn speculates, SHC-type phenomena produce *radiated* heat as opposed to direct flaming? Anything other than materials in direct contact with the body would not be ignited.

Decorator Albert Delnet thought he was entering another world when he stepped into 1200 Cherry Street that fateful morning. There was very little flame but quite an amount of smoke. In the hottest part of the fire there were flames licking up through the springs of the chair. All that remained of Mrs Reeser was a red smouldering mass.

Those who postulate a paranormal explanation for spontaneous human combustion, will note the depressed state of Mary Reeser immediately priory to her death. A number of similar victims have either felt ill, or suffered mental depression. Some suggest it is as if they unconsciously *will* themselves to burn. Would a rapid incineration explain the absence of any odour of burning human flesh, a smell very noticeable in normal fire deaths?

Nickell and Fischer refer to crime writer W.S. Allen. He wrote a piece for the December 1951 edition of *True Detective* magazine in which he alleges that a 'faint smell of grease' was present when the room was first entered. Almost certainly this was melted fat from Mrs Reeser's body. But where did Allen obtain his information? In his letter to Chief Inspector John Kelly, St Petersburg Chief of Police, J.R. Reichert remarks on 'the absence of odor of burning human flesh'.

Whatever the truth about this complex case, the verdict of accidental death glossed over a web of cracks and crevices.

In another sad twist of fate, the telegram delivered by Richard Bruce that morning contained a message from friends living in Columbia. They had at last been successful in finding an apartment for the doctor's widow.

6   A Fireman's Story

In our attempts to secure the views of those – literally – in the firing line of the SHC debate, we solicited many opinions. Often members of the fire service were reluctant to comment. Sometimes they had very definite ideas but were wary of repercussions. We have already met some officers who were prepared to speak out, and here we present an interview with one man with some years' experience in a relatively senior post. He not only has a firm viewpoint on SHC but has actually carried out some personal research.

Although he was recommended to us by the divisional officer of his brigade – who reported that he is considered 'our expert on the subject of spontaneous human combustion' – the man ultimately insisted that he not be identified, indeed that we not even name the location of his department.

Consequently, we have adopted the pseudonym of 'Terence Williamson' and note only that he works for a fire brigade somewhere in northern Britain. The reasons for his caution became apparent during our discussion. We asked Terence why he was interested in the subject.

> What really started me on the trail of this mystery was an article from a Scottish brigade officer who was attempting to predict where such events might happen next. I found this fascinating and it led me into deep research. But at the end of the day all I can say is that I am left with an open mind.

Why was this – was the evidence contradictory?

> Well, scientists quote the so-called 'candle' or 'wick' theory; that human fat will melt down and burn slowly. This might happen, but there are certain parts of the body that are very dense – such as the ball and socket joint. During cremation these remain and have to be ground down before the ashes are presented. Yet in SHC cases these are completely degraded to ash whilst softer tissue areas may remain. The amount of heat required to degrade these bones would be so intense that surrounding areas should ignite.

How often did potential cases of SHC occur?

The majority of them never come to public notice because coroners have a tendency to put all mystery fire deaths down to causes like asphyxiation merely as a means of expediency. Once upon a time they had the view that all such victims were gin-sodden and it was the alcohol that burned. Obviously that just does not bear weight in the light of modern scientific evidence. A more recent attempt to understand the process has been by proposing electrolysis of the water within the body producing gases that can ignite. From my experience that does not work either. So coroners are in a fix, really. They prefer to come up with any rational answer that avoids the need to speculate about things like SHC.

Did Terence have a personal view of what might be happening in cases of possible or alleged SHC?

Some years ago the Australians attempted to develop an oven that would burn very low grade coal extracted from open cast mines. A German company did produce drawings in an effort to design it. The concept had originated in World War Two as part of the Nazi's 'final solution'. They had then needed to destroy bodies as completely as they could and wanted to use the energy generated to create electricity. An enormous amount of thought and effort went into this research and the Australian development of it, but it proved very very difficult to entirely destroy a human body. To produce something that can both make and then retain such temperatures is even harder to achieve, as they are extremely high. Yet in cases of SHC there always seem to be body extremities left. Why? I think that however hard you try to explain it all away problems still remain if you are being honest.

So why was there such antipathy towards the subject within the fire service?

The majority of people in the service tend to think SHC is a bit of a joke. They really do not know a lot about it. It is certainly not researched much within the brigade. I found that out very early on.

When I give lectures on the subject – as I have from time to time – I see the seeds of doubt in people's eyes. Officers will say to me that up until that moment they had never taken the subject seriously. Now they are left in a quandary, unsure whether there really might not be something going on. Once they see the facts and hear the evidence presented to them in an unbiased way it can change a lot of people's minds. Too often when the media talk about it they do so either in supernatural terms – which is off-putting to serious-minded people. Or else they are ultra critical and err on the side of caution in their bias. I think the BBC TV presentation [Q.E.D.] of the subject did that. It was good in so far as it went, but it was rather one-sided. We need more objective appraisals that show the positive and the negative side to the question.

Is the same problem faced by coroner's departments?

Basically, I think, most coroners like to pigeonhole everything. They like to fit cases into square boxes. It is their job to an extent I suppose, but they seem to *need* to come up with an explanation that fits neatly. They don't want ends dangling. So when you come across a situation like you often find with SHC, it is a real dilemma – they simply cannot handle it. I guess when you need an answer and there is no answer that fits you have to call it something. If you label it anything understandable – rather than SHC – then it rids the problem. Having said that, I want to make clear that very often this is justified, in my view.

The majority of cases where SHC is suggested are no such thing. These really *are* mundane. For instance where someone has been smoking in bed or the electric blanket was faulty – or else someone had a heart attack and keeled over into the fire grate. There is very often evidence pointing to something of this sort and as none of us like loose ends when a death is involved, we all quite rightly try to tie them together and most times that is perfectly justifiable.

We wondered if he had ever faced such a case himself in his work and if he would estimate how common he thought possible SHC incidents might be? 'Nobody knows how common they are because the cases that may be possibilities are always written off as something else. The only way you would ever find out is to go through the FDR 1s at the Home Office. But I doubt you will be allowed.'

'FDR 1s' are fatal death reports. All such incidents from fires are on record.

Personally, I have never come across a clear-cut case in my area. I would estimate there may just be one or two a year per region, possibly up to a hundred for the country. But that is probably little better than a guess. Nobody knows the truth because it is all being obscured and nobody with access to the evidence is actually researching the matter. Those who are researching the matter cannot get access to the evidence.

I dare not even let you give my name or my brigade. If you talk about such matters in some places it can be detrimental to your career. I remember once I had a case where there was a fire in a kitchen. It seemed to start in a make-up drawer but there was no apparent cause. No flammable materials were present. It was weird. I suggested that maybe this was an example of spontaneous combustion and the ADA in charge of the area put me firmly in my place – 'You are *not* putting that on a report of one of my cases!'

Terence Williamson also expressed a view on the lack of animal combustions, and pointed out a problem in this regard.

If a cat bursts into flames while you are sitting next to it, in front of the TV, then of course you would *know*. However, if it happened when no humans were around, what then? Animals do tend to go missing. So do any of them become SHC victims? We also get cases from time to time where animals have been burned. Farmers claim they were struck by lightning – which in many cases is probably true. However, they do not have to show the remains and you do not have to carry out a post-mortem on a sheep or cow. Can you imagine what insurance companies would say if the farmer suggested SHC as cause of death? No – reasonably enough, farmers need the insurance compensation, so the death will probably always be attributed to a lightning strike. It's the easiest way.

In conclusion, we asked Williamson to summarize how he saw his position as an experienced fire-officer who is familiar with the evidence for and against SHC.

I would like to be able to say to you in all honestly that yes – SHC definitely exists, because I have seen it. That my brigade has records of such events. But that would be untrue. It could well have happened. Indeed I suspect it probably has. But, if so, then chances are that you or I would not be privy to the facts. You, because you have no 'need to know', and I because I was not by chance present at the incident. Of course, very probably it would then have been put down to some other cause and few of us would subsequently be any the wiser.

So, in my view, I would argue that it is impossible to say it does *not* happen. Indeed I might go so far as to say it is *dangerous* to presume that. Too many people seem happy to shut their eyes to the possibility. Yet it obviously needs more objective investigation. Frankly, whether it is proven or disproven it is all the same and all to the good. We just really ought to try to establish which is the correct evaluation of the facts.

However, if you push me [we did] then I would have to say that I am personally convinced that something is happening for which we presently have no understanding. We tend to think we know so much about the world but we are merely scratching the surface. When you think how a few solar flares millions of miles away can completely disrupt all our communications and we cannot do a thing about it, then you see we still have much to learn.

I suspect that maybe microwaves have something to do with the cause of SHC. But I retain an open mind. I honestly do not know the explanation. But I feel there may well be something going on which does still need an explanation. Indeed, my experience is that a lot of foremen share this view but most of them dare not say so in public.

Of the firemen who were prepared to speak out in public, one of them was Jack Stacey. He was David Niven's stand-in in the 1944 film, *The Way Ahead*. A full-time fireman, now retired, Jack was confronted by the bizarre one September dawn in 1967. He told his story for the first time on the BBC2 *Newsnight* programme, transmitted in January 1986.

Jack had been called to a fire at a derelict house, but when he arrived there were no signs of burning. On the stairs in the well-ventilated building, he found the body of a vagrant. Flames were coming from his stomach. 'There was a slit about four inches long in the abdomen. The flame was coming through there at force, like a blow lamp. It was quite warm, because it was charring the wood beneath the body.'

It was suggested to Jack that perhaps it was alcohol that was burning. After investigation, it appeared that the man had wandered in looking for somewhere to sleep. He had sat down at the foot of the stairs, where the conflagration had begun. Jack would not speculate on exactly what this might be.

The cause of death was asphyxia, due to the inhalation of fire fumes. This meant the victim was alive when his body began combusting. The actual cause of the fire was deemed 'unknown'. There was no gas in the building or electricity, and no matches, spent or otherwise, were found. Despite this, Douglas Leitch, Senior Divisional Officer of Strathclyde Fire Brigade, thought he had an explanation.

Mr Leitch speculated in an article published in the August 1986 edition of the magazine *Fire*, that in such cases, the greasy deposits on a tramp's clothing would encourage an accidental fire to burn. Once the abdomen was lit, it would create a slit-like wound, which might give the impression the flames were coming from within. However, no source of ignition was found in this case. As it was proven the victim was alive at the start of his incineration, if it was an accident, one wonders why he did not put the flame out?

Jack Stacey was an actual eye-witness to the phenomenon, and he is certain of what he saw, as he told journalist Steven Bradshaw. 'There's no doubt whatsoever that the fire began inside that body. That's the only place it could have begun.'

7   A Blazing Row

If we are to establish whether there is such a thing as SHC it will only be through careful study of contentious cases. But, as we have discovered, that is easier said than done.

Rarely are they presented as candidates for a taboo subject like SHC by official bodies. If by chance they are, the facts tend to get sensationalized or become media trivia. Other complicating factors of human tragedy and grieving relatives can intervene. The last thing they wish is to have the death of their loved ones turned into a supernatural side-show. As a result we are left attempting to piece together case histories often from fragments and with little assistance from the authorities. They much prefer that the spectre of SHC be pushed as far away as possible.

A baffling case occurred on 3 August 1978 in north-west England. Here are the facts. Judge for yourself what took place.

The scene was a block of flats at Harpurhey, a relatively poor district of north Manchester. As if to mock the idea of spontaneous combustion and the popular myth that older victims are most often claimed by its fiery clutches, the location was actually named Elderburn Drive.

Neighbours were alerted by a terrible commotion – screams that at first seemed like children playing, but which turned into something almost unearthly. One man insisted they did not sound human. Many people rushed out to see what was going on, and at least two were to wish they had chosen not to do so.

Victor Cunnington was one of the first to respond. He described the noise as 'agonizing' and the reason was quickly apparent. A middle-aged West Indian man ran out of one of the flats into the corridor, a mass of flame from head to toe. He screamed as he fled then collapsed to the floor.

According to one woman, the blazing man banged on the door of Mrs Betty Whiteside, directly opposite, screaming 'Help me! Help me!' Later the wooden door was found to be scorched black where the man's flaming hands had beaten repeatedly against it.

A group of stunned residents reacted swiftly. Ironically, one of them was named Patrick Furey. Furey was a nurses' officer and knew how to respond. He swiftly got hold of a rug and attempted to stifle the flames. Unfortunately he failed to get them under control. They would not go out. One brave man ripped off the victim's blazing trousers, oblivious for the moment to the serious burns this was causing to his own hands. Eventually someone had the presence of mind to call for help; although the burning man was now in a terrible state.

Then, horror on horror, emerging from the flat, running and screaming, came another human fireball – this time a woman!

Similar attempts were made to rescue her, but within minutes it was all over. An ambulance and the fire brigade arrived. But it left its legacy on the local inhabitants. One rescuer had to receive hospital treatment for burns to his hands. A woman fainted and needed attention. Another man was felled by the shock and also had to enter hospital for treatment. Beyond the injuries, the trauma and the horror, remained a real puzzle.

The flat itself was not apparently consumed by fire – only the two people. Charred bits of clothing littered the hallway between the second floor tenancies – pieces which had obviously fallen off as the victims ran into the open air, already ablaze. Once the flames were quenched the fire service had little work to do, except, of course, try to figure out what had happened.

As fire and police officers arrived on the scene they were confused. They had expected to see the interior of the flat badly damaged by flames. But there was no damage at all. So far as could be ascertained the tenement had *not* been affected in any way. The man and the woman had been the sole source of the inferno.

It transpired that the man – who was sadly dead before he could receive medical attention – was a 50-year-old railway worker called Edward Mason.* He had lived in the flat for several years and was married although his wife had apparently returned home to Jamaica some time before.

The woman – according to neighbours – was a frequent visitor to Mr Mason. She was one year younger and came from a nearby district. Her condition was very serious, with terrible injuries, but she had survived and was despatched immediately to the burns unit at Withington Hospital where she was placed on the critical list. Meanwhile, investigators were endeavouring to resolve the mystery.

Inside the flat there was no obvious source of ignition. A tin of inflammable liquid, said to be probably lighter fluid, was found, but there was no immediate indication it had been used to start the conflagration. A few smears of blood were found on the wall. These appeared to originate from the woman, who aside from her burns, had a small head wound. Whether this had preceded the fire or occurred when she banged her head on the wall in a blind panic to escape the room and reach help, was impossible to say. Detectives were sent to Withington hospital to take up vigil by her bedside, in the hope that she might be able to tell them the cause of the tragedy.

Enquiries continued among the neighbours, and these soon revealed that for some time before the terrible screams, what sounded like an argument had been heard. Voices were raised in anger, assumed to be those of the couple.

From all of this it was possible to piece together a scenario of what *might* have happened. Could the couple have argued and in the mêlée doused one another in lighter fluid, then set one another alight?

Of course, all this was pure speculation. There was no evidence to support the idea. The only serious hope of unravelling the issue lay with the woman, unconscious in a bed at Withington hospital. Unfortunately, this was never to be fulfilled. The following day the woman succumbed to her injuries and died. She did not regain consciousness and so said nothing to explain what had taken place.

The police were left baffled and guessing. They felt reasonably certain from the evidence of the neighbours that nobody else was involved. Their enquiries also led to no suggestion of some sort of horrible joint suicide arrangement. It all appeared most mysterious, unresolved and probably unresolvable.

To postulate SHC in this case is, of course, an option. One can easily play games with the facts and highlight the almost mockingly ironic names and coincidences. Apart from the location – Elderburn Drive, the nurse's name, Furey, has significance. 'Furies' are mythological demons who bring avenging death through fire and other means. In the current idiom, the word means 'violent argument' – a double irony.

Is it reasonable to speculate that the real cause of the tragedy was SHC? In truth it is an idea as vague as any explanation for this case. One should, we presume, pursue the most rational solution, but incidents like the above are blatantly irrational. With the facts at your disposal what would you decide? It is out of cases like this that the mystery of spontaneous combustion has developed. Indeed, in *Fire from Heaven*, Michael Harrison presents a case with interesting similarities.

This event took place on 18 September 1952 near Gretna, Louisiana, USA. The victim was a 46-year-old man called Glen Denney, owner of a successful business. Denney was apparently depressed at the time, when the fire department were called to his apartment by a suspicious neighbour. They had to break down the door to get in and found Mr Denney on the floor, a mass of flames. These were smothered by a quick-acting fire-officer with a blanket, although the victim was beyond rescue.

The room itself was virtually untouched by flame, although a pool of blood was found on the floor of another room. The fire-officer was quoted as saying he smelled nothing odd upon entry into the building, but speculated that the man could have been doused in some form of oil to burn as fiercely as he did.

It was confirmed that the fire had started whilst the man was still alive (carbon in his lungs and trachea could only have been inhaled from the flames). After much effort the typically reluctant coroner admitted in a terse statement to an enquiring researcher that in his view Mr Denney had killed himself. He had supposedly slit his wrists, then poured a can of kerosene over his body and struck a light.

One might have thought it more probable that the man would have poured the fuel over himself, got rid of the can (as it was not allegedly in evidence when firemen arrived – according to Harrison), then slit his wrists. Disposing of the evidence after cutting himself would surely have left a trail of blood from the wound. But why bother getting rid of the can anyway? And why was there no evidence of spilled kerosene?

In the end the circumstances of this Louisiana death are very similar to those at Harpurhey twenty-six years later; although there appears to have been no suggestion that either the man or the woman in Manchester had any reason to contemplate suicide – so the connections presumably end there.

The point we wish to make is that faced with the facts on offer in the Louisiana case Harrison apparently endorsed the views of the original investigator, Otto Burma, and the paranormal researcher, Vincent Gaddis. The latter published the case in *Fate* magazine in 1953. Harrison's book states firmly: 'No kerosene burned Mr Denney up ...' (p.89) The author goes on to suggest an idea that an attempt at suicide set up stresses in the victims 'etheric body' which had then unleashed SHC as some form of 'punishment'.

This may be valid speculation, but it seems unwise to conclude so much from so little. We need to probe the background of cases such as these as carefully as we can, although this is often all but prevented by bureaucracy. Only in this way can we hope to try to either demonstrate their fallibility as proof of some mysterious phenomenon or establish a more mundane cause.

Our efforts to explore the Harpurhey case took us initially to the coroner's office for the city of Manchester. Suspicion was immediately displayed by the person we initially spoke to. What 'need to know' did we have? Did we really expect to see any of their records on this matter? Were we not aware they were confidential?

Of course, we did understand all of these things. We put a simple request for the date when the inquest was held, commenting; 'surely this was not a secret?' In reply, we were told coolly 'well, it may well be.' This was not information at their disposal in any case. It would only be available through the central archives in Manchester. 'However,' we were dutifully informed, 'I am not sure I am at liberty to even give you their telephone number. I am not convinced you have a "need to know".'

In a nation without freedom of information laws this is a circumstance we faced quite often in our search for knowledge and official documentation. Fortunately, the woman in question, after due consideration, did give us the number of the archives. Our Kafkaesque journey through the dark corridors of officialdom could begin again.

After speaking with two more suspicious people who were equally unpersuaded they should help in our request, a little cajoling and discussion at least put us onto a records officer who seemed willing to listen. 'Why wouldn't the coroner's office assist you?' he asked. We explained their claim that they had no access to records on a 13-year-old case, but his department did have them. 'Oh – I thought they had their own records system and could have easily provided that information,' he mused. 'However, I can look it up for you. It will take some hours, and you will not be able to read the file, naturally.' Naturally. We explained that we appreciated his efforts, but would be grateful for any assistance he might provide. Specifically we wanted the date when the inquest was held.

In fact, the threat of several hours delay was not fulfilled. The call came back within the hour, prefaced with the words; 'This is all I can tell you.' We were informed that the inquest on the two people who had died in the fire at the Harpurhey flat was concluded on 24 August 1978. This is just twenty days after the second death – remarkably fast and suggesting little, if any, investigation into the circumstances of the tragedy. In any case the inquest reached an open verdict. It was officially decided that the cause of this double fire death was – and so presumably will continue to remain – a complete mystery.

We spent a day at the location where the incident had occurred. The chill winds and grey October skies some thirteen years later revealed an incongruous landscape of decaying tower blocks, overgrown greenery littered with the detritus of a careless civilization, and newly-built modern housing.

We wandered for some time seeking Elderburn Drive until we

finally realized that our cartographic skills were not deceptive. The green mound of grass, weeds and discarded bricks that swept before us was all that remained of the ill-fated tower block.

We entered into discussions with local residents at an old people's home, then moved on to a pub nearby. Here we found several people who remembered the incident. 'Oh yes – they threw petrol at one another, didn't they?' was one story we heard. Despite interrogation it became clear this was a rumour that had infested the area after the events. Nobody had any actual evidence to support the possibility that such a thing was true.

We discovered that the white flats – which were less than twenty years old when the tragedy occurred – had been hated by the locals. As with many buildings designed by planners who did not have to live in them, they were from an era when Manchester built high and crammed as many people into as small a space as possible. It seemed a good idea at the time, but the negative effects were foreseen by few and this area was only one of many estates around British cities that came to attract a fearful reputation. 'Legoland' – the Harpurhey residents termed it. Legoland had fallen to the bull dozers in 1989.

Another attempt to delve into this case took us on a merry-go-round of the local newspapers in the area. We knew that the *Manchester Evening News* had reported the story on their front page, but after twenty-four hours they had seemingly let it rest. At least, there was no account that we could trace of the post mortem on the victims, the police investigation or the inquest.

After many fruitless calls we finally spoke with David Edwards at the *Middleton and Blackley Guardian*. He was most intrigued by our story and felt sure they would have something to offer on such a major happening on their own patch. He checked the files by names and dates, for the incident, the post mortems, the inquests – everything – but there was nothing at all.

After consulting the weekly issues of the paper across all the relevant period it was soon apparent that a case of this magnitude in their small coverage zone, and which, one presumes, they could hardly have missed, had provoked not a mention.

David Edwards was clearly bemused. He told us: 'This is really very odd. We were very meticulous at the time. We covered every little chip pan fire that took place in the area but there is absolutely nothing about this. It did not even make a small paragraph!'

So surprised was he that he offered to devote some of his time to chasing up the former editor, now retired, and see if there was a reason why the paper might have chosen to leave the story out.

Some time later we checked back with the journalist. He told us;

'The editor was pretty vague, to be honest. He said he couldn't remember anything about it at all. I must admit you have got me really fascinated by this one. I just don't understand why we never reported it.'

Neither do we. We finally spoke to the coroner, who was quite happy to answer our questions. Leonard Gorodkin is H.M. Coroner for Manchester, and presided over the Harpurhey case. Apparently, the couple were having an affair. He saw no mystery. 'Petrol had been poured, more over the man than the woman, I think. At least both had inflammable material on them.'

In that case, why was an open verdict brought about? 'Because we could not tell if it was murder or suicide.'

Was lighter fluid the cause? 'No. I doubt very much that these injuries could be caused by lighter fluid.'

If it was petrol, then, or some similar inflammable liquid, were any traces found, on the victims or in the flat? 'Not as far as we were aware.'

How then were you able to conclude that petrol had been used? 'Because the distribution of the burns were consistent with inflammable liquid poured from the head downwards.'

There seem to be several problems with this supposition. Whether suicide or murder, petrol poured over someone in a furnished flat cannot fail to cause spillages over carpet, chairs etc. The result would be a conflagration of the occupants *and* the flat. No such thing occurred. And like the case of Glen Denney, the investigation could not find a container which had held the alleged substance.

8 A Rather Unusual Death

On the cold winter's afternoon of 6 January 1980, a little Welsh mining town near Ebbw Vale became struck by the tragedy associated with SHC. Experienced police officers who had attended many violent deaths stood open-mouthed and silent in the face of the terrible scenes spread before them. Rational, intelligent investigators were perplexed – even frightened – by the end result of what one of them likened to Dante's *Inferno*.

It was the sheer inexplicability of what had taken place that disturbed these hardened men. What they saw had – for some at least – no obvious explanation. Yet equally obvious was that it was a reality. The proof was right in front of their eyes.

John Heymer, now retired after twenty-five years as a scene of crime officer with the Gwent police, was called to the house because an unexplained fire had been reported. Nobody prepared him for what he was about to be confronted with. It was a 'rather unusual death by fire', he was coolly advised by one policeman. Words that were to prove a dramatic understatement.

As he entered the house, set in a council estate atop a little hill, he noticed first the pleasant warmth. No central heating seemed to be operating but the aftermath of the fire was still tangible in the air. He was shown into the living-room to see the 'body'. But there was no body – just a nightmare pile of ash and bone.

The ash was heaped with obscene neatness beside the undisturbed fire grate, and scattered in a small space on the carpet. Leg bones were calcified. Two human feet lay prone at the end, pointing away from the grating. The ends of the trousers were completely intact. There were undamaged socks on the gruesome remains of the feet. Further away still from the fire, out of place and presumably having rolled there, was a blackened skull without any trace of skin.

The fire had been astonishingly local. An armchair was close by. The victim had apparently sat in this. Whilst it showed signs of burning where it had been in contact with the man, the rest of it was unaffected. Less than a metre away was a settee. Despite the incredible heat that had consumed the victim's body this was fully intact. Loose covers were cast on top – highly inflammable in normal circumstances, but these were not even scorched. The carpet beneath the human remains were burnt, yet just centimetres beyond the heap of ash it was hardly singed. Below the carpet the floor was covered in plastic tiles. Even those situated directly underneath the remains were untouched by fire. The TV set across the room was still working, showing no more than a few warps in the plastic knobs. It was amazing.

Yet there was no doubting the terrific temperatures the room must have been subjected to. The walls were like a furnace that was cooling down, casting a sickly orange radiance. Thick black soot coated surfaces in the room. The plastic lampshades was melted but the glass bulb was covered in an orange shell of something sticky and indescribable.

The victim was a 73-year-old widower. We shall use the pseudonym Bert Jones* to protect his family from more suffering. They knew something was wrong when he failed to arrive early for Sunday lunch with his two married daughters. The sons-in-law went round to see what was wrong, got no answer from the front door and were forced to break in. They found the living-room sealed off with draught excluders and full of smoke that billowed into clouds as air now rushed in through the opened door.

Then they saw the pile of ash and struggled to take in the sheer incomprehensibility of what must have taken place.

A forensic team was called to the house in an attempt to establish what might have happened. John Heymer had read of spontaneous human combustion cases, but had never seen it first-hand. However, he had attended terrible fires in which the victims had been trapped within very high temperatures for some length of time. None had ended up destroyed in the way Mr Jones had been. Heymer felt obliged to moot the idea of SHC to the scientific team who arrived, but they gave incredulous smiles and insisted there was no mystery here. This fire – like all other cases of supposed SHC – would turn out to have an explanation. They would find it.

There was some burnt fibrous tissue on the front of the fire grating, Heymer was later to note in a paper he sent for publication in *New Scientist*. The expectation of the investigation team was that this would turn out to be human skin and that would fit their developing theory. This suggested that Mr Jones had fallen head first into a lit fire, struck his head on the grating and died as he lay there blazing.

However, there were problems with this hypothesis. There was no hint that the ashes within the grate had been disturbed. Also the fire damage to the chair itself suggested that it had come from contact with the burning man, begging the question: had he actually got up from the grate ablaze and, incredibly, sat back in the armchair to die?

The sticky orange substance on the light bulb was identified. This *was* undoubtedly human flesh that had been turned into vapour by the extraordinary heat levels.

In our efforts to evaluate this case we attempted to talk to the Gwent country police station involved. Our initial polite request for an interview with an officer who had been called to the scene was met with a suggestion that we adopt the standard policy where lawyers interview police officers. Part of this requirement was that we hand over a moderate sum of money to the police in payment. We were told this was normal practice whenever solicitors interviewed police spokespeople about non-criminal matters.

Our budget for this book did not allow us this luxury and so we pointed out to the Gwent station that we had for many years worked with police forces in the UK objectively probing all sorts of strange phenomena, and never before been asked to pay for interviews. In this instance a brief interview with a relevant officer was all that we required.

Some time later, on 11 October 1991, Sergeant Rodway from the station telephoned to apologize for the misunderstanding which had begun whilst he was away on leave. He accepted that his station may have been 'a little bit over officious', and he would now try to arrange an interview and bend the rules given the circumstances. We were very grateful to him for this and, true to his word, on 4 November 1991 we were able to interview one of those at the scene, Police Officer – now Sergeant – Russell. We asked if he recollected the case. 'Yes, I do remember it vividly,' Russell began. 'It is one of those incidents that when you first go to the scene you know it is not going to be as straightforward as it at first appears.'

Sergeant Russell confirmed the basic facts. Mr Jones was last seen alive at 6 a.m. on the previous night. His remains had been found by relatives at 9 a.m. and the police were called in straightaway.

> I was one of the first two officers to arrive on the scene. That would be at about 9.30 a.m. I was immediately struck by what I saw. The images were terrible. All I can say to describe it is that the man died like he was a candle. He was burnt from the head down with only the bottom of his legs visible. They were intact. The rest of him was ash. I had never seen anything like it before.

Sergeant Russell pointed out that John Heymer did not arrive until some time later. 'His job was really to take the photographs of the scene.' However, Russell and several others – relatives and police officers – stood about for some time, dumbstruck.

> There were a few of us in the room that morning, vying suggestions. The thing you are interested in – spontaneous combustion – that was certainly one that came up. But in truth, none of us could understand what had happened. Then the forensic science team arrived. They heard us talk about spontaneous combustion and they would have none of it. They told us it was not possible.
>
> The forensics officers did find some hairs on the fireplace grating, and in their 'wisdom' assumed them to be human. This affected their judgement of the case. However, in the end they did not turn out to be human hairs.

In fact Heymer alleges they were of bovine origin. We wondered how Sergeant Russell reacted to the eventual conclusions that were to be officially recorded about the man's death. 'Well there were other problems. The damage to the room was minimal. Why didn't it burn far more, given the heat needed to destroy the man's body?'

We suggested the idea that a sealed room may have been a factor, as discussed on the *Q.E.D.* programme, limiting the spread of the fire. Russell had evidently considered this.

> Frankly, it did not ring true to me as there was just no significant damage at all to the room when I got there. However, my senior officers weighed the evidence and dismissed from consideration any other suggestion. They took the view that it was a simple case and any other possibility might raise awkward questions.

As he accepted, it was a very difficult situation for the police. They had to be careful not to adopt wild theories or phenomena for which there was no scientific consensus. The preference for the easiest option was also motivated by the desire not to put the bereaved family through more unnecessary suffering. It is easy to understand why the SHC option, here as often in the past, was rapidly and officially frowned upon. As for his personal opinion, Sergeant Russell was clearly still affected by the memory of that winter's morning tragedy. 'Until my dying day nobody will ever convince me that it was a straight forward accidental death. There was something unexplained about it and we may never know what happened.'

The inquest followed just a month later. Officer Russell was not called. A CID detective who was present agreed that he was surprised to find so little damage in the room given the terrible state of the body. Pathologist, Dr J. Andrews, noted that Mr Jones had inhaled deadly carbon monoxide fumes from the fire as well as being consumed by the flames. Therefore, as we have discovered with so many victims, Mr Jones had been breathing after he had begun incinerating.

A neighbour told the inquest that he had seen Albert Jones sitting beside the fire on the previous evening. This reaffirmed the official view on his demise. Taken all together it led to the conclusion, reached by coroner Colonel Kenneth Treasure, that the man had probably been set alight whilst in his chair, and had subsequently fallen forward, struck the fire grate and died on the floor. This seems to be a very plausible solution – as indeed do so many at first sight in such cases. The verdict of accidental death may well be true and appears justifiable under the circumstances. But, of course, niggling difficulties remain.

Just how did the fantastic temperatures needed to incinerate Mr Jones's body form under the conditions found within this closed room? Why was the ash in the grate undisturbed? Did this mean, as the coroner implied, that the fire was *not* the source of ignition? Is this why the very limited fire damage to the room was more consistent with Mr Jones himself being the source of the fire, causing only items in direct contact with his body to burn?

Paranormal researcher Robert Rickard is editor of the journal *Fortean Times*. His interest in SHC cases led to an attempt to persuade coroner Kenneth Treasure to release the inquest papers and post mortem report. Despite the fact that the case was a matter of public record and local journalists took notes at the inquest, Rickard was to be denied access to the files. He was told by the coroner: 'I regret I do not feel able to give you the information you ask for as you do not appear to be an 'interested party' within the meaning of the appropriate regulations.' As we have discovered, the interpretation of these 'regulations' is often down to individual coroners.

John Heymer proposed his own possible theory that might explain the death of Bert Jones. He felt certain that the generated heat must have come from within the body and reminded us that human beings are between 70% and 80% water. What if this could spontaneously break down into the gases which combine to form water molecules; that is, hydrogen and oxygen? Hydrogen burns extremely well – and with a blue flame. Oxygen might catalyse the reaction. The spark – he suggested – could come from a build-up of static electricity within the body.

This is, of course, just another theory to try to account for a phenomenon still not even proven to exist. John Heymer recognized that, and it was received by readers of *New Scientist* with some caution.

Dr David Halliday, attached to the Fire Investigation Unit of the Metropolitan Police, was adamant that; 'all cases investigated by this unit have been resolved to the satisfaction of the courts without recourse to the "excuse" of "spontaneous" human combustion.'

He further indicated that in his experience obese people were often involved, providing a great deal of fat to burn. Also there were frequently long delays before the fire was discovered, allowing much time for near-total consumption to take place. That may have been true in this case.

An even stranger comment was offered by Sidney Alford, who was termed an 'explosives engineering consultant' from Wiltshire. He suggested that the fact that elderly people were often victims of SHC might tie in with a tendency of theirs to use liquid paraffin as a means of relief from constipation. This is indeed a practice adopted by certain people of an older generation who are known to us, but is it really so dangerous?

Alford spoke of reactions that might occur within the gut owing to the presence of such inflammable chemicals and mooted the idea that eating eggs might be another factor! These could generate gases such as methane which would further fuel the reaction. He termed such a process the 'dreaded phosphinic fart'! As evidence he was able to cite a case where a body was shown to display temperatures within the gut of 43°C some hours *after* death, owing to the chemical processes still occurring within the stomach.

Finally, Dr Dougal Drysdale from the Unit of Safety Engineering at the University of Edinburgh wanted to make clear that SHC was *not* receiving the kind of serious study within science he felt that it required. He was not convinced by Heymer's electrolysis of water arguments but proposed that tests using human fat wrapped in clothing so as to act as a wick could be carried out and may answer the question of the enormous and very localized temperatures apparent within such cases. These might, he felt, lay 'the ghost of spontaneous human combustion' once and for all.

As we have seen, the wick effect was to be demonstrated several years later by the BBC science programme *Q.E.D.* Far from explaining the mystery, it just lead to more controversy.

As a consequence the case of Mr Jones near Ebbw Vale remains typically frustrating. Something terrible occurred. Officially there is a rational explanation, but some (notably John Heymer and apparently Sergeant Russell) are not convinced by it. What is perhaps more worrying still is that, as in so many cases where SHC is never even considered, it should have been a candidate. It may never be proven. Ultimately it may prove wrong. But it deserves a hearing.

Unsurprisingly, John Heymer was another person *not* to be called to give evidence at the inquest on Bert Jones.

We have spoken with him on several occasions. At first he was reluctant to talk because he was engaged in his own research into SHC, but once we touched upon the common ground of our mutual concerns about the BBC television documentary in the *Q.E.D.* series, he opened up.

> I am not one to accept things at face value, but at least I do not have a career to worry about. Most of the officers who become involved in a case of possible SHC are career minded and dare not get mixed up in something as esoteric as that because it might jeopardize their chances. However, I do know one fire officer who went on TV once. On air he argued that a case he was associated with was probably not SHC. Since the programme screened he has changed his stance and is now willing to think about the option. He told me that he could not say so in public at the time for fear of the reaction that he might receive and what it would do to him.

This was pretty much the response we were finding from fire stations and coroner's offices all over the country. It was no surprise to hear it from a former senior police expert as well. But did he feel that in cases like that of Bert Jones the phenomenon of SHC had to be the answer?

> I don't say it was SHC as such. But what I do say is that having seen a body reduced to ash on a foam backed carpet with plastic tiles that do not melt, and with the carpet burnt only in the shape of the body – indeed when the carpet is removed you could not even tell where the body had been – then in those circumstances there has to be something strange going on.

But by strange did he mean paranormal?

> The assumption seems to be that the fire comes from the abdomen of the victim. I spoke with a pathologist who had passed off one case as merely a carelessly dropped cigarette. Afterwards he told me he dealt with a dozen or so cases a year which he interpreted in a similar way.
> This man would have nothing to do with SHC, but he agreed that in a dozen cases a year it was the abdominal area of the victim that had been destroyed. In such cases the torso burns away leaving the extremities. Whatever else it is that is not a normal situation!

John Heymer was understandably cautious about discussing the data in any detail. He explained that he had taken years to accumulate extensive information on five cases and intended to write full accounts for the journal *Fortean Times*. He was concerned about the number of paranormal researchers who had attached themselves to the phenomenon without any background or experience and who were simply interested in using it as a vehicle to propound their own exotic theories. He felt what was needed was an *objective* debate of the facts. In conclusion he told us:

> I do not know what is happening. But I do know that in every single case of apparent or alleged SHC that I have examined the pathologist who studied the body judged that the victim was alive when he was burning. This is very significant as it tends to dispose of one of the most common explanations we see offered. That these victims have been near a fire, suffered a fatal heart attack, and then slumped forwards to be consumed. The cases I examined did not involve people who had suffered heart attacks and had fallen into a fire. Whatever else they were the fire seems to have come from within themselves. That is what makes SHC so puzzling.

9   A Fireman's Investigation

Tony McMunn has been a serving fireman for twenty-three years. He spent time as Assistant Divisional Officer, lecturing to colleagues at the Fire Service College, Gloucestershire, about Fire Prevention, and unofficially on spontaneous human combustion. Currently he is Senior Divisional Officer for the Fire Safety Service based at Kent Fire Brigade. Tony's inauguration into the SHC controversy was a true baptism by fire. At the time he was attached to the Lancashire Fire Brigade. 'Around twelve-thirty midday, on 4 March 1980, I received a call to go to a 'person's reported' incident. That is fire brigade jargon for someone trapped in a house fire, or a fire fatality.'

The address was a terraced house in Chorley, inhabited by an elderly lady. When Tony arrived, he expected to see lots of smoke and flames but strangely there was no sign of the fire he had come to see. A police officer who met him there, said: 'You've got to see this to believe it!' Tony entered by the front door and walked into a back sitting-room which contained a bed. What he saw on the floor left him aghast. It was the remains of the old lady.

> The woman was found with part of her body in the fireplace and the lower part on the carpet. The knees to the skull were just calcined remains – in other words; pure ash. From the knees to the feet the legs were intact. There was no damage by fire to the surrounding area, although there was smoke damage from the upper part of the walls to the ceiling.

The approximate time of death was deduced by the fact that passers-by and neighbours had noticed a large volume of smoke and sparks issuing from the chimney at approximately 9.30 the previous evening. However, it was almost fifteen hours later before a neighbour called round to see the pensioner and discovered the bizarre tragedy.

> There was a bucket in the room. We presumed that while she was relieving herself, the victim had collapsed into the hearth where there was an open coal fire. When I first saw the phenomenon, I was taken

aback. I had never seen anything like it before, neither had the ambulancemen nor the police, although like all other fire brigade personnel, I had attended many fatalities involving fires. Even the bones were gone, yet when you look at nearby objects such as a brushed nylon footstool and clothes to the right of the remains – these were just stained.

At the time I hadn't a clue what it was. Someone mentioned to me it was 'spontaneous human combustion', and I naïvely accepted the explanation without knowing exactly what the terminology meant. It was later that I began to wonder exactly what the phenomenon might be.

The inquest was held at Chorley Magistrates Court. A verdict of accidental death was brought about when it was determined that the deceased had fallen head first into the coal fire.

Tony learned that the phenomenon was split into two categories; spontaneous and preternatural combustion. In the latter, the body burns unnaturally in its own substance after being set alight *by an exterior ignition source.*

Could someone really burn in this way, he wondered? Had there been any other cases? Was anyone carrying out research? He decided to investigate. What resulted was several years' intensive investigation funded out of his own pocket. He had applied for a research grant from The Institution of Fire Engineers in 1986, but it was refused.

Tony was not impressed by what he initially found.

I picked up the usual publications and quickly realized they were all copying off one another and regurgitating the same old cases over and over again. I found out how gullible some people are who accepted things at face value without digging deeper into the subject matter. During my research I also found that obstacles were placed in my way – for what reasons I'm not clear. People promised me countless photographs of incidents they had attended, and valuable documentation on cases, but they rarely materialized. Little information came from fire brigade personnel. I can safely say that the majority of my information came from other professional bodies.

His position at the Fire Service College gave him access to the British Museum Library. There he uncovered documents which referred to SHC dating back to the mid-eighteenth century. Historical references were also discovered and sent on to Tony McMunn by Bob Skinner, a researcher into 'curiosities of natural history'. Tony wrote to every conceivable person he could think of to aid him in his research. As a starting point, he looked up the meaning of the term itself, 'spontaneous human combustion', and discovered it meant: 'A biological or chemical reaction which produces its own heat, resulting in combustion'.

> Could a human body create an internal biological or chemical reaction producing sufficient temperature to bring about combustion? Being naïve about the internal workings of the body I wrote to the British Medical Association and the Clinical Research Centre, and asked them both the same question: 'Are our internal organs capable of producing so much heat that it could not disperse, and so could ignite through contact with gases that build up inside the body?
>
> Both these organizations replied they could not help me as they did not understand the subject. They hadn't a clue what I was on about! So here was my first hurdle – a subject documented for hundreds of years, which the two leading medical associations of Great Britain did not even understand.

During his research, Tony spent a day at a crematorium and spoke to experts there, and visited Harwell to question scientists about nuclear particles called neutrinos. He looked at some of the 'classic' SHC cases more closely. 'I spoke to Dr William Krogman about the Mary Reeser case, and discovered he did not support the SHC explanation at all! I realized that not only had many writers regurgitated the same stories, some of them had actually moved the goal posts.'

But Tony knew he was dealing with a real phenomenon.

> In normal fire fatalities, the flames 'rip' the top layers of skin from the body, but do not *penetrate*. Sometimes flames 'wave' over the body and even clothing survives. You can see bones, still make out the outline of a body. What happens to bodies in a fire is it *chars* the surface, but the flames don't actually penetrate.

Tony came across a booklet dated 1922, called *Forensic Medicine and Toxicology*. Like many scientific publications, it was not prepared to consider SHC, but, realizing there was a phenomenon to address, discussed the less esoteric option of preternatural combustibility. The booklet concluded: 'It is evidently due to the formation in the body of some substance which is capable of burning alone when ignited, not in a smouldering way but with a luminous flame'.

The more he delved into the subject, the more Tony favoured preternatural combustion as the likely avenue of research for an explanation. During his investigations he uncovered a new case which we present here for the first time.

London Fire Brigade answered an emergency call and appliances were dispatched from Clapham Fire Station. It was a few minutes to nine in the morning of 22 February 1964. The caller was a neighbour of 72-year-old Janice Campbell*. Mrs Campbell lived in a ground-floor flat. The fire brigade found her remains in a back room.

The room itself measured eight feet by six. There was fire damage in the vicinity of the 'body' to the timber flooring, and the ceiling was partly stripped of plaster by the intense heat. This is indicative, Tony McMunn told us, of a quick flash fire which dries out plaster, breaking its bonding, and allowing it to fall away from a wall or, in this case, the ceiling. The structure of the room was otherwise undamaged. Fire-officers determined that twenty-five per cent of the room contents were severely damaged by fire, and the rest damaged to a lesser degree by heat and smoke. The remainder of the flat was just slightly affected by smoke.

When fire-officers arrived in response to the call the conflagration was already out. A thorough investigation was mounted, and in answer to question one, 'Supposed Cause' of their 'Report of Fire' form, was written; 'Unknown'. On page two, under the heading of 'Nature of Injury' was typed; 'Severe burns to body'. To say this is an understatement is an understatement itself! Tony showed us a photograph of the room, and remarked: 'I call this one "hunt the body".'

There is no body. Hardly anything remains of the human being which once was Janice Campbell.

Another, more recent case which Tony has been able to obtain documentation for involved a student. In deference to the parents, and the investigating fire-officer, we have omitted many relevant details which might otherwise lead to the identification of the victim. The incident took place in an accommodation block situated in Birmingham. While a natural explanation seems at hand, it is stalemated by the total bizarreness of the other components of the mystery.

It began in the early hours of Tuesday 13 May 1980, at just after 3.30. On the twentieth floor, two men were awoken by screams. They emerged into the corridor and discovered the cries were emenating from room C2. There they discovered 20-year-old Jeremy Rackham* ablaze on his bed. They went and got their own pillows and used these to put out the fire. Rackham, in shock, was somehow moved out into the corridor.

In the meantime, the fire brigade had been alerted by Ambulance

Control that there was 'a man with electrical burns' in the block. An appliance arrived at 3.42 a.m. headed by a sub officer. When he and his crew reached the twentieth floor and found that the fire was already out, the fire officer decided to investigate the possible cause. In reports later made to his divisional commander and West Midlands Police, he made the following observations.

On reaching the twentieth floor the casualty was discovered lying in the corridor outside flat C2. He was suffering from severe burns to the neck, back, chest, lower abdomen, both arms and legs. First aid was rendered by the ambulance crew. After checking the victim the officer entered room C2 which was set out as follows.

The bed was in the far left-hand corner with a small foot-mat in the centre of the floor. Behind the door in the near left-hand corner stood a desk. On the right-hand side there was a wash-basin, and lying folded in the right-hand corner was a bed quilt which was slightly burnt. He made a check of the room and found a piece of paper which had been neatly folded into a taper lying on the foot-mat. One end of this taper had burnt, and the mat also showed scorch marks.

He checked the bed and found the sheet thrown to the end. When he pulled it back he discovered scorch marks on the sheet which corresponded with a person lying asleep; head, back, backside and one leg. In a metal waste-bin he found various pieces of burnt paper. These included newspapers, magazines and small pieces of torn notepaper. In a cupboard on the far right of the room a bottle marked 'surgical spirits' containing a small amount of liquid was found. The officer then went out into the corridor and into the kitchen area to check for signs of where the taper might have been lit. But there were no signs of burnt paper on the cooker, neither were there any burnt paper droppings in the corridor.

He asked the ambulance driver if the victim had said anything. He said 'No', then asked Mr Rackham how it had happened. Rackham replied: '*I was lying in the bed, and I awoke in flames.*' Then he went back into shock and was conveyed to hospital, where two days later, he passed away, having suffered 70% burns.

After this, the officer went back into the room to ascertain the cause of the fire, but could find no ignition source such as matches or a lighter. A friend of the student told him Rackham did not smoke.

Following procedure, the officer contacted his headquarters, and requested the attendance of the duty divisional officer, because of the 'doubtful origin' of the fire, and the absence of any source of ignition. The assistant duty divisional officer duly arrived and took over the investigation.

The fire brigade had been called out to a 'man with electrical burns'. Was this because of the lack of general conflagration in the room? But there were no signs of any electrical faults, and from experience, the officer thought the burns to the victim were caused by flames and not anything electrical. The sub officer thought the seat of the fire was the metal wastepaper-basket under the sink, but in his statement to his divisional commander, under the heading, Supposed Cause, he had written; 'Doubtful pending police enquiries'.

We do not know the details of the subsequent police enquiry, but the inquest was held on 31 December. On the inquest report, the 'Nature and Cause of Occurrence' is put down as 'fire, cause unknown'. Even though it was agreed that the cause of death was 'burns', the inquest could find no explanation of how this came about, not even a theoretical one. Because of this an open verdict was arrived at.

So what caused the fire death of student Jeremy Rackham? As usual, there is conflicting evidence to prove any particular scenario, but there is no doubting there is a mystery. But is this mystery indicative of SHC, or is it due merely to a lack of facts? Let us take a closer look at room C2.

The fire investigation revealed that there was no damage at all to the structure of the room. The conflagration was almost entirely confined to the bed, and its victim of course. Bedding was 50% damaged by fire. The evidence seems to back up the victim's claim that 'I was lying in the bed and I awoke in flames.' It does seem that Jeremy Rackham was asleep when he caught fire. As we have seen, the scorch marks on the sheet corresponded with his body, and even the pillow suffered 10% fire damage. But what of the other, lesser, damage in the room?

The fire-officer thought the metal bin might be the original seat of the fire. As there was no evidence of an ignition source in the room, it obviously occurred to him that the victim had made a paper taper, walked out of the room to the communal kitchen where it was lit, then returned to destroy the contents of the bin. But as we have seen there was no evidence to support this scenario. Even if this was correct, how had the fire transferred from the bin to Rackham, sometime later, after he had gone to sleep? Perhaps hours later? What was the taper doing on the mat, which itself was slightly scorched, between the bin and the bed? The scorch marks on the mat and the folded quilt across the room, could have been caused by Rackham after he had awoken in flames and panicked, perhaps moving haphazardly about the room.

Were we dealing with a suicide or even a murder?

Some emphasis was placed on the discovery of the bottle marked 'surgical spirits' containing 'a small amount of liquid'. This was found in a cupboard. If the innuendo was that the inflammable liquid had played a part in the fire, why was it then put carefully back in the cupboard? Was Mr Rackham supposed to have doused himself with it, then, after burning some papers in the bin (perhaps their contents a reason for the 'suicide') set fire to himself *after climbing into bed and covering himself with a sheet*? It does not really make sense, especially when one bears in mind the victim was wearing pyjamas which were destroyed by the fire. And surely the bed sheet would *prevent* a fire. A normal fire anyway. Blankets are thrown on to fire victims to cut off oxygen and smother the flames.

Could it have been murder?

There was no sign of forced entry to the flat. Perhaps someone who had a key let themselves in, lit a taper with their cigarette lighter, set fire to the bin to make it look like an accident, then applied the flame to the sleeping student, covering the body up with a sheet.

Is it feasible? Surely the murderer ran an enormous risk of waking up his intended victim as soon as he/she entered the room, and especially when the fire was lit. Murderers normally kill their victims in a conventional way, such as with a fatal blow to the head, and then try to disguise the crime with fire.

The truth is that *none* of this makes sense. Of course Jeremy Rackham could have burned the papers earlier in the evening, and it was just coincidence (or synchronicity) when his own body burst into flame some hours later. But why burn the papers anyway? Why not just throw them out ...?

Accident, suicide, murder ... spontaneous human combustion? Those who believe that SHC is paranormal, cite spontaneous fires which occur as part of general poltergeist activity. In their view, the fire in the bin, the odd bits of scorching on the rug and the quilt across the room, were caused by the same phenomenon that combusted Jeremy Rackham. These items aside, certainly there was an obvious lack of fire damage to the room, considering the state of the young man.

After studying the reports, and talking to some of those involved in the investigation, what did Tony McMunn think?

It's a real mystery. There was no evidence of a break-in, no ignition source, nothing to explain how the young man came to wake up in the early hours of the morning to find himself ablaze. The examination which was carried out was just for a normal fire. When I spoke to Home Office scientist, Roger Ide, about the case, he said if only he had known about it they would have done a full forensic examination.

Tony's second personal involvement in a case of alleged SHC came in 1986. On 5 February, Lancashire County Fire Brigade were called out to a terraced house in Preston. Two youths, arriving at the address to complete some work started the previous day, found they could not get into the house and alerted a neighbour who had a key. Inside they came across a horrifying spectacle. 61-year-old Charles Pimm* was lying prostrate across the hearth and living-room carpet, reduced to a head, three limbs and a heap of ashes. He had last been seen alive the previous day at 4.30 p.m.

Although there was a lot of smoke damage to the room, a settee, just inches away, was not even scorched. The room *was* ventilated. Nearby was an open fire, by then extinct, and the grate appeared to be disturbed. This caused the investigating officer to conclude that the victim, who suffered fits, had fallen into the fire, then lay on the carpet ablaze.

What did Tony think about SHC – does it exist?

There is a phenomenon of which no one has been able to explain. The only way to attempt an explanation would be for someone to be present when it happens. The nearest I've been to that was when I was confronted with the calcined remains of a human being. I can't give you an answer as to why most fire victims just suffer surface charring, and why a very small number are almost totally incinerated. People may say it's because there is a slow smouldering fire, but the truth is that no one really knows. There is something present in these cases that is out of the ordinary and unexplained.

With some of the cases the victims seem to have fallen head first into an open fire. But there is not a lot of flesh or fat on the head, and the fire should have gone out. The wick effect is only viable in terms of the torso. I think the surroundings are only usually scorched because we are dealing with an intense radiated heat, rather than direct flaming.

10 Who Flamed Roberta Rabbit?

Do animals suffer spontaneous combustion? Or more accurately; do *other* animals suffer spontaneous combustion? After all, we are just highly developed animals who have used our intellect to claw to the top of the food chain. If SHC is a reality in humans, then surely there should be examples in dogs, sheep and rabbits?

Other researchers told us there were no known cases of spontaneous combustion in animals. We wondered why. Taking an esoteric view, if SHC is a psychic phenomenon, did a lack of 'spirituality' in 'lower' animals provoke this? Or, as one wag remarked; is it because animals do not become drunkards? If the wick effect *is* a viable mundane explanation for some instances of SHC in humans, where are the cremated remains of Ben the beagle or Pinky the cat? Show a dog or a cat a fire, and that animal will get as near to it as it can. The animal will lie panting, its fur hot to the touch, moving only as a last resort. As far as candidates for the wick effect are concerned, family pets should be at the top of the list.

Similarly, if SHC is the product of an external natural phenomenon or energy field entering the body surely that should affect animals just as readily? Indeed, as there are more animals in the world than human beings, this should happen frequently.

Perhaps a lack of animal combustions would imply that SHC does not occur at all. Yet, as noted, even the wick effect as a substitute solution should affect animals. Or does this lack mean that something unique to human beings is involved in the condition? Even if it were a phenomenon mainly occurring inside buildings domestic animals should be subject to the same freak event from time to time.

Without doubt the question of this missing spontaneous animal combustion evidence is of great significance.

We tried to solicit information on animal victims through the letters' pages of farming and pet magazines, but with absolutely no success. The RSPCA said they kept no records. Did this mean there *were* no victims, or could there be other reasons for the silence?

If someone out for a walk in the country came across the calcined remains of a sheep, what would be their reaction? Would they go running for the police? No. Would it be reported to *anyone*? Probably not. They would presume the animal had died, and the owner had set fire to it to save burial. What would a farmer do, finding a sheep or a cow incinerated in this way? Would he call in police forensics experts to determine how the animal had died? Unlikely, as we reported previously after talking to a senior fireman.

The officer suggested that suspected spontaneous animal incineration gets reported as something else by farmers. When filing insurance claims it would be more expedient to write down 'lightning strike' rather than 'spontaneous combustion' – thus preventing a lot of awkward questions and a delay in payment. Imagine having to justify death by spontaneous combustion to an insurance investigator.

Given this, is there any evidence that animals suffer the same fiery fate as allegedly visited on some human beings? We found some examples, although the claims are at best sketchy and anecdotal.

Michael Harrison reported in his book the case of the Dawson family, who lived on Thorah Island, Beaverton, Ontario in Canada. They adopted an orphan called Jennie Bramwell, who suffered meningitis shortly after she moved to the house. During her illness hundreds of small fires reportedly broke out. What is of interest here, is that on one occasion, the family cat spontaneously burst into flames. When it ran out of the house in a panic, the flames mysteriously went out, and fortunately for the animal, only its fur was burnt and there was no permanent injury.

A clipping from the *Newcastle Journal* was passed on to us regarding an incident which occurred on 6 February 1978. Reputedly, a dog belonging to a Mrs Jean Payne was discovered out in the street with its stomach on fire. A man, passing by, had the presence of mind to roll the animal in a nearby puddle and put out the flames. We were intrigued, and attempted to contact Mrs Payne, who at the time lived in Jarrow, Tyne and Wear. We failed, but if true and the dog survived, what did a vet make of the incident? Of course there could be a rational explanation for the fire, such as the work of a vicious sadist. Sadly, at present we are none the wiser.

One case where we made slightly more fortunate enquiries was reported to us by a truck driver and long-term army man who was so determined to retain confidentiality that we had to meet him covertly at a spot on the M6 motorway! Such clandestine arrangements aside he did have a fascinating story to relate. It occurred on 9 February 1988 when he was looking for work as a farm labourer near Oswestry in Shropshire.

The day was fine and sunny and it was just after breakfast. Whilst walking back from an unsuccessful interview he saw a car parked off the road and a woman with a spaniel which was off its lead and running freely. In fact it was running straight towards a small cloud of yellow vaporous mist that was close to ground level but glowing with angry ferocity. A vibrating sound came from it as the 'mist' apparently rotated and the grass and bushes nearby shook as if in response to massive air pressure.

The witness told us that during the two minutes or so that this phenomenon was visible, he felt the air charged with static electricity. His hair was literally standing on end. In addition a musky, sulphurous odour was present which may conceivably have been ozone. This can form when the atmosphere is ionized by a strong electrical field.

The dog had seen the cloud and was running into it oblivious to any danger. Within seconds it was swallowed up inside the glow. The woman was now in hysterics and the man had to calm her down. Moments later the glowing cloud vanished and the utterly prone body of the dog was seen to be on the ground beneath the now dissipated mass.

Going to pick up the dog the man reported that it was alive, possibly unconscious but panting heavily. Its eyes were red and fiery and its skin was soaking wet and almost scalding hot to the touch. He covered it with a blanket and lifted it into the woman's car. Whilst the man was still in a state of shock, she drove away.

Investigation was limited by the refusal of the woman to cooperate with us; although she insisted the story was true. The dog was never examined by a vet, but seemed to recover fully after three days only to pass away a few weeks later. She felt it died from old age and did not connect it with the incident.

Whilst not an example of spontaneous combustion, *per se*, the connection is obvious. In fact the case has parallels with a number of others that have come to light within ufology. Indeed, the truck driver reported this phenomenon to us as a UFO, although nobody is suggesting that this was a spaceship, of course!

A very interesting example was the one that befell a man on the beach at Sizewell in Suffolk on the evening of 24 February 1975. Here a similar cloud-like mass (coloured greeny-yellow and described as a pumpkin by the postal worker who saw it) 'attacked' a dog and its owner, making a buzzing sound and generating an electrostatic field. It was said to look like the cathode-ray tube of a TV set, which may be significant. The dog cowered behind its master and then fled. The man stayed put until the object vanished, but he suffered a long spell of ill health afterwards and we have been led to believe that he had to give up work as a consequence of this.

Hearing of our ongoing researches in this area, we were contacted by Raymond Reed, who related an incident he and others encountered during his time serving with the 9th Battalion of the Royal Welsh Fusiliers, stationed at Weymouth in Dorset during World War Two.

> At that time, units of one officer and two men used to patrol the coastline to keep in touch with the coastguards. One night we were crossing open downland where there were lots of sheep grazing. It was pitch black. Suddenly, without warning, a fire erupted about a hundred yards away. The officer said: 'What the hell's that?' We approached carefully and discovered it was a sheep on fire.
>
> The animal was on its side. From its stomach area issued blue flames. The colour took me back to my boyhood, when I used to set fire to sulphur. Then [the] flames would suddenly flare up yellow [as they did here] when the fleece started burning. We were absolutely astounded. The sheep was a large animal, in no way decomposed, in fact quite fresh looking. I think it was dead, but cannot be certain. We extinguished the fire by throwing earth and clods onto it.

Mr Reed went on to be selected for the 'Phantoms', a secret military organization of wireless operators whose job it was to get information from the very front line back to Army command, bypassing all normal lines of communication.

An even more intriguing report reached us from a reader of *New Scientist* magazine, which published our uncontentious and simple request for comments on SHC (as did those fire, police and medical journals we approached – the only clear refusal being from the best-known publication of mainstream science, *Nature*). Bernard Beeston included a clipping with his covering letter, from the *Sunday Express*, dated 29 January 1989. Cleverly entitled: WHO FLAMED ROGER RABBIT? it told of 'the bizarre case of the blazing West Country bunny being investigated by Home Office forensic scientists'.

It told how Police Sergeant Colin Price came across the wild rabbit in the middle of a quiet country lane outside Bristol. At first he thought it was a ruptured gas main, and was astounded to find instead a dead rabbit blazing fiercely on the tarmac. Using a shovel he tried to move the animal to the roadside when 'a sheet of fire three foot high burst from its carcass'. Sergeant Price told reporter, John Vincent: 'It's the weirdest thing I've ever encountered in twenty years on the force. This seems to have no logical explanation.'

The report said that the Home Office laboratory at Chepstow were examining the remains. We wrote to the laboratory, requesting a copy of the forensic report, and learned of two other newspaper accounts. These added further details, although, as we were to subsequently learn, many of them were somewhat inaccurate.

The *Daily Telegraph* of 24 January, said that the police were linking an 'exploding' rabbit 'with the apparently motiveless attacks on three vehicles'. Two days later, the *South Avon Mercury* stated that 'during the previous night' two cars and a lorry – all at different locations – were discovered burnt out, by mystery arsonist(s). One can just imagine the leader of a gang of yobbos yelling: 'Right lads, that's enough cars for now, *let's start torching rabbits!*'

The *Mercury* quoted 'police spokesman' Inspector John Jones as stating that 'the dead rabbit had been gutted, stuffed and set alight'. They added that a forensic examination had revealed that the carcass had been filled with 'an accelerant'. Our enquiries showed that none of this was apparently true!

Dr A. Ian Grant, Principal Scientific Officer of The Forensic Science Service at Chepstow, kindly replied to our letter. He enclosed a full forensic report and informed us that the rabbit had been found on the B3128 in Failand, burning 'with sparking flames a few inches high before erupting into flames, three to four feet high'. We have summarized the main points from the report, dated 9 February 1989, and added emphasis.

This was a dead rabbit with its fur and the outer surface of skin burnt and blackened, and part of the intestine protruding from a split in the vulvar area. A petrol residue was detected on the item. X-ray examination and limited dissection of the rabbit showed that:
1. It had not been cut open and eviscerated [gutted].
2. There had been *no burning inside the body cavity.*
3. *No foreign materials or objects were present inside the body.*
4. The spine and one leg were broken.

The general injuries to the rabbit have been caused by impact with a vehicle. The presence of petrol residue would suggest that the rabbit's fur had been soaked in petrol and ignited. *Nothing was found to explain the reported feature of initial burning with small sparking flames.* There was nothing to suggest evisceration and packing of the carcass with any form of incendiary material.

So Roger – or rather 'Roberta', as the rabbit was actually a female – had been doused with petrol and set alight, although Dr Grant and his team could not explain the 'small sparking flames' initially observed by the police officer. Whichever way you look at it, the incident is bizarre. However, as proof of SHC – which many researchers at least initially took it for – the case has a lot to be desired.

The evidence, and indeed lack of evidence, for the spontaneous combustion of other animals is tantalizing and inconclusive. It also leaves a number of serious questions outstanding about the reality – or even the non-reality – of spontaneous *human* combustion.

11 The Survivors

Although the first rule of investigation is to find a *rational* explanation for allegedly paranormal incidents, sometimes such 'explanations' are in reality only suppositions. Often it is easier to adopt a supposition as 'fact' than to admit that there is no rational explanation.

This seems to crop up predictably in the realms of mysterious human fire tragedies. Victims, not in any condition themselves to challenge suppositions, 'obviously' suffer heart attacks and fall against lighted cookers or fires. Sometimes, if victims are smokers, they 'obviously' have fallen asleep smoking a cigarette in bed. Although proof is lacking, to the rationalist, *these are the only possible answers.*

The late Harry Price tells of the mysterious and tragic burning of Mrs Madge Knight, who awoke the household with her screams in the early hours of 19 November 1943.

Her back was so badly burned that the doctor anaesthetized her before applying medication. Incongruously, none of her bed sheets were burned, and there was no smell of fire in the room. A Harley Street specialist who was called, asked the poor woman what had happened. She replied she 'had no idea'. Mrs Knight died of toxaemia on 6 December.

In addition to the coroner there were four doctors present at the inquest. Incredibly, although it contradicted and ignored many of the salient factors, these learned men contributed to the official line that 'the burns might have been caused by some corrosive fluid'. This conclusion was arrived at even though the police found no evidence at all to support it.

Dead men tell no tales, but there are people who have caught ablaze and survived. They know there was no source of ignition in the immediate area. They know there are no easy answers.

On 5 January 1835, Mr James Hamilton, Professor of Mathematics at Nashville University, walked home in the intense cold. According to John Overton MD, in the *Transactions of the Medical Society of Tennessee*, while checking a hygrometer hanging outside his house, Hamilton felt 'a steady pain like a hornet sting, accompanied by a sensation of heat', in the thigh of his left leg. Looking down he 'distinctly saw a light flame of the extent ... of a ten cent piece ... having a complexion which nearest resembles that of pure quicksilver'. The flame was several inches high and flattened at the top.

Instinctively the professor slapped at the flame but to no avail. Then, bringing cool scientific methodology into practice, he cupped his hands around the area to cut off the oxygen. Whether this was what succeeded in extinguishing the flame is open to conjecture, but the fortunate man survived a fire, which, Dr Overton claimed, after treating Hamilton, was *internal*.

Even though the flame had gone, the pain continued, and seemed to emanate from deep within his thigh. Inside the house, the professor removed his clothing and examined the wound. It resembled an abrasion just under an inch wide and three inches long, extending obliquely across the lower portion of the thigh. The burn was livid but dry.

His underpants had a hole in them that corresponded with the flame, yet the edges of this hole were not scorched. Even more amazing was the fact that his trousers were not burned at all, although the fibres in contact with the underpants were tinged with a dark yellow fuzz.

Dr Overton found the burn very unusual. The muscles around the area were sore for a long time, and the wound itself was deep and took thirty-two days to heal. When it eventually healed, the scar was unusually livid. John Overton described his patient as a victim of 'partial human combustion'. If the professor had not kept his head, would he have succumbed to the full fatal fury of total combustion?

What is interesting here is that the flame penetrated the trousers without causing damage to them. Curiously, whilst researching this book we came across a recent case which depicts the same anomaly.

In a village near Farnham, Surrey, in 1976, a young couple, Mr and Mrs Andrews*, climbed out of bed one Sunday morning and went downstairs for breakfast. Their gas cooker, a 'cordon bleu' model, featured an eye-level grill. Mrs Andrews cooked some sausages and bacon under the grill, turned it off, then she and her husband went into the dining-room to eat. After they had finished the meal and drunk some tea, an act which had taken 'less than an hour, and a *minimum* of fifteen minutes', they carried their dirty pots into the kitchen, and stood talking, looking out through the window.

Mr Andrews stood two to three feet away from the cooker. He

was wearing a dressing-gown with nothing underneath. As he turned to go and shower, his wife suddenly noticed several blue flames, about six inches high, shooting out of the shoulder of his dressing-gown. Mr Andrews was totally unaware that he was on fire. Instinctively, his wife batted the flames out with her bare hands. Curiously, she felt no sensation of heat whilst doing this, and an examination of the dressing-gown and Mr Andrews's bare shoulder showed no evidence of burning at all.

Rationalizing the experience, the couple turned to the grill, presuming that somehow this strange fire had emanated from there. However, not only was it confirmed that indeed the knob was switched off, the grill itself had cooled down since it had been used some time before. Still hanging onto the only possible explanation, Mrs Andrews reported the cooker to the Gas Board, explaining that she thought the grill was faulty. An engineer arrived and could find no fault with the control knob, nor the grill itself.

A similar story with more tragic consequences involved a 53-year-old woman names Mrs McDougal* of Wythenshawe in south Manchester. She was also beside a gas cooker when she found herself ablaze one day in January 1980. This was during a fateful ten-week-period in which we have uncovered half a dozen little-known cases that are potential SHC incidents merely from our search in Britain alone.

Mrs McDougal survived this accident with 70% burns to her body, but she died the next day. However, before doing so she told a neighbour that the emission from the gas cooker must have somehow suffered a blow-back effect and ignited her as the flames had suddenly erupted.

Given the circumstances that appears a reasonable proposition. However, at the inquest on 3 March 1980 this theory was rejected by expert testimony from both North-West Gas and the fire brigade.

The cooker was evidently not lit at the time, but Mrs McDougal was trying to light it. Tests had apparently indicated that the kind of accident she had speculated about to generate her massive injuries was just not feasible. As a result only speculation was left open to those trying to discover the truth. This centred on the option that the woman had unfortunately ignited herself by error with the match during her fruitless attempts to light the cooker.

As coroner Leonard Gorodkin was quoted as saying when pronouncing the verdict of accidental death; 'It is not really clear what happened'.

Almost exactly 150 years after James Hamilton's lucky escape another tragic case involving cooker flames served to pour oil on already contentious waters. Minutes after leaving a cookery class at Halton College of Further Education, a Widnes teenager suddenly became a 'human torch', according to eye-witnesses. With 13% burns she seemed to make an amazing recovery only days after the incident, sitting up in bed, chatting to friends and relatives.

Tragically, the girl died fifteen days later, on 12 February 1985, through inflamed bronchials, septicaemia and 'shock lung'.

The young woman was as much in the dark as regards the source of the fire as anyone else. However, after discussing possibilities with her friends, she reasoned that perhaps she had been leaning against a lighted gas-ring before leaving the classroom. This was a line of enquiry favoured by the Home Office, although most witness testimony at the inquest did not seem to us to support it. Nor did the Cheshire Fire Brigade agree with this explanation. For reasons we could not discover, their thirty-page report, compiled using research by the Shirley Institute in Manchester, was not allowed in presentation. The jury, ignorant of what (to us at least) seems a very important piece of expert analysis, brought about a verdict of accidental death.

For a full report of our very detailed investigation of the case, including our attendance at the inquest at the invitation of a police source, please see our book, *Death By Supernatural Causes?*

In another case, Thomas Murphy, owner of the Lake Denmark Hotel, Dover, New Jersey, discovered his housekeeper, Lillian Green, burned and dying. Apart from consuming her clothing, the fire had done little damage to the carpet. In hospital, Mrs Green also could not find a satisfactory explanation for what had happened to her.

Computer operator, Paul Castle (some sources refer to Paul Hayes, others to Paul Castile), survived a mysterious fire which he claims attacked the upper part of his body whilst walking home in Stepney Green, London, on 25 May 1985. We have tried to trace Mr Castle/Castile (or Hayes) without success. However, on 23 July 1985 the American tabloid newspaper, *The National Enquirer*, published what they claimed was Mr Castle's first-hand account of his terrifying experience. In part he alleged:

> It was all so sudden. It sounded like a huge gas flame suddenly being lit. I could feel the flames burning, as if I'd been doused with petrol and set on fire. Paul's arms felt as if they were being prodded by fiery pokers from his shoulders down to his wrists. He pressed tightly against his eyelids. At the same time his cheeks were red hot, his ears numb and his chest felt as if boiling water had been poured over it. The torture was indescribable, he said; like being plunged straight into the heart of a furnace.

Paul shouted in panic, and instinctively began to run, as if he could outpace the flames. After just three or four steps he fell onto the pavement and curled into a ball, thinking he was dying.

It was over very suddenly after about thirty seconds. Opening his eyes, there were no flames or smoke. He lay immobile and terrified, shivering in shock. Paul adds 'I ... gingerly felt my face, hair, arms, neck and chest. I was numb in some spots, white in others.'

Paul 'staggered' through the emergency doors of nearby London Hospital where he was kept overnight for treatment to his injuries. They were described as extensive though superficial. British newspaper reports said that police were puzzled, and his mother was quoted as saying that her son did not smoke. Paul, pushed for an answer, wondered if the fire could have been set off in some way by a passing car. Pictures appeared showing the young man's injuries and his badly-scorched shirt.

There are similarities here with the Halton College case, only Paul was far luckier than the victim there. But something at the start of his account strikes a chord with the description of a witness called Mrs Viner who contacted us. Paul Castle said: It sounded like a huge gas flame suddenly being lit. Mrs Viner, in describing a similar phenomenon, told us: 'I heard a very loud rushing noise best described as a roar from a bunsen burner.' We will be returning more fully to Mrs Viner's case later in the book.

Paranormal investigators Harry Price and Vincent Gaddis, noted that in the majority of mysterious fires the victims almost always cannot explain what had brought about their predicament. Nothing seems to amplify this point more clearly than the classic case of the world's best known SHC survivor – Jack Angel.

However, our investigation into this affair discovered that there is serious confusion about this much-debated story. We shall try to offer you the full facts and both sides of the argument as these tend not to be seen together in most brief accounts.

Angel, a well-salaried salesman, met his appointment with the unknown some time around Tuesday 12 November 1974, according to SHC researcher, Larry Arnold. After parking his motor-home, which doubled as a garment showroom, at the Ramada Inn, Savannah, Georgia, he donned pyjamas and retired. At about noon, *four days later*, Angel awoke. His right hand was charred black on both sides from wrist to fingers. 'It was just burned, blistered,' he later stated to Arnold. 'And I had this big explosion in my chest. It left a hell of a hole. I was burned down here on my legs and between my groin, down on my ankle, and up and down my back. In spots!'

Angel's reaction to waking up and discovering this catalogue of injuries was unexpected. Feeling no pain, he climbed out of bed, showered and dressed. Staggering 'like I was drunk,' he left the motor-home and entered the motel's cocktail lounge, where a waitress remarked on his condition. 'Yeah, looks like I got burned,' he understated, half aware of his injuries, but still insensitive to pain. He ordered a whisky, thinking it would help him, although he claimed normally not to touch alcohol. Then he collapsed. 'The next thing I knew,' Angel told Larry Arnold, 'I awoke in the hospital. And there's a doctor ... with a pair of tweezers pulling skin off my arm.' One doctor, he remembered, 'explained to me I wasn't burned externally, I was burned *internally*.' He was initially treated at the Memorial Medical Centre in Savannah.

Angel's wife examined the motor-home but found no evidence of a fire. Just as in the Madge Knight case, even the bed sheets were unmarked. In the meantime Jack Angel transferred himself to a Veterans Administration Hospital which specialized in burns. After examination, Dr David Fern told him: 'This is a third degree burn which damaged the skin severely and most of the underlying muscle of the hand, causing a total anaesthetic hand.'

He added that the ulner nerve was 'completely destroyed', with the median nerve showing 'questionable viability'. In other words, Angel's hand was so badly damaged it was as good as dead. He decided to have the hand and the lower forearm amputated rather than face months of painful surgery.

A firm of Georgian lawyers, hearing about the case, decided that the cause of the fire must have been faulty electrical equipment in the motor-home. They told Angel they would sue those responsible for three million dollars on a contingency fee basis (i.e. they would take a cut of any winnings). Thinking a thorough investigation might at last get to the bottom of the mystery, Angel gave them the go-ahead.

The investigation began with a detailed examination of the wiring, but nothing untoward was found. Neither were there any scorch marks around electrical sockets. Then weather records were scrutinized for a lightning strike, and the possibility of arcing from overhead power lines was explored. All of these areas drew a blank. In final desperation, engineers completely dismantled the vehicle. Not a single clue indicating an electrical cause for the incident could be found, despite Dr Fern's reported comment that: 'The description of the burn and the findings in surgery are very typical of an electric-type injury. This generates a high-powered heat source because of the resistance of the skin and the underlying tissue.'

Dr Fern and a Dr J. Madden were two of four physicians,

according to Larry Arnold, who signed medical documents attesting to the likelihood of the cause being an electrical source.

All this allowed Arnold to conclude that the only remaining option was of spontaneous human combustion. According to the popular American science magazine, *Omni*, of December 1981, even Dr Fern attributed the burns to SHC, although he later denied to Larry Arnold that he had ever said that.

But was SHC the only other option? Three researchers who support a more prosaic answer, are Philip Klass, Joe Nickell and John Fischer (we met the latter two when looking at the Mary Reeser case).

Klass is an aviation journalist and well known as a debunker of UFO reports, and with the aid of analysts Nickell and Fischer recently wrote a damning and excellent analysis of much-touted official documents supposedly describing a secret military and scientific think-tank on crashed alien craft. Ironically, it was American ufologist, Jerome Clark, who suggested that Nickell and Fischer turn their attention to the Jack Angel case back in 1984.

The pair had already published the results of a study of thirty alleged SHC cases in *The Fire And Arson Investigator*, the journal of the International Association of Arson Investigators Inc. They concluded that everything they looked at could be explained in rational terms. Applying this logic to the Angel case they made several observations.

They pointed out the incongruity that, in the worst cases of SHC, the extremities were what remained. Here, it was the hand which was consumed while the rest of the body survived relatively unscathed. Leading on from this, they speculated that therefore it was the hand which had come into primary contact with the source of the injuries, which had then radiated out across the body. Finally, because of what was (to them) Angel's irrational behaviour after the incident, where he ordered whisky instead of seeking medical assistance, the investigators wondered if he had been in a 'stupor' earlier, which led to an accident.

We find this final speculation to be a little vague and unproven.

Jack Angel had told Arnold: 'I'm not a drinker but I thought that would help me.' This seems a not unreasonable explanation of his actions, and as far as we know, Nickell and Fischer have no evidence to the contrary. Whatever the cause of the injuries, obviously Angel must have been in shock upon their discovery.

In his articles for *Fate* and *Fortean Times*, Arnold introduces, and then discards, the theory that Angel was *scalded*. Apparently, the motel maintenance man was the first to bring this up. The injuries reminded him of scalding, and so he theorized that Angel had been sprayed with boiling water after loosening his radiator cap. But a check showed that the cap was tight. Neither were there any ruptured pipes which might have poured steaming water on the slumbering salesman, but they did discover a slipped drive belt on the exterior-mounted hot-water-pump. According to Arnold, the engineers employed by Angel's lawyers saw this as the only viable option if they were to bring about a successful court action.

They compiled an engineer's report. Arnold says this *speculated* that the next morning after retiring, Angel arose to shower but found the unit not working. Dressed still in his pyjamas, he went outside to investigate, removed the water heater's metal cover and opened the safety valve which released a scalding jet of pressurized hot water.

Larry Arnold discounted the theory because access to the valve entailed the removal of a metal plate first. If he had been scalded, it would seem inconceivable that the victim would then have remounted the plate before returning inside and losing consciousness. Angel was not impressed by the 'theory' when interviewed by Arnold. He repeated that he had been told by someone that he had been burned *internally*. Nickell and Fischer, in their article in response published in the May 1989 issue of *Fate*, criticize Arnold for accepting Angel's word for this. But Arnold has told us that he knows the name of the doctor who made the pronouncement. However, he chooses to withhold this.

The lawyers told Arnold that to test their engineers' theory, they had Jack Angel put under hypnosis by a psychologist and regressed to the accident. Nothing emerged, Larry Arnold says that after two and a half years' research, 'Angel's attorneys withdrew the case from the court's docket just one week before coming to trial'.

It should be recalled that for the case to succeed these attorneys had to prove an engineering fault was to blame and so as a result inevitably disprove SHC. Presumably they did not continue because they felt they could not clearly establish a fault as the cause. Withdrawing the suit does not, therefore, argue against SHC.

However, this seems different from what Nickell and Fischer say.

In fact they challenge Larry Arnold on a number of points after independent research by Philip Klass, who handed over to them the alleged engineers' report and also, they say, various court records.

First of all there seems to be a muddle over the dates. According to Arnold, Jack Angel went to sleep on Tuesday 12 November and 'slept' until noon 16 November – almost four days. In the civil action suit procured by Klass, the date given for the incident is 21 November. However, this should not be accepted as necessarily correct, because the date which appears on other documents including two engineering reports is apparently 15 November. To add further confusion to this bemusing saga, Arnold has recently stated to us: 'By cross-referencing many sources (one of which contains internally contradicting dates), we have concluded that Angel retired the evening of 11 November 1974; that he awoke around noon on 15 November, with no recollection of the intervening time.'

In preparing their case for court, Larry Arnold stated that the engineers had *speculated* that Angel arose the following morning, went to check the heater unit when discovering that the shower was not working, and in the process received severe scalding. In Nickell and Fischer's report, they recount as apparent fact, without explaining how they had come across this information, that Angel arrived 'on or about November 13', awoke to have a shower, but then could not say what happened next from that moment until noon, two days later.

As far as these sceptical researchers are concerned, the scalding was more than speculation. In support of this, they quote directly from the suit presented, they say, by Angel's lawyers in the Superior Court for Fulton County, Georgia (i.e. this is presumably the one later withdrawn pre-trial, according to Arnold):

> On November 21 1974, Plaintiff was attempting to take a shower in said motor-home which was parked on a motel parking lot in Savannah, Georgia. While Plaintiff was in the process of taking a shower, the water suddenly stopped flowing from the shower plumbing.
> Plaintiff, in attempting to discover the reason for the loss of water pressure, exited said motor-home and attempted to inspect the hot water heater. In making said inspection of the hot water heater, the pressure valve on the hot water heater released and as a result, scalding hot water under tremendous pressure was sprayed upon plaintiff.

The suit was designed to prove that the manufacturer was negligent. As if to counter the thought some may have that what started out as just legal speculation had been adapted as fact by Angel and his attorneys, Nickell and Fischer come up with additional corroboration, gleaned from the engineers' report.

Apparently it contains a statement from an Ed Jonikens who saw Angel in hospital and also thought his injuries looked like the result of scalding. He had driven the vehicle home for the salesman and in doing so found the panel on the water heater was 'extremely hot'. The engineers not only noted the drive felt was off the unit, but discovered the safety release valve was in the *open* position.

There seems little doubt in the minds of Philip J. Klass, Joe Nickell and John F. Fischer that Jack Angel's injuries had nothing to do with spontaneous human combustion. That begs the question of why Angel has been presented to the world by numerous commentators and many times over as a survivor of this bizarre phenomenon. This is especially so if his civil action suit was dismissed for costs when transferred to the Federal Court, as alleged by some sources.

This is once again something that Arnold totally denies; 'Despite what Nickel would like the world to believe, and what Klass claims, Angel vs. AVCO was *never* tried in court,' he says.

But what do these sceptics actually claim? We asked Klass and he seems to agree about the lack of trial. In a letter received as we go to press he says; 'You ask why the case never went to court. The reason is ...' followed by his speculation about why the lawyers did not proceed with the suit. On the face of it this seems plain enough.

However, what of the dismissal for costs reported before? Do we assume that the attorneys for Angel had to pay costs when withdrawing their claim? Is that the same thing in legal terms as their action being 'dismissed for costs' when in Federal Court, as alleged elsewhere and by others? The matter remains very confusing.

Unfortunately, we were unable to work out this confusion as Philip Klass apologized that he was a very busy man and under medical advice to take at least four hours sleep per night and one day a month as free time. He regretted that he may not find himself in a position to retrieve the Angel case files from their location in his home until perhaps several months after our book had to be completed. We naturally sympathize with Philip Klass's situation, but as a result (of this rather puzzling explanation) are unfortunately left facing unresolved questions.

Which of the dates for the incident are correct? If Angel really was unconscious for four days, why was no one suspicious, and what of the problems of dehydration?

Inversely, if Angel really did receive his injuries whilst checking the outside heater unit, why did no one see him get scalded, or hear him scream out? Was the 'metal plate', referred to by Arnold, replaced after the alleged accident? According to Arnold, Angel had a shower and dressed in a traumatized condition *after* receiving his injuries several days later. If the drive belt was off the hot-water-pump, how was this possible?

Or, we may wonder, in his confused mental condition, had Angel sandwiched the last thing he could remember – the curtailed shower – with his next memory of discovering the injuries and getting dressed?

On this point, Larry Arnold told us:

There could have been residual pressure in the motor-home's plumbing that provided a small amount of water for a brief shower, at least the start of one. Additionally, AVCO motor-homes had a dual-type heater system, the water heater being under the driver's seat. There is no recorded evidence that this water heater malfunctioned. Furthermore, Nickell's sprayed-hot-water scenario mandates that the pop-off relief valve rupture; it did not.

Angel told us he attempted to shower but there was inadequate water pressure. He proceeded to wash himself as best he could.

We asked Larry Arnold for a reply to the allegations contained in Nickell and Fischer's article on the case. He directed his remarks at just one of the authors, after making a general comment.

The debunkers who (in America at least) most vigorously oppose SHC have, in truth, not investigated first-hand classic SHC. One of those debunkers – arguably America's most vocal SHC naysayer – has rebuked in print our investigation of the Jack Angel case, claiming instead that Angel scalded himself. Yet he admitted to us that he had never interviewed Mr Angel. Nor had he spoken to Angel's physicians, who likened their patient's burns to high-temperature, electrical-type injury; nor to his lawyers who, despite assiduous effort, could find no evidence for an external source of injury; nor to the service technicians knowledgeable about motor-home hot water systems, technicians who laughed and said 'Impossible!' when told about the debunker's scalding water theory.

Who are these technicians, we asked? Larry Arnold readily provided the information. 'Earl Witsil, motor-home service manager for ten years, Dick Beaver, retailer of motor-homes since the late 1960s, Dale Dentler, an RV service technician, Tommy Hippensteel, owner of an RV dealership and who serviced AVCO motor-homes in the early 1970s, and Wayne F. Schweitzer, a former AVCO dealer.'

This complex case is not as clear-cut as either side in this protracted debate may believe. However, the investigations from both perspectives show the sort of work that needs to be carried out if we are to hope to get to the bottom of any reported incident of alleged SHC. Even then much confusion may well still remain.

Perhaps he will never learn what really happened to the one man best known in supernatural records as a survivor of spontaneous human combustion – a man who rather ironically is named Angel.

Of course, if this much-researched case can still remain so contentious it must inevitably pose questions about other examples which have had far less rigorous or probing investigations from so many angles. How reliable is the evidence for those events?

PART TWO
The Theories

Senior Divisional Officer for the Fire Safety Service at Kent Fire Brigade, Tony McMunn has spent more than ten years researching cases of alleged SHC, in his own time and at his own expense.

A contemporary photograph of the two houses occupied by the Kirby
sisters, who both burst into flame at the same time on the same day.
Hargreave Terrace is in the foreground, and 45 Wakefield Road, across
the Calder Valley, is the second house from the left in the row of terraces
level with the chimney pot

The entry in the Sowerby Bridge cemetery register for 1899, recording the deaths of Amy and Alice Ann Kirby

Fireman Jack Stacey was called to a derelict building, but the only fire damage was to a vagrant inside. Flames were jetting from the dead man's stomach like a 'blow torch'

All that remained of a twelve stone woman and a well-stuffed armchair.
The 'classic' case of Mary Reeser was even stranger than is
popularly believed

Fireman Tony McMunn's inauguration into the SHC controversy was a
true baptism by fire. On 4 March 1980 he was confronted with the
calcined remains of an elderly woman

In his unofficial lectures to other firemen, Tony McMunn calls this
picture 'hunt the body'. The victim is an elderly woman who was found
on 22 February 1964, at an address in London

The room in the Midlands where a student awoke in flames in the early hours of 13 May 1980

SHC survivor Jack Angel displays the stump where his right hand had been. This was lost after a mysterious fire in his trailer home. (This photograph is a screen shot from a TV appearance made by Mr Angel)

Meteorologist and physicist Dr Terence Meaden measures ground damage from an electrically charged vortex near Warminster in Wiltshire, August 1990. What would happen to a person standing in this same spot when the force struck?

(Below) This photograph shows the gruesome results of fire on a human body. The anonymous airman was trapped in his cockpit when his aircraft incinerated. The head, torso, and one arm are visible, plus the remains of wires, twisted metal and even a pair of spectacle frames (centre left). Yet despite the intense, protracted heat the body outline remains recognizable and the bones are not destroyed in any way. The appearance is in marked contrast to those images of reputed SHC victims found elsewhere in this photographic section, where the destruction is of a completely different and remarkable order

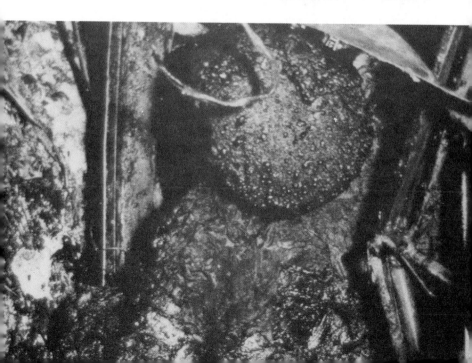

Head cremator, Peter Thornley, operating one of the five cremators at Overdale. Temperatures up to 950°C are required here to incinerate a human body. Even so, bones still remain

(Below) After cremation, the bones are put inside a cremulator together with eight iron balls weighing several pounds each.
A drum revolves, and the bones are pounded into ash

12   Chemical Reactions

Harry Godfrey is a resident of the state of Victoria in Australia. He recounted the following story to us which is based on his own experiences.

> During the summer of 1942 I was flying with the 108 Squadron in the canal zone of Egypt. Occasionally, for no apparent reason, an aircraft would blow up. Sabotage was suspected, but we could never go much further than suspicion. Anyhow, once I happened to be inside an aircraft during the middle of the day when I suddenly smelt smoke. I turned towards the front of the kite (as we called the aircraft) and I saw smoke coming from the front gun turret. I nearly crapped myself, thinking that it was a thermite device or some other type that had misfired and was likely to blow at any second. I dropped down to the ground, stopped, looked up and I now reckoned I could beat it! The smoke was coming from the ammo and I ripped out those canisters (normally a two-man job). Then I discovered that the incendiaries (but they may have been tracer ammunition) were smouldering due to sun-driven high temperatures of the metal part of the aircraft.

Disaster here was narrowly averted, but as this frightening tale with a happy ending clearly demonstrates fires can occur in nature without apparent cause and with potentially devastating effect. Here one is left to assume that the volatile chemicals in the weaponry were merely set alight by the intense temperatures. These would be magnified by the hot desert sun and the heat conductivity of the metal within the systems.

But some chemicals are capable of interacting with each other in perfectly cool surroundings and yet they generate heat as a consequence. This is because heat is simply one form of energy and certain chemical reactions do release energy as the various constituents blend together to form other substances. This energy has to be conserved (i.e. remain the same amount) in some manner and occasionally, in the right circumstances, some transforms into heat.

Spontaneous combustion occurs in flammable elements such as coal, oil and hay without a source of outside ignition. It generally results as oxidation when the oxygen in the air combines with reactive surface particles. In the beginning there is a slow smouldering until enough heat is produced to spawn fire. As a chemical process, spontaneous combustion is hard to detect since almost no light or heat is evident in the initial stages. The fire ignites when the material reaches its flash-point.

Botanist, Christopher Perraton, told us of his experience of spontaneous combustion. 'Once I had a splendid fire in a chemical store through the spontaneous combustion of linseed oil soaked rags. These had been used to treat bench tops and then dumped in a heap inside a cupboard. Fortunately there was a student dance that night so the fire was detected before it had spread.'

But spontaneous chemical combustion has practical advantages. One can buy body warmers for use on camping trips to remote areas. These rely upon a plastic seal which can be easily broken. Once it is broken the chemicals inside the plastic tubing begin to react and heat is produced from the energy exchange. This gets trapped within the seals as if a magical hot-water bottle has been created.

It is a rather more serious story in Australia's Northern Territory as one of us discovered on a September 1991 visit to the vast wastelands and tropical regions east of Darwin.

Here, as in many regions further south, the bush fire is a real hazard. The weather has only two seasons – the Wet (from November to March) and the Dry (April to October). The fiery red terrain is alive with spear grass that pokes up in spiky masses in great profusion. But in late September the chemicals within this produce a major threat. They can interact in such a way that heat is created within the living system of the plant. By this time of year there has normally been no rain for many weeks and the ground is so dry that a tiny spark could ignite an inferno. This chemical reaction can thus very easily set alight a patch of spear grass which within minutes envelopes huge areas in a travelling sea of flame.

The problem is made even worse by the awesome electrical storms during October which herald the arrival of the wet season and its prospect of vicious tropical monsoons. One of these flattened Darwin in recent times. The huge levels of electricity in the atmosphere coupled with the spontaneous combustion within the spear grass and the high winds that may also appear can wreck hundreds of square miles in hours.

As a consequence it has long been common practice in the area to purposely set fire to regions of wasteland just before sunset, allow these to burn throughout the night and create islands of safely carbonized woodland within the spear grass. Should the grass then spontaneously ignite the damage from the resulting fires will be limited and will not spread across the parts already destroyed and which act as barricades.

Dr Peter McCartney, a hyperbaric physician in Tasmania, pointed out to us that the baobab tree, native to western Africa, spontaneously combusts when chemicals produced in two of its separate chambers combine. Through his work with divers Dr McCartney learned that cannonballs from ancient shipwrecks, brought to the surface after long submersion in salt water, can also generate heat.

Of course, we may speculate that if inorganic chemicals and organic products within botanical systems can spontaneously combust, the theory can be extended to include spontaneous combustion within bio-systems like human beings, producing similar chemical reactions.

As we saw earlier, Sidney Alford – an explosives engineer – speculated in *New Scientist* in 1986 that abnormal quantities of highly inflammable gases such as methane might theoretically result from freak internal chemical reactions. Methane – actually hydrocarbon – results through anaerobic bacterial decomposition of vegetable matter. Outside of animal digestive systems, it forms in swampy ground where it is called 'marsh gas'. Coal miners know it as 'firedamp', because when it mixes with air it becomes combustible. It is a major constituent of natural and coal gas.

Alford spoke of the effects of too many eggs and high concentrates of certain liquids (e.g. paraffin), although neat alcohol in excessive quantities is a favourite of the SHC sceptic.

Another gas which is produced during the rotting process of organic matter, is phosphine. Phosphine ignites spontaneously in contact with air. In marshy areas where it is produced, including graveyards, observers know it as 'Will o' the Wisp'. It is found in the body as phosphates, and conceivably a freak activity in the digestive system would result in the production of this gas. Indeed, retired industrial chemist, Cecil Jones has postulated that this could be the explanation for cases like those of the teenager at Halton College. In that case, Jones told us:

It is possible that the victim had passed wind containing phosphine. The mixture would be confined by her clothing, but would rise up her back, partially igniting in the restricted amount of air available, giving the initial sense of heat, then escaping at her shoulders and bursting into flames with the phosphorescent glow seen by the two witnesses. This would account for the extensive burns to the back and buttocks, but nothing to the front of the body or legs.

This bizarre, if unproven, phenomenon has been termed elsewhere the phosphinic fart! It may be less amusing than it seems, if true.

The stomach and surrounding areas of the body are full of a complex cocktail of chemicals, from the acids produced within the digestive system to the numerous natural and artificial constituents of the food we consume. We eat food to produce energy in order to survive and part of the energy that the body creates from processing this food appears in the form of heat. Without food we stop producing energy (and heat) and eventually will die through a lowering of body temperature and other factors.

The speculation is that for some reason SHC cases involve a malfunction of the digestive system whereby almost all the energy within the gut is transformed into heat and ultimately such high temperatures are created that they pass the ignition point of the fatty tissues within the body. Naturally, obese people and both the elderly and females tend to have a high fat content. Once aflame and with a plentiful supply of fuel within the stomach this process will continue for some time and – being internal – be very difficult to extinguish. Emitted gases may well burn with a pale blue flame such as sometimes reported in SHC cases.

In *Fortean Times*, issue 50 (1988) reader Barry Singleton noted that if SHC was a result of a chain reaction in a closed energy system then it ought to be simple to calculate what would happen and whether this was theoretically possible within a human being. He appealed for someone to do this work.

In issue 52 an interesting response came from Hugh Stiles, a Dutch chemical engineer who had spent five years researching the destructive distillation of chemicals within paper and wood.

Stiles showed several things. Firstly, that the very high volume of water in the human body (up to 70% in fact) is not a problem; at least in the sense most people might envisage. The water would not 'quench' the flames of any hypothetical SHC fire that began within the body.

Stiles noted that the carbon within the soft tissues of the body would oxidize in the standard way when set alight. These tissues are, of course, reputedly incinerated in the classic SHC cases apart from the odd leg or arm. But then extremities in a fire often do not burn. The ends of logs in a grate stay intact the longest. This process would turn the tissue into carbon dioxide gas and generate heat, perhaps adding fuel to the self-combusting cycle. A massive

365 megajoules of heat energy would emerge as a result, of which less than one third would be the required amount to evaporate all the water within a human body. This certainly leaves enough heat energy left over to complete the SHC to its alleged levels of destruction.

However, there is an unexpected problem from these calculations, as Stiles himself found. He suggested we recall a bathroom after hot water has poured into a bath. It becomes filled with steam which condenses onto all cool surfaces such as mirrors. The steam generated by evaporating all the water content of a human body would be enough to condense back to some ten gallons of water. By all expectations the scene of an SHC event should show clear evidence of this.

One speculation was that this is not a commonly reported feature of SHC cases because the body is discovered hours after the process is completed, by which point the humidity of the room has reverted to normal. However, not all SHC victims are found so long after the fact.

We might add another possibility, that secondary fires within the room or the long-term burning process itself has maintained the water as steam for long enough for it to escape, as gases can readily do, through ventilation holes such as a chimney flue. A problem here is the apparently cool surface temperatures of large parts of a room involved in SHC incidents, as shown by their typical lack of minimal fire damage. If cool, then these surfaces should have condensed the steam, and excess water vapour in a room really ought to be a more common sight than it is in the numerous reports now to hand.

Of course, whatever the cause of the near total destruction of the soft tissues and bones of a human body within these cases (be it SHC or some other more mundane process) the water vapour would still presumably be released and so should be evidenced somehow at the scene. The exception might be when the water content of the body is perhaps electrolysed during the SHC process and split into constituent gases that would be less easy to detect after the fact than would condensed water vapour.

Whether or not there was even a possibility of a chemical reaction within the human digestive system was a question we put to Dr Joyce Nelson, a Cheshire GP. She had never come across any case like this and reminded us that as a general practitioner she was not an expert in the field. But we merely requested her personal opinion as to the medical feasibility of the sort of physiological concepts proposed to account for SHC. She did not find it impossible to conceive that such a thing might theoretically occur, but was cautious and pointed out that this is not the same thing as saying it does.

Dr Nelson explained that there are certain processes that take place within animals, notably cattle, where excessive amounts of methane gas build up and bloat the stomach. The only way for a veterinary surgeon to release the pressure is to make an incision so that the methane can escape.

As we have seen, once mixed with oxygen, methane is a highly inflammable gas and within the human body normally finds a natural outlet. There could just possibly be a medical situation whereby a freak combination of events might generate gas as well as excess heat energy. If it does then there are potentially horrible consequences.

However, this remains nothing more than speculation. Whether it will ever be established as medical fact is quite another matter. Of course, it also begs the question as to how frequent SHC in cattle must be if this build-up of methane is known to be relatively commonplace in these animals. The question is particularly valid because, as we found, there appear to be no established reports that we could trace of SHC events in cattle.

Could inflammable gases produced in the stomach and bowels be the cause of SHC? During our search for evidence, Mrs D.G. Viner of Banbury, Oxford told us of her intriguing and frightening experiences.

I used to be a cigarette smoker, and last thing at night I would bank down the fire with slack coal. During the night I would get up to make my sick husband a hot drink, and it was nice to wait beside a warm fire for the milk to boil.

On this particular night I thought I would have a last cigarette, only to find I had left my lighter upstairs. So using the silver and tissue lining paper, I made myself a spill. As I leant towards the fire and lit the spill I felt a minor explosion in front of my face which startled me into dropping both spill and cigarette.

I thought I had trapped a small amount of coal gas in the loose sleeve of my crimplene frock, and that had caused the 'plop' of the explosion. There were no signs of scorching on my clothes or my skin.

The second incident involved a cheap throw away lighter, so there was no possibility of coal gas. It was a worrying time, coping with the death of my husband, a wedding and preparation for Christmas. Feeling very tired in body but not in mind, I took a flask of hot tea, a book and my handbag upstairs and got ready for bed. Sitting up I decided to have a cigarette while reading and drinking. As I leant forward to light my cigarette, I heard a rushing noise like the roar of a bunsen burner, although many times magnified.

As the gas inlet was metered under the stairs, I thought perhaps it had ruptured. Suddenly I realized my mouth and throat felt very sore, and the sound was coming from me. I quickly clamped a hand over my mouth only to find this channelled the sensation through my nose. I pinched my nostrils together, and this stopped the rushing feeling and the bunsen burner sound. Gradually I lessened the pressure on my nose and nothing happened, except it felt very sore, as did my throat. The soreness persisted over Christmas, and I had to use my handkerchief a lot. My grandson remarked on the scabs around my mouth and nostrils.

Thinking back, I did have a lot of gastritis – belching up wind. I've had it since, but I always keep away from naked flames and I've given up smoking. I'm sure that if on the last occasion I'd blacked out or panicked, I'd have been one more unexplained fire death put down to careless smoking.

13   A Shocking Suggestion

Many people have probably experienced the curious sensation of the electric kiss.

When two people meet in a romantic close encounter it is possible to get a mild electric shock from the embrace. This happens if their lips touch together under certain circumstances.

This is not a mystical experience; although it might seem like it at the time. In fact it is just the result of simple physics working out as expected. Human beings do contain electric fields in their bodies and their strengths vary from individual to individual as well as from time to time.

A simple way to demonstrate this is the old party trick of 'charging' a toy balloon by rubbing it vigorously against the sleeve of a nylon garment. This builds up a static electric force which you can feel as a soft tingle when the balloon is brought close to the body. Your hair may stand on end or the balloon stick to your skin as both human and balloon fields of energy attract one another.

The same effect can be demonstrated by holding your arm against the TV screen shortly after it has been in use and then turned off. A heavy static charge has accumulated on the surface and the fine hairs on a person's arm are attracted towards it. Gentle crackling noises can probably be heard as the charge runs from screen to arm. In fact what you are doing is simulating lightning and thunder on a very small scale.

The electric kiss is similar and occurs if a person has built up an excess of static electricity for some reason. Because the act of kissing involves moisture from the saliva in the mouth, this makes an excellent contact. Your partner may literally feel the earth move as a consequence!

Fortunately (at least in our limited experience) this effect is rarely strong enough to cause more than a tiny jolt of surprise. Indeed it can even be an enhancement to the mood of the occasion. However, there appear to be some people and some situations when the build-up of electrical energy within their bodies run amok and goes far beyond such basic levels.

The London Times in their foreign correspondent's columns of 1934 reported on the bizarre story of Anna Manaro, a woman from Pirano in Italy. She was for a short while a celebrated medical phenomenon under study by a team of doctors because for no apparent reason a strange blue glow would emerge from her body whilst she was in deep sleep.

Various attempts were made to link the apparition to an asthmatic condition, from which she was known to suffer, and ideas about bioluminescence and electrical fields were all contemplated.

'The luminous woman', as Ms Manaro became known, was the subject of a report to the University of Padua Society of Doctors and Surgeons in early May. The reporter was Dr Protti, who had been present on 11 April with five other medical men when the effect began to emerge from the woman's breast area. They were prepared and had a cine camera ready to film what took place so that later they could study the results.

In total fifty-four frames of film were taken depicting 3.6 seconds of the puzzling spectacle. Some felt that the result had to be psychosomatic. It was noted that she was a deeply religious woman and had just engaged in an extensive fast for Lent. Could this glow be a product of the same process by which people willed themselves to have stigmata – the alleged wounds of Christ – gouged onto their bodies? This speculation was never verified.

What was discovered was that during her brief spells as a human glow-worm Anna Manaro's heartbeat and breathing rate doubled. This led Dr Protti to propose a mechanism connected with the 'radiant power of her blood'. He had already seen that this was three times the normal level. He suggested that it generated ultra-violet radiation which was known to excite any sulphide chemicals in the bloodstream. If Anna had built up an excess of these then they could be triggered into a form of luminescence by her super-radiating blood (which he argued would be even more active during the periods of increased heart rate). This in turn would serve to raise the combustion energy levels of the body.

In the end the unexplained medical condition just stopped, the mystery dribbled away and was consigned to yet another page in the discarded scrapbook of science. It was of little evident meaning – just one of those things where experience sprints ahead of knowledge at such a pace that knowledge seemingly gives up the chase.

In modern times the effects of an excess of electrical energy within the body can have damaging consequences, as so much of daily life now depends upon highly technical equipment. For some, presumably important, reason young women appear to be far more prone to this problem than men.

After four years, Jacqueline Priestman of Stockport, Cheshire, had had enough of her experiences. Frequently when she passed the TV set it would switch channels automatically. If she tried to use electrical equipment it would overload and every so often when she put a plug into a socket sparks would leap out. Her husband was himself an electrician and was baffled by this series of disasters. Knowing that the circuits blew through an energy overload was no substitute for understanding the source of the energy that flowed into the circuit in the first place.

Oddly, throughout childhood Jacqueline had suffered no problems. Only when she reached the age of twenty-two did these begin. They manifested themselves in a variety of forms. Apart from her inability to control electrical appliances she would often receive electric shocks whilst outdoors, merely from touching metal objects like handrails on stairways or at road crossings.

Her doctor was unable to help, but by a stroke of good fortune Mrs Priestman eventually found Dr Michael Shallis, a physical sciences lecturer at Oxford University. He was an expert in electric shocks and had been studying people with large amounts of static electricity in their bodies. He concluded that Mrs Priestman was one of this rare band. In fact she had over ten times the normal level of static electricity bottled inside and was literally capable of transmitting small lightning bolts destroying the fuses of the equipment she handled.

By mid-1984, after several years of this, Jacqueline's electric touch had put paid to so many devices a housewife takes for granted (over two dozen vacuum cleaners, for example!) that local service engineers were refusing to keep up. A move to Sale had not eased the situation. But something else that Jacqueline did may have done. She changed her diet.

As soon as she began to eat large quantities of green vegetables the effects of the electric charge seemed to drain away and by the end of 1984 she was relatively stable. Dr Shallis had no real answers for what was happening but felt it possible that something about diet might tip the scales in individuals prone to this electrical build-up. When it did take place it allowed the static to accumulate in the body and wreak such havoc.

A similar dilemma was reported in 1988 by Pauline Shaw, a London housewife. Her super-charged self had overpowered equally numerous pieces of domestic equipment, ranging from video recorders to ordinary lightbulbs – which showed a terrible proclivity for exploding with a sudden surge of power when she walked underneath. Worst of all was the time when she reportedly leant against the computer at her bank, creating chaos.

A number of offices have stories of electric people whom they prefer to keep away from key equipment. Usually the claim is that these individuals are 'jinxed' because malfunctions follow them around. In many cases the effects are linked to a poltergeist. Indeed there are classic cases in the records of psychic research where house lights fail, radios churn out massive static crackles, telephones go crazy and all these things are blamed on the interference of a ghostly force.

It now seems more likely that many of these instances are a natural result of human beings like Jacqueline Priestman or Pauline Shaw, pumped full of body electricity. Innocently they are creating mayhem through the simple laws of the universe. Indeed, it may well be the case that this phenomenon is much more commonplace than has previously been recognized, lurking within the shadowy world of the discredited and scientifically suspect; in other words the field of parapsychology.

The study of such a phenomenon is in its infancy, battling the prejudice that all seemingly paranormal events face. Sometimes this disdain for the supernatural has due cause, but occasionally it impedes progress. Wholesale rejection may seem a wise precaution but it can act to the detriment of science. The chances are that a perfectly reasonable solution for these assorted happenings will emerge in time and electric people will help resolve questions about many other subjects.

Some animals, such as eels, can generate very intense electric fields that render prey temporarily unconscious. As all human beings are known to possess electricity within their bodies there are clearly good grounds to feel that biological and perhaps environmental reasons exist as to why this normality can run riot once in a while.

However, we suspect that scientists grappling with the data will rarely contemplate the importance of hidden evidence within paranormal literature. Or if they do, they may be afraid to take account of it.

Of course, the problem they face is that much of this evidence is spurious. Also to credit it may diminish their scientific rigour in the eyes of colleagues. One atmospheric physicist of some repute told us he could not take home verified film evidence that we offered his team, despite it being of potential relevance, because if he was seen to be spending time and effort on something reported in a supernatural context it would weaken him critically at the time of his next grant funding application!

But records of poltergeist activity probably do mask some cases of genuine value to research into body electricity. Similarly we have personally come across a number of significant cases of apparent concern to this area whilst investigating another badly tarnished field – ufology.

For example, we spent a good deal of time investigating an incident which occurred at Risley, Cheshire in March 1978. Here – by tragic irony considering the problems that Jacqueline Priestman faced with service engineers whilst living in Sale – a service engineer was himself returning from a union meeting in that same small Cheshire town when he encountered a glowing mass of energy. This form (which he very specifically interpreted as a figure) drifted across the road in front of him, before discharging 'energy beams' into his vehicle.

Forget for a moment the understandable emphasis placed on such events by the tabloid media, starry-eyed ufologists and occasionally by the witnesses as well. We live in an era where unknown phenomena are often 'obviously' UFOs and where UFOs are 'clearly' delusions or else 'spaceships'. Years of indoctrination make it hard to break the mould of such suspect evaluation.

Boiled down to its juices after much investigation it was apparent to us that this man on a quiet road at Risley *did* have a real and frightening encounter with something that provoked potentially destructive consequences. The witness, in fact, died a couple of years later, still a young man, after contracting multiple cancers. There was never any proof that these were triggered by the electric force that struck him head-on one winter's night. But can we disregard it as a possibility?

The force was very real. His fingers were 'sunburnt'. His radio transceiver overloaded with energy and literally blew apart from within. Jacqueline Priestman and Pauline Shaw will empathize. His watch stopped at the moment of the event and would not work again whilst he wore it. Yet when someone else picked it up later it began to operate perfectly.

Cases where a witness cannot wear a watch after being struck by a beam from a UFO are not uncommon. But all such people recover very quickly and normally the watch is not found to be damaged in any way.

A perfectly reasonable scenario in cases like these is that some kind of electrical phenomenon discharges into the radio aerial on an isolated car as it travels along a lonely road. Such features recur in a very high percentage of cases the world over. The observed phenomenon is not surprisingly called a UFO (rather than an unknown type of electrical energy discharge) and any subsequent effects resulting from the incident are almost certain to be put down in ufological and media folklore as the actions of an alien intelligence. In fact what may simply have occurred is that the body of the human being unfortunate enough to be involved was topped up with static electricity after the discharge of some energy source. It is this which creates difficulties with the wearing of wristwatches; at least until this excess static charge drains away.

Indeed, we have come across several cases where witnesses to a 'close encounter' with a UFO also report 'poltergeists' in their home after the event. They describe lights or TV sets switching on or off all by themselves or hearing odd noises. The reaction of ufologists is either to reject these phenomena as irrelevant to the study of 'alien landings' or ascribe them to some psychic force which may also be behind the UFO encounter.

One interesting case involved a man at Halewood on Merseyside who was returning from a night-shift duty at the giant car plant in December 1979. A white 'balloon-like' mass floated towards him along a deserted path and drifted by. The hair on his neck was set tingling by its close proximity, but the oddest feature was his own appearance upon arrival home. His wife remarked on the 'goose bumps' on his arm and that his hair was literally standing erect as if shot full of electricity. This charge apparently, remained in his body for forty-eight hours until it leaked away gradually and he returned to normal.

In the light of what we have just discussed it may be plausible to suggest that a lot of the supposedly supernatural occurrences that are alleged in the wake of seemingly alien UFO encounters are really just the after-effects of excess static electricity that is somehow pumped into the body of the unfortunate witness by a natural energy source.

A very typical story is an impressive close encounter that occurred in Nelson, Lancashire at 3.10 a.m. on the morning of 9 March 1977. Here two night-shift workers were returning to a factory after dropping off canteen staff when they saw an object emerge from cloud above Pendle Hill. The object was a mass of swirling light, made a humming sound and was seemingly attracted to their moving car. At close proximity both the engine and lights of the vehicle failed as if drained of power by the floating mass. The men jumped from the car in panic. Both describe a tingling sensation pressing on their heads and shoulders (the man at Risley described it as like two hands pressing down on his head). Their hair stood erect as if attracted by a magnet and they noted that their eyes watered and their heads pounded (after-effects which persisted for some hours as did tiredness and nausea). The object drifted away and both car engine and lights returned to normal.

One is at liberty to reject such stories as meaningless anecdotes or even as falsities. However we believe from first-hand experience that they usually stand up to scrutiny – especially when stripped bare of the illusions imposed by society. Once we realize that the spaceship and alien imagery which dress up these tales are candy floss that disguise the essence of the account, then we see that the evidence cries out that some interesting natural phenomenon is probably involved. And it is one with powerful static electric fields surrounding it.

In the Nelson case the car owner had arranged to put the vehicle up for sale at a modest price. It hardly takes a genius to work out that it is not recommended sales practice to spin a yarn to your prospective purchaser that the proffered car has just stopped working for no good reason.

No – in this case as in hundreds of others now on record – it seems that a powerful static electric field can manifest itself as a glowing energy force and descend on people and cars from above. When it does so it appears to charge human beings with static electricity as a consequence.

Of course, all of this is interesting, but seems far removed from the question of spontanoeus human combustion. However, what we seek to do is eke out clues that might work toward a mechanism to explain what SHC could be – one that science can eventually turn into a testable theory.

If, as suggested, human beings can suddenly find themselves charged up with huge levels of electricity with rather damaging results are there further extremes of this phenomenon where the process might evoke SHC?

One additional story was reported by Paul Priestman about the electrical adventures of his wife Jacqueline. She was holding an iron one day when she presumably passed energy into its circuits. It immediately burst into flames. As you can see – electrical energy can easily be converted into heat energy, creating fire. A bridge between excess static electricity within the body and spontaneous fire may now be appearing.

We have a strange story picked up second-hand in Australia. It reportedly occurred in about 1961 somewhere in a state we will not divulge. Three men from the local electricity commission were in a vehicle with a movable tower which allows access to overhead power lines. The box in which they worked was fully insulated to provide protection from the live wires. But on this day something unexplained went terribly wrong.

After having worked in close proximity to the very strong fields surrounding the wires for several hours the tower was lowered towards the ground. One man, perhaps eager to clock off before the others, leapt out of the insulated box and on touching the ground burst into flames. A second man reacted without thinking, and perhaps in panic to escape also leapt out to get away from whatever was occurring. Exactly the same thing happened to him. He became a fireball. There was pandemonium and the third man stood in the cradle refusing to move. Checks were made. Nothing was found. He was reassured but only after several hours gingerly coaxed out of the cage. He suffered no ill effects at all, unlike his unfortunate colleagues.

We will make clear that this was a story which came to us via an employee of the company concerned, not a direct witness, but appeared to us (and to the source) to be a reliable account. However, we were unable to find anyone in Australia who could verify that such an incident had ever occurred, including those at the electricity commission involved.

For that reason it has to be treated with some caution. However, if it were true then it might suggest that enormous static charges had built up inside these two men (perhaps they were prone to this in the first place). Such was the intensity of the field to which they had been subjected that when it earthed itself through their bodies as they stepped out, the energy shorted in a huge burst of power and created the fires in their clothing. The third man presumably either did not suffer an internal static build-up or this drained out slowly as he waited in the cage.

This is, we stress, just speculation, of course. It is possible that the incident is a folktale. But it matches other data we will examine later.

Better verified is the case of a small boy in China's Hunan province. In April 1990, at the age of four, according to the *China Youth News*, he started smoking. Unfortunately this was not merely a bad social habit for which he could be chastised – because he was not smoking cigarettes – he was quite literally smoking!

The grandmother of Tong Tangjiang first noticed smoke pouring from his trousers and he was rushed to hospital. A hole of one-inch diameter was burned outward from his skin through two layers of clothing. During the next two hours he self-ignited four times from different parts of his body, producing burns on his skin as a result of the clothing set alight.

Only when naked was Tong able to cope. The internal heat build-up then had nothing to ignite; although people he came into close contact with were said to be understandably wary as he had wrecked a mattress and a couch and had narrowly averted causing his grandmother's hair to burst into flames.

Dr Hsing Peng was bemused by this phenomenon, which almost certainly was very temporary (at least, past experience suggests it is not likely to be a long-term problem). The doctor saw the possible connection with spontaneous human combustion, but from his study of the youngster had concluded that the electricity within his body was at huge levels and that this was the trigger for the hot spots under the skin.

There was some debate about chemicals within the body of the young boy, perhaps generating these excesses of electricity. Michael Harrison also cites a report in the June 1920 issue of *Electrical Experimenter*. This came from Dr Julius Ransom, chief medical officer at Clinton prison in New York State. Thirty-four prisoners there were hospitalized with severe food poisoning. The botulism toxin had to be cleared from their bodies over several days. Yet a remarkable and unexpected side-effect was that these patients had unusually strong static electric charges imposed into themselves. One man could attract pieces of waste paper to himself. Compass needles could be made to spin. Dr Ransom claimed that *every* patient with the bug in his body developed the excess static electricity. Those with the most severe doses had the strongest charges. As they got better the static charge drained out. When they were well again all the victims returned to normal levels.

If this chapter has led us any closer to an understanding of what might be happening (as usual always assuming that SHC as a phenomenon *does* happen in the first place) then we can see several clues emerge.

Firstly, all humans have electrical currents inside their bodies. Possibly when affected by strong outside electrical fields of some origin these are temporarily boosted. Also, possibly, the food we eat might be relevant to the fuelling process in some unknown way.

If a particularly susceptible person finds their body electricity is dramatically increased they may cross a threshold. This energy needs an outlet in order to be discharged. That seems to be readily available today through the overloading of domestic equipment which surrounds most people's lives. Maybe this is a defusing process and a means of preventing SHC from occurring.

In the days before electrical appliances were commonplace around the home perhaps another escape route was needed for this excess electrical energy. Even today some people may not have frequent contact with electrical circuits. Elderly people living alone, for example, may not be able to 'earth' on a regular basis through electrical appliances and any charges inside their bodies may be retained long enough to build up toward dangerous intensities. Possibly this accounts for the percentage of cases with more mature

SHC victims that we find in the database.

Of course, if true, it poses the question as to whether SHC should be common in the primitive tribal societies of countries without electrical equipment. The evidence of such SHC epidemics seems scant, to say the least.

This may be connected with another factor to emerge. It could be that diet is involved; either helping to create the increased charges in some way or when certain combustible gases are generated as a consequence of body chemistry. Perhaps the non-fatty, cholestrol-free diets in primitive societies have an added advantage. They are thought to contribute to very low cancer rates. Maybe they also help keep SHC at bay!

On the other hand, a super-charged person unable to find a way of releasing the electricity may find that it becomes the spark that ignites inflammable gases trapped inside – producing a violent and sudden eruption of fire.

At this stage these thoughts should be treated as nothing more than ideas emerging from the data as we accumulate the evidence. They are certainly not intended as coherent solutions to what may be taking place.

14 Bolts From the Blue

In a small town in New South Wales, Australia, there is a teenager who is lucky to be alive. His almost fatal mistake was to answer the telephone.

The phone call came amidst a ferocious thunderstorm. Holding a plastic receiver as lightning bolts flash from the sky outside may not seem an especially foolish thing to do. But he was about to find out that it was.

Some distance away the phone lines were struck by a bolt of lightning. At the speed of light an incredibly powerful surge of electricity sped through the wires and the phone exploded. Seconds later the youth was writhing in agony, the plastic phone now mangled and twisted as if hit by a nuclear device. One of his fingers was blown to smithereens in the process.

In a sense he was extremely fortunate. Despite the loss of a digit and relatively minor burns to his hands he survived. There are cases of people who have been killed in similar circumstances and Telecom Australia now carries a warning in the front of its phone directories.

Ellen Taylor, from a small town in Nova Scotia, Canada, lives in a valley which attracts terrible storms. She vividly recalls one day when a lightning bolt hit the power lines outside her home. The energy shot through the wiring, fusing everything as it passed. But it did not ground itself. It continued on its path and an instant later relieved its enormous surge of energy on the next building along the way.

Ellen saw it happen. The house exploded like a bomb, transformed into an inferno within seconds. The power of the raging storm was turned into fire energy with terrifying consequences.

Such awesome power has made some argue that lightning triggers SHC, if indeed SHC can happen. It may represent one very likely source for the vast energies that bring down fiery doom. So we need to consider it carefully.

Is it possible? Look at the facts. At the very moment you read these words – indeed at any moment of any day – there are some 1,900 thunderstorms raging somewhere on earth. Sixteen *million* of them brew up every year. The earth is struck by lightning approximately 100 times every single second.

When you think about these figures it is inevitable that people will get in the way from time to time. Between 100 and 150 individuals a year are killed by lightning in the USA alone. In Britain (a country with a quarter of the population of the US) the total is far smaller than that – only five or six per year on average. There is also something which seems peculiar about the distribution of such strikes.

In the September 1991 issue of the *Journal of Meteorology* Paul Brown wrote to point out that he had noted an odd feature in the fifty-six deaths in England and Wales officially recorded for the years 1974–89. A surprisingly high percentage (eighty-six) involved males. He wondered if lightning found the male body a better target or whether there were sociological reasons.

Men are more likely to engage in outdoor pursuits – such as football or fishing – and these are high-risk occupations during a thunderstorm. Women, on the whole, are probably less likely to place themselves outside in this way, retreating to the safety of a building if a rain storm breaks when they are not at home, rather than daring to sit it out under a tree so that the game can restart when the weather clears. The vast majority of those killed by lightning are in the open during a storm. Very few die indoors.

We mention this partly to issue a cautionary warning that statistics can suggest things which look mysterious at first glance but which are probably created by less obvious and yet readily explicable factors. This is a lesson worth applying to the study of SHC.

Because we know that lightning is a very visible method by which energy from the sky can be transformed into heat, it has been proposed by some that SHC victims are struck down by the proverbial bolt from the blue. We should assess whether this is feasible.

A thunder cloud is like a vast factory generating negative charge through the motions of heat, wind and rain. This is so strong that its internal field actually repels the electrons in objects on the ground as the cloud moves by. This includes the earth, buildings, people, trees – in fact anything over which the cloud drifts. As it passes, a shadow of positive energy forms underneath and trails in tandem across the landscape.

We cannot see this shadow beneath a thunderstorm but many can feel it. An approaching storm is detected by people and animals as it affects the electrical fields within their bodies. In response animals adapt their behaviour and prepare to get out of the way. Particularly sensitive human beings (seemingly those with strong electric fields inside them) say that they feel depressed, their head starts a dull ache and their skin and hair prickle. These are partly psychological but mostly physical reactions to the electrical changes that are being induced by the gathering storm.

Positive and negative charges are equally matched in any object in the absence of a storm, but the cloud bodily repels negative energy from anything below it, upsetting the normal balance of neutrality. An object that is tall or thin and needle-like is affected far more than other forms. The closer to the passing cloud the greater the positive charge induced within it.

This is the basic principle on which the lightning conductor operates and it is also why radio or TV masts on hilltops or skyscrapers like the Empire State Building in New York regularly attract lightning.

The air between cloud and ground is a good insulator and normally will not break down, but eventually the pressure becomes overwhelming and, aided by an upward flow of energy attracted from the ground toward the cloud, invisible feelers meet, a channel is forged and billions of negatively-charged particles can rush to the earth in a torrent of energy. The stream of energy merges with the area free of negative charge down below and returns it to a state of neutrality and balance. The result is a mass of lightning flashes raining down so rapidly they appear to the slow responses of our eyes to be just a single brilliant stroke.

Most people killed by lightning are not hit directly. If they shelter under a tree and the tree is struck the lightning grounds itself in a wide arc around the base and some of this energy enters a person through their feet. Humans have a very low tolerance of even moderate electric charges. In the same way animals are frequent victims of a strike possibly some distance away from them. Up to fifty sheep and twenty cattle have been felled by one bolt at a time, although it actually hit none of them. In a known incident one cow was killed 300 feet from the impact point.

According to W. Lee of Manchester University human deaths in such circumstances are caused by factors such as paralysis of the nerves controlling breathing or the heart. Burns are not extensive. Often a victim seems to have no mark on them. This was confirmed to us by the crematorium operators whom we consulted. In all the cases of lightning deaths which they had handled no victim had been seriously burnt. Death occurred because the nervous system was destroyed.

The temperature at the core of a lightning bolt is extremely high – up to 30,000°C – but this dies away to almost nothing in a tiny fraction of a second. As a result heat energy is supplied to a human body for no more than a few microseconds – and there simply is not sufficient time for extensive burning to occur.

As a consequence we can note several things. Lightning strikes can create fires, but usually when electrical equipment is fused by the bolt igniting surroundings. Animals and people who get struck very rarely catch fire and in fact show little heat-related injury. The vast majority of strikes occur outdoors, the reverse is true of SHC. These do allegedly happen outdoors, but SHC commencing in the open is seemingly quite rare.

One might envisage a situation whereby a lightning strike has triggered off something within the human body (i.e. a build-up of inflammable gases sparked by the surge of electricity). But in such cases one would expect to find strong evidence of the lightning in the area immediately around the witness (e.g. extensive blast damage to the house).

Of course, what we have been discussing is ordinary lightning relating to severe thunderstorms. However, just as the human body has electric fields constantly circulating inside, so the atmosphere is a permanent dynamo producing invisible waves of electric force. Very occasionally the difference in charge between a pocket of air and the ground is sufficient to envoke a true-life 'bolt from the blue', lightning out of a clear sky.

At other times the electricity within the atmosphere can produce all manner of spectacular events. St Elmo's Fire is an eerie blue glow that forms on the masts of ships, aircraft wing-tips, radio towers and tall buildings on land, even occasionally around power lines. It seems to be a dancing sheath of flame. With the blue colour it is visually similar to the descriptions sometimes given by witnesses to the flames of SHC.

In fact this effect is a coronal discharge caused by the air ionizing as the electricity breaks it down. It looks more dangerous than it is.

Yet this living mass of electrical energy which envelops all of us seems capable of doing things which we do not yet understand. The phenomenon of ball lightning will be discussed in detail in the next chapter. It is a fine illustration of the limits of our present knowledge. But other things do occur which hint at electric fields or ionization and yet are not as simple to reconcile with what science knows.

A case in point is the fate of York minster.

The facts are these. At about 2.30 a.m. on the morning of 9 July 1984 some youths reported observing 'lightning' streaking from the sky and striking the famous old cathedral in this ancient Roman city. It caught alight and by the time the fire brigade arrived the entire south transept was ablaze. By daybreak they had the fire out but the tons of water used to douse the flames had caused the 500-year-old timber frames to collapse. Three million pounds worth of damage was the result. As a major tourist attraction and significant part of English heritage it was a disaster, although eventual restoration work did repair much of the damage.

However, the real question posed by this night was the actual cause of the fire. How could a building highly protected against lightning receive such a devastating blow? Locals had claimed to see strange lights (possibly coronal discharge) on the rooftops of the area several hours before the event. The air was electrically active that night, it would seem. However, meteorologists said that there had *not* been a thunderstorm in York. There were some minor ones elsewhere in Yorkshire and the air seems to have had enough charge within it to have created them, but how did a relatively common situation provoke the fearsome lightning strikes that were apparently necessary to lead to the destruction of the minster?

Public debate was less concerned with the physics of what had gone on than with the rapidly developing view that the fire was divine retribution. Less than seventy-two hours earlier David Jenkins had been created the new Bishop of Durham in a ceremony at the minster. It occurred amidst a bitter public row stemming from the man's earlier appearance on a religious television programme. Some observers interpreted him as saying that he did not believe in the virgin birth or the actual resurrection of Jesus.

There was no doubting the churchman's basic Christian beliefs. The Church itself obviously agreed and confirmed his appointment despite some doubts from the public about allegedly unorthodox views.

Inevitably this simmering row surfaced during the July investiture of the Right Reverend Jenkins at York minster. When the flames struck so soon afterwards media headlines screamed about the 'wrath of God' (usually barely disguised with the addition of a question mark).

Most senior church figures were quick to condemn the stories as ludicrous, including the Archbishop of Canterbury himself. A small minority were more open-minded about the possibility.

Of course, there was the thought that the fire was the work of an arsonist; perhaps as a twisted act of protest. However, this would have been very difficult considering the high vantage point where the fire began. In the end investigation uncovered no possibility apart from that the fire started 'spontaneously' – ignited by some external force such as lightning.

The only trouble with that explanation was the absence of any sign that there had been a local storm severe enough to produce lightning.

Some days after the fire two men came forward to claim they saw what had happened. A taxi driver and a van operator allegedly made their reports without the knowledge of each other; although why they delayed doing so we do not know. An object, described in the media as either dark or orange and projecting rays onto the minster roof – according to which source you read – was blamed for the fire. Inevitably this was labelled a UFO in popular conception and the press had a field day. Headlines ranged from 'Was the minster zapped?' in the *Daily Mail* through 'Church fire blamed on aliens' (a local Yorkshire paper) and on to the amusing if perhaps a tiny bit presumptuous 'Ray gun zapped the minster say UFO men' (the *Daily Star*).

A fire-officer responding to these claims reported 'certain leads' but insisted that 'a UFO attack is not one of them!' However, an interesting story in the *Northern Echo* on 19 July quoted one of the two witnesses as saying; 'I only saw it for a couple of seconds ... It was over that quick that I am not so sure.' The other witness later told the paper that the 'UFO' had fired 'bolts of lightning' at the roof (which are *not* alien rays)!

In fact the whole matter comes down to a game with words. What the men claim they saw was a dark mass over the rooftop for a very brief period out of which emerged orange/yellow coloured bolts of electrical energy which earthed onto the roof of the church and ignited the fire. Now you are at liberty to refer to this as a UFO firing a ray gun and zapping the minster into oblivion, but less emotive terminology does spring to mind.

Eventually the fire brigade sent their conclusions to the Home Office and these were reported by the media. UFOs and heavenly retribution did not figure in them. Instead it was alleged that satellite photographs taken from space at the time of the events showed that an unusual 'cloud formation' had apparently drifted over the city at the appropriate time. It was the sort of cloud known to be electrically charged but not known to divest itself of energy in any ferocious manner. The assumption had to be that for just this once it had done precisely that.

Presumably the truth is another delicious irony. God had indeed sent down a thunderbolt from heaven at the conclusion of this stormy time in the English church. Or, to phrase this scientifically, the air that night was teeming with electricity and by chance York minster was singled out to be the one and only place for a passing isolated cloud-mass to relieve itself of all that pent-up negative charge. It did so suddenly and catastrophically and ignited the fire, before dispersing back into the heavens leaving human beings suitably bothered and bewildered.

Donald Lampson from the USA told *Fate* readers of yet another unusual electrical display that he personally witnessed.

It was August 1973 and he was on the road east of Demming in Washington state one night when he spotted strange blue flashes pulsating across the sky in front of him. Beside the road was a railway track and he had assumed there had been an accident, felling power lines and creating a short circuit. The truth was stranger than that.

For about sixty seconds he was able to watch bolts of lightning in reverse climbing from the metal rails of the trackbed at the rate of three a second. They rose to a height of about 100 feet and then disappeared. After a minute the process simply stopped.

Obviously the rails were involved in some sort of exchange of charge with the air above them, but the mechanism by which this might occur is not so certain.

Things like this are going on all over the world. The evidence trickles in to collectors of stories of ghosts or UFOs more often than it does to scientists. However, it is to science that these pieces of data may contribute the most.

On 19 June 1969 an East Anglian radio and television engineer had the following experience. It was well investigated by researcher Peter Johnson.

Robin Peck, then aged twenty-eight, was driving from Kings Lynn towards Docking in Norfolk. It was 12.25 a.m. At Bircham Newton his van lights dimmed and the engine failed. Being trained in the field he sniffed the air to try to detect any short circuit, then as the effects became worse pulled to the side of the road and suddenly lost all power. He could not restart the vehicle. The battery was dead. Stepping out to investigate he felt the air charged with static electricity. Hair on his arms, legs and head all stood up, attracted by the force. Also the luminous dial of his watch was glowing twice as brightly as normal, evidently excited by the charge in the air. At the same time he saw a glow above an electricity transformer in an adjacent meadow. The glow was a dazzling blue and in the shape of an inverted mushroom. After a minute or so this seemed to drift away. Robin Peck got back into the van and after composing himself tried the ignition. The vehicle worked perfectly and he returned home. Next day he made a statement to the police but noted that his watch no longer appeared luminous. He even checked it with a geiger counter but it still gave a normal emission reading.

Around 9 p.m. on 16 September 1974 Mrs Richards and her two young daughters were returning home from Launceston, Tasmania, on a dark night. Approaching Ansons Bay bridge the car radio filled with static – which was unusual. At the same time the sky in front of the car became brightly illuminated. Crossing the bridge all power drained from the vehicle and engine and lights failed. The woman could not restart the engine but as she was attempting to do so a powerful vibration hit the car. As it did so painful electrical shakings were felt coursing through their bodies. It lasted a minute and was followed by a smell which made them choke. The three jumped from the car and ran home, abandoning the vehicle on the bridge. Stopping at a house two miles down the road the owner, his brother and Mrs Richards drove back to the bridge. There was no sign of any problems and the car started first time. It was taken to a garage at St Helens the next day but had no electrical faults. The engine, lights and radio all worked perfectly. At the same time Mrs Richards's arms and fingers were swollen, her face had a red patch on it and she was numb on one side (suffering a minor upset of the nervous system presumably). The two children suffered no ill effects.

Both the cases just recounted were reported as UFOs, despite the fact that neither incident seems likely to be more than some sort of unusual process going on within the atmosphere. They serve as typical examples of the urgent need to break down the barriers between science and parascience. Those who care about establishing the truth concerning strange happenings that stalk the borderlands of accepted knowledge and so help kick science into the future, all have access to cases such as these. We believe that scientists researching atmospheric physics would find this material of considerable help. To do so, of course, they must exorcize the ghost which the supernatural invokes within their minds.

As we have seen, lightning is undoubtedly a frightening phenomenon, perhaps more so as it has various rather unusual forms. But is there any real evidence to propose it as a cause for SHC?

We spent some time studying examples of the alleged SHC phenomenon to establish whether lightning might have been a factor. It has been mentioned on occasions in connection with various cases. For instance, in the Mary Reeser story the Florida skies were electrified the night she died. But how frequently does this pattern occur as a rule?

We checked twenty-five of the recent British cases (dated 1978 to 1987) against the monthly weather report of the Meteorological

Office. Of these we found four that might potentially have a link with lightning.

On 2 August 1978, night of the Harpurhey, Manchester, double fire tragedy a major depression was sweeping across Britain. On the night there were severe storms in Scotland which cut electricity supplies and a girl was struck by lightning in East Anglia early on 3 August. Manchester sits midway between these events in the path of the depression.

On 6 January 1980, when the terrible death in Ebbw Vale, Gwent, took place there was what was termed freak lightning recorded over mainland Britain. A woman on the Wirral peninsular was walking with her young daughter in a pram when lightning struck and hurled her backwards. Somehow the child was unharmed.

On 13 May 1980, when there was an SHC death in Birmingham, it was in the middle of an intensely hot spell of weather. Records were set in the West Midlands on 12 May and much static was in the air, causing TV interference.

Finally, there is an interesting tie-in with a case of reported SHC survival on the night of 3 May 1981 see case 101, p.208. This somewhat debatable case occurred near Rotherham in South Yorkshire and on the same night Princess Diana was involved in a frightening incident. She was aboard a Boeing 737 jet flying from London to Aberdeen. Some minutes into the flight they flew through a severe storm and the plane was struck by lightning, fortunately to no ill-effect.

None of these cases are close enough as correlations to prove anything and it is unclear how relevant we may claim a ratio of four from twenty-five examples to be. But there is enough to suggest further research might be called for.

From what we have seen in this chapter, it is very unlikely that lightning is ever directly the cause of SHC as might at first have seemed credible. There is some possibility that it might be a trigger for other methods in unknown ways, but there is as yet no real proof even of that.

More plausible is the idea that the atmospheric conditions that make lightning form may also be conducive to the occurrence of SHC by some other – perhaps loosely related – effect. This is at least an option to bear in mind.

15 Balls of Fire

A married couple from Edinburgh, Scotland, reported to us a rather 'ghostly' experience undergone shortly after the woman's mother had died. One evening a lightbulb fell out of the socket on the ceiling of the room with an almighty crash. Bemused by this odd event they swept up the shattered glass and sat down to watch television when a second extraordinary thing occurred. In the words of Mrs Sandra Black, the narrator; 'We both at the same time saw a small ball of light enter through the living room window and in slow motion float across the room to where I was sitting. We do not know whether it stopped at me or seemed to go into me but it disappeared completely.'

This amazing phenomenon is linked with the seething mass of electricity inside our atmosphere. It is often, not surprisingly, taken as something supernatural when observed. Mrs Black might connect these happenings with her mother's death. But she sensibly remains open to the possibility of a more mundane solution.

Another Scottish case (this time at Blairgowrie) was investigated by BUFORA. It took place a year later on 25 April 1984 and was very similar – a ball of electrical energy forming above a garden on a warm and sunny day, floating gently across and 'entering' the body of a woman who was then engaged in doing a tapestry. Her dog apparently reacted to the ball. She was temporarily blinded by a flash as it went 'inside' her and had a feeling of calm and peace which she attributed to the incident. As in the Edinburgh case no thunderstorm was raging at the time and so 'lightning' never suggested itself to the witnesses.

In fact at Blairgowrie the woman regarded her encounter in somewhat spiritual terms, which under the circumstances of her strong religious background is quite understandable.

However, if we remove any interpretations imposed onto such events we are left with simple accounts of a real occurrence. Electrical phenomena can form as tiny glowing balls and float freely in the atmosphere. They can also apparently 'enter' (or discharge into) a human body without ill effect. Occasionally when this happens witnesses refer to electrical tingling sensations which they may even interpret in a supernatural manner. However, in essence what took place was a strange if natural event.

Needless to say, if electrical energy can enter the human body in a more gentle, apparently less destructive form – or on other occasions strike with the terrible violence of a lightning bolt – the question is whether it can sometimes follow an intermediary route.

Can it enter quietly and then unleash its raw power *after* going inside the body? What if it enters a person who may be prone to combustion – e.g. through a build-up of internal gases or excess fatty tissues?

In the incident at Widnes, Cheshire, which we fully investigated in 1985, one eye-witness at the inquest made a remarkable statement. It was virtually ignored at the time. We wonder if it is of unexpected importance.

Karena Leazer passed the teenage girl on the stairs moments before tragedy struck. She told the inquest that she saw a small ball of light appear over Jacqueline's right shoulder and 'fall' down her back.

Ms Leazer added that her fellow student seemed to recognize what had happened and cried out loud; 'It's gone down my back – get it out!' Just seconds later the teenager erupted 'like a stuntman on TV', as another eye-witness graphically described the terrible occurrence.

Walking with Karena Leazer at the time was her friend, Rachael Heckle. She confirmed the story at the inquest; although initially said that Karena had referred to a cigarette falling down the back of the tragic victim. Karena denied this and eventually both girls appeared to agree that all they had seen was a small light appear in mid-air, which fell down and seemingly entered the clothing on the victim's back just seconds before she burst into flames.

The inquest let this claim pass by with little evident consideration. Conceivably this has no relevance to what happened to the teenage girl that morning. But it is remarkably similar to the incidents from Edinburgh and Blairgowrie.

In those cases two women claim a small ball of light formed in mid-air, drifted towards them and apparently entered their bodies. Is such a bizarre claim as ridiculous as it appears on first sight?

Once we start to ponder such questions the possible answers with regard to SHC can loom disturbingly large. For they may suggest that the conditions which generate this awesome and horrendous phenomenon could be more commonplace than anyone had previously imagined.

In fact what all the witnesses above may be describing is ball lightning. The literature of many surprising fields is full of it – from ufology to hauntings and from astronomy to meteorology. Yet incredibly ball lightning is a phenomenon that many scientists have refused to accept until very recently. There are still some who cling to that position.

In his 1972 volume *The Lightning Book* published by MIT press, Peter Viemeister called it 'The most controversial form of lightning' and cautioned 'some scientists do not believe that ball lightning exists'. In this he was referring to a popular view, as expressed in B. Schonland's 1950 book *Flight of the Thunderbolts*. This reported how some felt that most cases of alleged ball lightning were really just an optical illusion. Such an illusion, the theory went, may be created by the dazzling effect on the retina when the eye sees a brilliant, yet quite ordinary, lightning flash.

Whilst it may be true that this illusion can sometimes lead to spurious reports, there are now few scientists who reject the phenomenon out of hand. Sometimes it also appears in the total absence of ordinary lightning. Furthermore, the potential links with SHC are impressive, as we shall see. We need to give ball lightning the most detailed consideration.

The evidence for the phenomenon has established itself past the scepticism of demanding researchers, because it had been consistently reported. It is also ongoing and its cases are global in nature. Yet it has not yet allowed science to determine what it is. The debate is as intense and fractionalized as that surrounding any field of the paranormal.

Indeed, many reports of ball lightning are made to supernatural investigators and ignored by science. It sits uncomfortably between science fact and fiction. Yet like SHC it reflects a dangerous natural force crying out to be better understood. As a form of trapped energy it may even be harnessed one day and prove financially lucrative in some technological sense. This may explain why the Japanese are so fascinated by it.

The best way to come to terms with ball lightning is to review the evidence. The following brief accounts are summaries of ten documented events selected almost at random from a huge and constantly expanding database. They give the essence of this mysterious phenomenon and illustrate just how common yet diverse it is. References are given to the full report.

1920 Parkside, South Australia

A hissing noise was heard in the sky and a ball of about one foot in diameter descended slowly down an adjacent fence. It was smoke-like and had small 'worm-like' shapes inside that wriggled, flickered and sizzled. The ball hit a cement porch and 'bounced' at walking pace along a thirty-foot path, rolling slowly the rest of the time emitting sparks from its edges. On the three or four times it rose it did so to a height of some one-two feet and formed an egg-shape by 'squashing' at the base before returning to a perfect sphere as it climbed into the sky. At the end of its final bounce it took off at an angle over a tree. Seconds later it hit some houses, exploded and badly damaged them. (*Science Frontiers*, 33, William Corliss)

1941   Basingstoke, Hampshire

A family was dining during a violent thunderstorm when a clap of thunder was followed by a small ball of light a few inches in diameter, first seen by a witness delighting in the apt name of Mrs Rumble. It rushed through the garden and entered the room through the open French windows to then move about in front of the startled diners. It resembled an electric lightbulb and was a violet or purplish colour inside. A strong hissing noise was emitted. It passed the back of Mrs Rumble (then a young girl) within a few inches but she felt no heat sensation. Then it crossed the room and left the house via the rear door. A faint sulphurous odour remained. (*Journal of Meteorology*, 1990, report on ball lightning, Mike Rowe)

Late World War Two   Shetland Islands, Scotland

During a very violent storm late one night a small ball of fiery colour entered a secure radar station by the feeder lines and moved slowly around the room for several seconds. It did not earth on the huge metal transmitter equipment around which it moved freely. Instead it hit a small wall-mounted lamp with a metal bracket. The disappearance, in a flash of light, resulted in the complete destruction of the glass bulb. Every piece of glass was literally evaporated. But the room displayed no other evidence of heat or scorching. (Letter to the authors, November 1986)

September/October 1969   Gee Cross, Hyde, Cheshire

During a late-night autumn thunderstorm the radio mast on Werneth Low was struck by lightning, causing damage and power loss. A bungalow in the lee of the hill experienced the storm directly above it, waking the man and wife who lived there. An orange ball of light like a beachball entered through closed and double-glazed windows. It was some three feet in diameter and emitted little sparks as it rolled along the floor. It moved in an arc into the room, round the side of the bed, then reversed its path (the direction of emission of the sparks changing also) and went out of the room again, travelling very slowly. The couple got out of bed but could not understand how it got in or out of the house. A slight smell of electric arcing was left but the nylon carpet over which it passed was not touched. (Personal investigation by meteorologists Mike Rowe and Dr Terence Meaden of TORRO)

20 September 1973   Margate, Kent

At 5.30 a.m. after a night of torrential rain and violent storms a couple in their house observed a small ball of six inches diameter appear literally out of their TV screen! It materialized as a shimmering blue glow and drifted slowly across the room a couple of feet above the ground. Then it streaked up into the light-fitting in the middle of the room and vanished. The only damage was a blown fuse in the television's plug. (Mike Rowe in the 1990 ball lightning report from the *Journal of Meteorology*)

6 June 1977   Barnards Castle, Durham

During a heavy downpour without thunder a teenage motorcyclist was enveloped by blinding light which emerged from a purplish-pink mass that had formed just a few feet into the air. A car was overtaking on a slight incline and observed this also. Both driver and motorcyclist felt power drain out of their engine and lights, but they continued moving during the few seconds of this effect. The oval vanished and steam was pouring from the leather clothes worn by the motorcyclist, although he had felt no heat. His clothes were, in fact, now bone dry (as was his motorcycle) despite the incessant downpour, implying a lot of water was rapidly vapourized. Both vehicles halted. The motorcyclist felt the tank of his machine and found it scalding hot to the touch. Car and motorbike now had full power and no after-effects; although the motorcycle brakes (applied instinctively at the moment of power reduction) were badly worn. On arrival home the mother of the motorcyclist commented on how red and flushed his face was. (A UFO investigation by the group CHRYSIS in UFO Investigators Network files)

4 August 1977   Irlam, Lancashire

A mundane ball lightning case which involves Edna Randles, mother of this book's co-author. It was above the roof of the author's home (unluckily when she was away). Mrs Randles was in the garden talking to a neighbour on a warm, sunny evening. They both heard a loud buzzing noise 'like an electricity sub-station'. After fifteen seconds it ended with a 'pop' like a gun being fired. The women looked round but saw nothing. However, the neighbours' children who were playing nearby came running to report an oval about the size of a streetlamp over the roof-top. It was a deep yellow blending into orange and was stationary. The pop corresponded with its disappearance amidst a white flash. The house was on the edge of open farmland and it is reported that at this time the rest of Irlam suffered a sudden short rainstorm which missed only this small area. (Personal investigation)

3 December 1979   Fleetwood, Lancashire

At 6 p.m. on a night with an intermittent thunderstorm a sphere of six inches diameter entered the room down the sealed chimney. It was not unlike a soap bubble, i.e. semi-transparent, and purple in colour covered with furry spikes. It drifted between a man and his adult son and headed towards the TV screen (the set had been switched off shortly before so the screen was presumably still ionized). When about eight inches from the screen the ball vanished with a loud crack or pop and a smell like an electrical arcing was left behind. (Letter in *Journal of Meteorology*, May 1986)

3 July 1986   Winchester, Massachusetts, USA

At 2.20 p.m. on a wet afternoon a woman saw a red ball of light over trees in her neighbour's yard. It remained stationary for some seconds and as she shifted position she heard a tremendous explosion as if a bomb had struck her house. The burglar alarm and lawn sprinkler were set off but the house lights were unaffected. Outside she found the cover on the meter for the sprinkler had been blown off and was blackened and smoking. The fire brigade were called and said they had seen the ball when driving in the area minutes before. Substantial other damage was done to electrical circuits and a nearby tree was stripped of its limbs and bark. Weather records show that thunderstorms were in the area at the time. (Investigation by astronomer Walter Webb in *MUFON UFO Journal*, January 1987)

26 August 1989   Sedgeley, West Midlands

On a cloudy but dry evening a man and dog in fields outside a nature reserve saw a 'soap bubble' just larger than a golf-ball drift past with the wind. It went into the field and swooped as if caught in a downdraft and flew round some horses (who took no notice). After a couple of minutes it headed into the wind and flew at the man, climbing over a wire fence and then stopping right next to him. He saw a white feather-like blob inside its semi-transparent surface and a small dark patch which he thinks was his own reflection! He was tempted to touch it but perhaps luckily for him the little ball 'kicked' into motion and vanished. (Authors' investigation)

As you can see ball lightning has some commonly reported features. It is rarely very big (a couple of feet would be a large example and most are only inches in diameter). It is free floating and seems to have no problem entering well-sealed rooms – indeed it has a tendency to do precisely that and has even been seen on several confirmed occasions passing right along the aisles or cabins of moving aircraft. Yet, so far as we can discover, it has never been seen inside a car. This is important because there is no verified case of a car ever being struck by ordinary lightning. The metal body creates an environment called a 'Faraday Cage' which offers near-perfect protection to its occupants. Excellent advice if you are scared of lightning is to sit in your car until the storm is over.

The colour of ball lightning varies considerably, although yellow/orange and bluish/purple are both common. It can avoid electrical equipment or earth into them. When it vanishes it can do so silently, with a huge explosion, a fizzle, crackle or pop. It is sometimes silent in flight, other times fizzes, buzzes or hisses. It can be very brilliant or dull and semi-transparent, being likened to a soap bubble on a number of occasions. When seen at very close quarters internal structure is sometimes reported, other times not. From time to time it drains power from cars underneath it, blows electric wiring and puts out house lights as it passes by. Or else it causes unlit house lights to glow as it drifts past or again it may have no effect at all on electrical equipment just inches away.

Although it is very rarely said to emit any heat, even when extremely close to a witness, on several occasions it has turned water into steam, warped metal, and evaporated glass completely – indicating considerable heat energy must be present, even if trapped inside.

Ball lightning, as you will appreciate, is almost impossible to fit into a nice simple box. This is a key reason why science has had real problems coming to terms with it.

It is not even possible to say whether it needs a thunderstorm to appear. It does form during violent storms but quite often happens when the weather is merely wet, or hot and sunny, or just plain dull. In the UK and USA scientists usually argue that ball lightning is by far more common during thunderstorms and rarely forms in their absence. Yet UFO organizations in these same countries regularly get cases of what look like non-thunderstorm ball lightning (usually regarded by witnesses as UFOs).

Are scientists wrong to assume ball lightning is rare in non-thundery weather? In an investigation by Professor Yoshi Hiko Ohtsuki – from Waseda University in Japan – he found that out of 2,060 ball lightning events collated in his country an amazing 97% did *not* occur during a thunderstorm.

It is no wonder some scientists face all these conflicting reported properties and statistics with a modicum of despair and may wish that ball lightning was just an optical illusion!

Indeed, such are the conflicts of evidence that some theorists seek refuge in quite astonishing ideas.

Vincent Gaddis is an American writer who in many ways rediscovered SHC. This was in his reports during the early 1950s for *Fate* magazine and his later book *Mysterious Fires and Lights*. This was not about SHC as such but it did incorporate media stories that he had picked up in his research.

In early 1991 the now very elderly Gaddis was interviewed by Mark Chorvinsky for *Strange* magazine (issue 7). He spoke of his long interest in ball lightning, saying; 'I consider that there are two types ... There is a natural type which explodes when it is through manifesting. The other is smaller in size and much more vivid ... It runs around exploring everything, and in addition it exhibits intelligence, which I think is innate ... There hasn't been enough emphasis on this.'

Leaving aside the astounding concept of intelligent ball lightning, most scientists have rather more mundane yet hardly less controversial theories to try to deal with the phenomenon.

For example, in the science journal *Nature*, 19 March 1971, Ashby and Whitehead from the UK Atomic Energy Authority research laboratory at Culham, Berkshire, questioned whether miniature meteorites formed of anti-matter might enter the atmosphere and create ball lightning. However, they held back on the premise of the apparent tie-in with thunderstorms which do not seem likely to produce more such particles.

Physicist Dr Roger Jennison in a letter shortly afterwards asked how could such micro-particles penetrate the sealed hull of an airliner in flight as a floating ball of light?

This was no academic question. Jennison knew they did because he had been on an Eastern Airlines jet above New York when precisely such a ball chanced to drift past him and dozens of other passengers right down the aisle. It was in fact one of those cases that had finally persuaded science to accept ball lightning.

As the debate continued in *Nature* further letters followed, including one on the subject from the aptly named UMIST, Manchester professor, Dr Charman. Also Professor Paul Davies (then of Cambridge, later Newcastle, and now Adelaide University in Australia) was alert to the similarities between UFO and ball lightning data.

Paul Davies has experience of the serious UFO data, which may explain his astuteness. In fact, he has, since 1971, published two papers about how we might resolve the difficulties of understanding ball lightning.

In *Nature*, 15 April 1976, he wisely uses the disguised phrase 'transient aerial phenomena', but notes how the properties of this floating energy phenomenon (be it UFO or ball lightning) are 'puzzling and bizarre'. He adds, very perceptively, that the 'situation would be greatly improved if the aura of mystery and superstition surrounding unusual aerial events were dispelled'. From our research into SHC and its potential links with such 'unusual aerial events' we wholeheartedly agree.

In *New Scientist*, 24 December 1987, Davies wrote an article entitled 'Great Balls of Fire' and reviewed the various attempts to recreate ball lightning in the laboratory. As he phrased it, 'nature can do something that we cannot yet'. Although minor success is reported, often by accident, nothing long-lived or stable has been produced, according to this report.

British UFO researcher Ralph Noyes followed this up with a paper in *MUFON UFO Journal*, June 1988, entitled 'Paradoxical Energy Levels'. He has developed an interest in the possibility that some UFO sightings reflect unknown natural energies which could be used for technological purposes.

Jenny Randles gave a briefing lecture to politicians in the Houses of Parliament in 1980 and was told by one senior figure that official interest in UFOs continued because of this very possibility; i.e. that the perceived unusual energies could be ensnared and turned into weaponery. In that one statement may lie the real truth about the so-called UFO 'cover up'. It seems a lot easier to believe this idea than the cries from the media and UFO buffs about alien invasions hidden from a terrified populace.

Noyes briefly reviewed the recent scientific attempts to work out the cause of ball lightning and showed how its contradictory status leads almost all theories astray. He drew no real conclusions but did point out that the paradoxes encountered in trying to understand UFO data and poltergeist activity have much in common with those faced by scientists struggling to get to grips with ball lightning. We might now add SHC to the same list. He remarked that 'progress in understanding any one of these very different phenomena may conceivably throw light on the others'.

Perhaps the most detailed theoretical attempt to resolve the dilemma came in an article by Altschuler, House and Hildner of the National Center for Research at Boulder, Colorado. This was published on 7 November 1970 in *Nature* and asked 'Is ball lightning a nuclear phenomenon?'

From case histories where water barrels have boiled dry and logs split asunder they suggested that one hundred million joules per cubic metre was trapped in some fireballs. Such an incredible degree of power is hard to explain in terms of chemical processes. Furthermore, microwave or electric currents did not work especially well, they claimed, as they could not enter a sealed system like an aircraft hull.

As a result they felt a steady release of energy is needed and only a form of radiation appeared to fit that possibility. A problem immediately arose, as they put it, because, 'an observer standing within 2 metres of high energy ball lightning ... might receive a radiation dosage of a few hundred rad; enough to cause radiation sickness or death'.

They anticipated the argument that *no* cases of ball lightning show this effect. However, that could be a misconception based on the limited data available to ball lightning researchers. We can argue quite well that the strangest examples of ball lightning are never reported to – or found within – the province of science, but reach paranormal researchers. There are some undeniable indications that illness and even fatality has been reported after a close encounter with 'ball lightning' in these fields.

Altschuler, House and Hildner argued that the apparent lack of radiation effects on ball lightning witnesses is explained because very energetic forms are rare. Indeed we may add that such 'super' ball lightning is widely reported as a UFO because of its extreme range of features. As a result science is barely aware of its existence.

Even UFO buffs doubt that their 'spaceships' could be exotic forms of electrical phenomena.

Presuming less energetic ball lightning of between ten and one hundred times lower power were all we had, Altschuler, House and Hildner indicated that much reduced radiation counts would then be expected on close proximity witnesses – hence the missing cases of severe illness. However, was anybody actually quizzing ball lightning victims about whether they suffered after-effects over the subsequent days, weeks and months which might even be consistent with radiation sickness? We doubt it.

In a reply to *Nature* on 5 December 1970 C.R. Hill calculated expected dosages from such a low energy ball lightning event. These still came out at several hundred rad and he said that 'it would be surprising if there had not been reports of close observers developing signs of radiation sickness'. He suggested these be immediately sought in the records.

It is not clear whether many researchers bothered with this, but on 15 November 1974 Fleming and Aitken from an Oxford research laboratory reported to *Nature* on tests they conducted into bricks taken from the archway of a house in Berkshire which had ball lightning pass through it on 8 May 1970. They predicted from the environment that twelve rad should be detected within the bricks. In fact they found thirteen rad, a quite routine amount that was in no way suggestive of serious irradiation. This proved nothing except that if this small-scale ball lightning event some years earlier had given off radiation then it was of a pretty low order.

On 15 April 1976 a new case was reported in *Nature* that offered hope of a breakthrough. The reporter was physicist and ball lightning researcher Mark Stenhoff (who, like Paul Davies, had been wise enough to see the value of UFO data and had for a time worked with BUFORA). He described an incident which occurred at 7.45 p.m. on the night of 8 August 1975 when a violent thunderstorm struck the Warley area of Smethwick in the West Midlands. In fact it was to suggest a possible direct link with SHC.

A woman cooking in her kitchen observed a ball of light about four inches in diameter appear in the air above the cooker. It headed straight towards her. It was bright blue/purple and surrounded by a flame-coloured ring.

She heard a noise like a rattle, smelt singeing and felt a burning sensation as she was hit below her midriff. She instinctively brushed the ball away. It then simply vanished. We do not know if the smell and heat were directly associated with the ball lightning or secondary effects that were created by it. It is these effects which make the case so important.

Her hand quickly turned red and swelled up at the point where it had contacted the ball. Her gold wedding-ring (which had not been in direct contact but was nearby) was so hot that it was searing into her finger and had to be removed. Furthermore a hole appeared in her dress and tights where the ball had struck. Her leg underneath was not burnt in any way but did become red and numb and felt like pins and needles.

The hole in the dress was approximately two by five inches and the synthetic fibre was shrivelled around the edges. E.R. Wooding analysed it at Stenhoff's workplace, the Royal Holloway College, and told *Nature* on 29 July 1976 that the damage plus the red mark on the victim's skin (less red than from a scald apparently) all pointed to a temperature of no more than about 100°C coming into contact with the woman and that this indicated that the energy within this ball lightning event was only about one thousandth of the extremely high estimates researchers had speculated previously. It was not high enough to generate radiation sickness effects and none were evidently reported by this woman.

Indeed, this was presumably a contributary factor to comments from Mark Stenhoff which he offered when we asked him for an opinion. Could accidental encounters with ball lightning such as that reported by the woman at Smethwick perhaps lead on in some instances to deadly SHC cases?

He told us firmly; 'I am of the opinion that the energy of ball lightning is only about one kilajoule and that most of all cases where damage is reported whose severity implies much higher energy are better explained by the effect of ordinary linear lightning. I would thus conclude that ball lightning is not the explanation for SHC.'

Which is fair enough. However, we do wonder about those cases where no linear lightning could be involved. In addition the similarity between the Smethwick incident and the ball of light allegedly seen to fall down the back of the Halton College teenager with such tragic consequences ten years later do seem noteworthy. This may be coincidence or not. Particularly as we have reason to suspect that ball lightning can be far more powerful than that rather small example which appeared over the West Midlands cooker.

Certainly one must ponder the now well-established phenomenon of miniature ball lightning, forming suddenly in the midst of a storm or clear skies, seemingly oblivious to confining walls and discharging itself instantly with tremendous heat or rapid loss of enormous energy levels.

If this was what struck the two women in Scotland did the

Halton teenager have the misfortune to catch a rare form that discharged all its energy in one burst, transforming this into a destructive fire?

Recall also the engineer at Risley who met something on a lonely road and then contracted fatal cancers. Was this by tragic coincidence or not?

A large fiery object also wreaked havoc when it hovered in front of a car in Huffman, Texas. The two adult women and a young boy who were inside suffered serious 'burns' as a result. We might now see this in a slightly different light from the normal 'starship' imagery of similar happenings.

This terrifying incident occurred at 9 p.m. on 29 December 1980. The conical or triangular mass was radiating heat at such intensity that the inside of the car in which the three witnesses were travelling became unbearably hot. The 7-year-old boy was in hysterics and his grandmother could only inform him she thought it was the end of the world and Jesus would be coming soon. They sheltered in the car – with the door open – for much of the encounter. The other woman, Betty Cash, got out and stood in front of the bonnet, directly exposed to whatever radiation this thing was apparently pouring out. Later, when she returned to the car she had to use her coat to touch the door handle as the metal was scorching hot.

One feature remarked on by Betty Cash is potentially very significant and familiar in the light of the Smethwick case. She felt her gold wedding-ring grow very hot and begin to burn her finger. This was later red and swollen, as were parts of the bodies of all three victims; although most particularly Betty Cash, who had been out of the car for the longest period.

The child and his grandmother who stayed inside were ill for some days (the boy vomiting all over his bed the same night). Both had severe burns to their skin. Their eyes were affected with blisters and illness and diarrhoea persisted for weeks.

But it was Mrs Cash who was so ill that she nearly died. By morning her skin was blistering and she could not even keep down sips of water. Although her friend cared for her for three days her condition rapidly deteriorated and she was rushed into hospital almost in a coma. Here she stayed in intensive care for two weeks. Huge clumps of her hair just fell out. She also developed breast cancer and over the next three years had five spells in hospital. She survived but has never been fully fit. One could well suspect that the phenomenon produced these effects, although no link can be proven.

This wedding-ring 'burn' found at Huffman and in the

Smethwick ball lightning report has appeared in several other cases. A similar effect was reported in an incident between Exhall and Haselor in Warwickshire at 7.50 p.m. on the cold, clear night of 13 March 1980. Once more this is amidst the three month spell we have traced when SHC incidents were oddly frequent.

A man driving his car was passed at close range by a white object which glowed red at each end and was a cylindrical shape. It took only a couple of seconds to pass but left a legacy. The steering wheel suddenly became very hot. The driver nearly lost control and suffered a nasty burn on his hand.

Only the steering-wheel was affected. The man himself felt no radiated heat. Jenny Randles published the story in a UFO magazine and solicited responses from qualified readers in seeking to establish how this effect might have occurred. The view from several physicists and engineers was that the metal ring inside the steering-wheel had become electrically charged by the radiating field emerging from the object but only during its very brief passage across the plane of the car's path. This circulating field had been partially transformed into heat.

Physics teacher Paul Stevenson made some calculations. About 5,000 joules per second was added to the wheel with a current as high as 18,000 amps from an evidently very powerful radiating source.

We also got a letter from a Mr J.W. Goodes who operated massive spot welding equipment. This had an overhead transformer and two long arms, with a core of copper and a rubber casing and water-jacket to insulate. When the arms were brought into contact a huge field was generated for a very brief time and the magnetization of the two arms forced them apart. The operator once tried an experiment to prevent this effect, putting a metal ring around the two arms to stop the magnetic field separating them beyond a certain point. However, he soon began to smell burning and had to drop the expensive equipment as his hand was growing intensely hot. A huge electric current had been induced into the metal ring. As with the ring-like car steering-wheel or the gold wedding-bands this could circulate freely and could only release energy by creating heat, melting through to burn the operators' hand.

Another case of what looks to be ball lightning but which was not reported as such came at 9.30 p.m. on the dry night of 17 September 1977. A young couple were restoring an old stone post-office in the village of Newmill in Cornwall. As researcher Terry Cox found, they got rather more than they expected.

As the woman prepared to leave the house she sensed something odd (very possibily the static charge in the air). By the step was a hazy green mist in the form of a ball. She ran back inside to bring her boyfriend and he also saw the form, now floating just above ground level up the steps towards the building. The ball eventually drifted upward and hovered by a tree before it meandered away and disappeared.

Within days both witnesses, who came within a few feet of this object, began to feel ill. The symptoms included vomiting, headaches and muscle pains. Both were admitted to hospital. The man was given extensive tests and released when the illness appeared to clear on its own. No cause was ever apparently discovered. His fiancée (who had been outside the longest period of time) did not improve as quickly and it was decided she must have appendicitis. A perfectly healthy appendix was thus removed. Again the symptoms eventually vanished on their own over the next couple of weeks and she was discharged from hospital with no lasting ill effects.

If nothing else these cases might suggest to researchers such as Altschuler, House and Hildner that a radiation theory for ball lightning is possible. Meteorology may not have such data, but ufology apparently does.

Given the characteristics of ball lightning that we have discussed its possible relationship with SHC should begin to emerge. However, there are three cases where the two phenomena blend together with even more frightening coincidences.

In *Fate* magazine (April 1961) American Reverend Winogene Savage reported a story from a friend. Allegedly this man awoke at 5 a.m. to hear his wife screaming. He ran to the living-room and found her on a rug, a mass of flames. A small ball of light was seen briefly in the air just above her. The man was badly burnt trying to help, but she died from her injuries. It is not clear where the 'ball lightning' went, but, as in many SHC cases, the fire was extremely localized. Not even the rug underneath the woman was burnt.

Slightly better documented is a case from the USSR. This involves a horrific accident which befell five climbers whilst on the Caucasus Mountains on the mild night of 17 August 1978.

They were at about 12,000 feet on the mountainside and had made camp for the night. A mountaineering teacher with the party was Victor Kavunenko. Like the others he was in his sleeping-bag awaiting the dawn to continue their trek when the air began to feel strange.

This effect was possibly an intense electrostatic field, as noted in other cases. Looking around him Kavunenko was horrified to see a yellow ball of light just a few inches in diameter which was hovering in mid air inside the tent. Then it drifted *into* the bag in which one of the climbers was asleep. Seconds later that man screamed in agony.

The ball emerged from the bag and entered an adjacent one with similar results. Kavunenko describes being frozen with fear awaiting the arrival of this object at his side, which occurred moments later. It seared a hole right through his sleeping-bag. Kavunenko says it gave him an intense pain like a welding torch and he lost consciousness. He 'came to' soon after to see the ball still darting about the tent, occasionally entering one of the bags. It 'attacked' him again, he lost consciousness once more and later, when he recovered the ball of fire was gone.

Kavunenko talks of being paralysed and feeling as if his body was on fire. His comrades were also howling in pain. When they could move they found that one of the team, Oleg Korovin, was so badly burnt that he was dead. The others had multiple burns but struggled down the mountain and eventually alerted a helicopter rescue team. They were rushed to hospital.

In hospital the injuries to the men were found to be very severe, with huge holes burned into their flesh, even exposing muscles in some places. It was speculated that Korovin was the least fortunate because his sleeping-bag had been insulated from the ground by a rubber mat and so he had taken the full brunt of the attack.

Finally, a horrific case that is still under investigation was first reported by ball lightning researcher Dr George Egely of the Physics Institute in Budapest, Hungary. This was in a paper to an international science symposium in June 1990. We have had help from British physicist and meteorologist, Dr Terence Meaden, who attended the conference, but Dr Egely has apparently changed jobs in the new political climate in his country and has not responded to our questions. Here is the basis of the case.

On 25 May 1989 a 27-year-old engineer stopped his car on the roadside some seventy miles from Budapest near a village called Kerecseud. He intended to urinate into the bushes. His wife remained in the car and suddenly noticed that he had become surrounded by a blue aura, apparently akin to coronal discharge, on the perimeter of his body. He opened his arms out wide and moments later collapsed onto the ground.

Obviously distressed, his wife leapt from the car and ran towards the man. One of his trainers had been stripped off by a blast of energy and had a hole burnt into it. The man's wife tried desperately to revive the lifeless form. Then, by quite amazing fortune, a vehicle passed by. It was a bus filled with medical men on the way home from a convention! Several came to the aid of the man, but it was too late.

The autopsy later revealed that the man had a hole in the heel of his foot coincident with that in his shoe and his stomach and abdomen area were literally turned to carbon. He had evidently been 'combusted' through some sort of intense electrical charge inside his body.

The weather on site was dull and dry with no thunderstorm; although the couple had driven through an electrical storm some thirty miles before.

The hole in the foot shows clearly that a strong electric current had earthed itself through the man's body, although the blue glow and the apparent combustion of his stomach area are more puzzling if one seeks to ascribe this to some mundane form of electrical discharge.

We were grateful to meteorologist, Sheldon Wernikoff, from Skokie, Illinois, who has studied the case for the Tornado and Storm Research Bureau. He remains unconvinced that it is directly connected with spontaneous human combustion or ball lightning.

Instead Wernikoff proposes that overhead power lines might have lead to the incident. He notes that in rural areas of the USA 'where public utilities have quietly exceeded the capacity of their lines', huge discharges have been known to spontaneously 'leak' from the cables to the ground and suddenly electrocute unsuspecting cattle.

Indeed, the scenario he is painting of sudden breakdown (either through overloading or some malfunction) might fit the Australian power workers' case discussed on pages 126–7 where two men 'caught fire' after earthing themselves into the ground following maintenance work on overhead lines.

Wernikoff suggests that the case of the 'urinating Hungarian' opens up a potential danger that few people will have given thought to. In fact he thinks the man may have literally been electrocuted through his own stream of urine, which was acting as an excellent conductor for the build-up of electricity! Not a pleasant thought.

Wernikoff describes a case involving a friend in eastern Canada around 1961. Some new power lines had been installed and a group of men were working nearby. Afterwards 'they cleaned up at a wash basin on an outdoor table about 100 yards from the overhead power lines beside the road. After [one] poor fellow had washed up he emptied the basin on the ground and was immediately electrocuted'. The cascade of water poured from the basin fulfilled the same function here as the stream of urine. Apparently he also had a very similar hole burnt into his foot and heel of his shoe (a feature we have ourselves discovered to be commonplace in outdoor lightning strike victims). Although the Canadian survived for a few minutes he also died.

The meteorologist proposes this as a timely warning to anyone who may think of relieving themselves in open country beneath power lines. Invisible yet very intense electrical fields surround them. You may well be better off holding on until you find a better insulated place to carry out your ablutions!

Of course, this solution to the Hungarian case has not been established. We have been unable to confirm that there are power lines at the site and Wernikoff does not know either. A freak discharge may still have been possible even without them. The nearby storm suggests the atmosphere was saturated with electricity. Dr Meaden told us that Wernikoff's theory 'seems reasonable to me'.

However, there are some scientists working on the possibility that the atmospheric conditions that were present may have created ball lightning literally inside the body of the unfortunate young man. Once it had formed it calcified his internal organs and then electrically discharged through his feet, with only the blue glow as any external sign of its presence.

This is far from proven either, but we know that such a thing may be possible. Ball lightning has a significant tendency to form as very small balls of energy and to appear out of nowhere *inside* confined spaces (incidents in rooms, chimney-stacks, TV sets, aircraft cabins and cupboards have been frequently recorded).

What if a small example of ball lightning were able to form *inside* a cavity within a human being? What if it could not ground itself in any way and had to discharge energy more slowly over a period of time – thus generating tremendous and continuing levels of heat?

Such frightening questions have no answers, but do need to be asked.

16　May the Force be Within You?

On page 125 we told the story of two men 'attacked' in their car by a strange glowing force. Afterwards they reported various odd effects; notably tingling sensations, hair standing on end, pounding heads, red and watering eyes and nausea. These were evidently not psychosomatic disorders, so what caused such problems to occur?

In his 1986 book *Earthworks*, biologist and anthropologist Dr Lyall Watson described the results of various recent studies into the sensitivity of human beings subjected to high strength electrical fields. These forces may only be visible if they ionize the air and make it glow. However, many people placed inside one experimentally do become aware of it. Indeed they complain, as Watson says, of 'a tingling or crawling sensation of the skin and a stirring or prickling of fine hairs on the arms or in the nape of the neck ... [also] fatigue and dizziness'.

As we can see, this matches the symptoms expressed by those who come into contact with ball lightning, or indeed often by those who believe they have been confronted with a UFO. If our suspicions about a link are vindicated the symptoms may even be considered warning signs of potential risk from an outbreak of SHC!

Although ball lightning can be seen there can often be less visual evidence for the presence of an isolated, intense, electrical field. We noted how in the Hungarian combustion tragedy of May 1989 it is possible that electrical fields generated by overhead power lines (if such were present) could have been responsible for a major catastrophe within the man's body. To an observer sat at quite close quarters all that was visible was a faint blue glow – intriguingly akin to the pale-bluish flames said to accompany some SHC incidents.

There has also been research into the effects of electromagnetic fields on human beings. In 1961 Robert Becker, an American surgeon, produced a claimed correlation between severe mental disorders and magnetic storms which sent showers of cosmic rays and atmospheric ionization to earth.

In a world which has become increasingly high-tech, with microwaves used for cooking food, energy-leaking computers in most officers or homes and magnetic resonance scanners checking your ailments in hospital we are all exposed to a regular flood of hidden energies. There are growing indications that those people who come into contact with such forcefields more than others may be running the risk of physical and mental disorders.

A growing number of studies in recent years have begun to probe the unexpected dangers of power leakage from electricity pylons. Correlations with both suicide and leukaemia have been allegedly traced; although the evidence is still disputed by other researchers.

A case in point is the delightfully-named village of Fishpond Bottom in Dorset. When examining a map of the county so as to describe its proximity to rather better-known towns we saw with a smile that it is just south of both Ilminster and Chard – rather appropriate as it happens!

Certainly for the people of the village itself it is no joking matter. Not only have they had the quiet tranquillity of this hamlet shattered by the intrusion of a row of high-tension wires and pylons marching through the countryside, now many of those living close by claim they have since had a more tangible payment to make.

There have been stories of sickness, sore eyes, headaches and strange 'blackouts'. Demonstrations show that a florescent light-tube illuminates when held underneath the pylons, apparently from the intense ionization and electromagnetic field filling the surrounding air. Exactly this effect was also reported to us by an RAF man and his wife living at Katong in Singapore (see full report in *Crop Circles: A Mystery Solved*). Ball lightning drifted through their kitchen during a torrential downpour and passed by an unlit house's light-tube, making it glow eerily just as at Fishpond Bottom. As we saw in the last chapter witnesses to ball lightning have also reported the same ill effects as claimed by the people in Dorset.

Official views are that there is no cause and effect relationship between the illnesses and the power lines, but villagers have fought on and won some support from some scientific studies. One was carried out in the area by Professor John Taylor, a physicist from King's College, London. He found that 75% of the residents who lived within 300 feet of the power lines alleged serious health complaints which could have been related.

Although this is far from proof, the locals pointed out that freak electric discharge from the lines had incinerated a cow and there were other possible incidents that might be associated.

At the very least this argues for more research into the potential hazards of living within vast seas of energetic forcefields. This is in fact exactly what we all share our lives with, usually in unsuspecting ignorance. If the Hungarian SHC case does turn out as Sheldon Wernikoff proposes then the risks are all the more horrific and starkly displayed.

There are some remarkable cases we have tracked down that seem to relate to even more baffling energy fields of no discernible cause. They again point out the increasing risks brought about our modern scientific world and reveal the hidden hazards of environmental pollution.

A woman trying to enter a new car park in the centre of Durham in 1975 reported the dilemma of finding that an invisible forcefield seemed to push it back. It was as if a giant magnet was resisting all attempts to squeeze the car into this small area. Yet subsequently local officials had no trouble at the site and when the woman attempted to repeat her experience for the TV cameras she also had no more difficulty at all.

We were tempted to smile, but came upon an even stranger case in Australia. It occurred in 1979 in the Armidale region of New South Wales and involves a farmer who had a traumatic experience one fine and sunny day.

He went out for a look at his sheep – or rather he tried to do so. Instead his vehicle hit an invisible barrier just like that claimed by the woman in Durham. This seemed to be spread around his 100 acre farm and although he tried several ways to get out it was as if the air was solid and was preventing movement beyond a certain point. He attempted walking and it was reputedly equivalent to stepping into a 'plastic wall'.

Evidently there was no problem with electricity supplies reaching the farmhouse, but this may be because the field was intermittent. It was there for a minute or so, then it disappeared only to return some minutes later when he tried another escape. After forty-eight hours the effect disappeared for good and never returned. Apparently the farmer was so disturbed by this that it took him several months to return to any sort of normal life.

A peculiar moving barrier was reported to us by an engineering PhD student from Hampshire who experienced the phenomenon in June 1935. He was on a farm at Osmaston, Derbyshire with two friends. At about 11 p.m. they were walking towards the road to catch the late bus back to Ashbourne. Suddenly there was a crunching sound as if something was touching the gravel on the path. This came up behind them, the noise stopped and the invisible field of energy literally passed right through them.

The physical sensations that were felt by the men were a deep clamminess and also their hair standing on end, suggesting that an electrostatic field was involved. There was also a brief muscle paralysis.

Interestingly, the same engineer had a second experience in August 1938 whilst cycling from the youth hostel at Dunblane in Scotland and heading up the slope of Glen Almond. It was an overcast day but with some sun filtering through. However, suddenly he became aware of a dark swirling cloud, almost like a tornado without the vortex tube. It was already overhead and an intense oppressive sensation was filling the air. Within moments it was surrounding the man on his bicycle and a high-pitched 'piping' noise was filling his ears. After a few seconds it simply vanished.

With the benefit of fifty years' experience the engineer now suspects that the metal bicycle traversing a lonely moor was a perfect attraction for an energy cloud of ionized air. How it was generated is quite another matter.

Intriguingly, some suspect that these ionized fields descending from the sky also produce the so-called crop circles as found in cereal fields. We should stress that most of the circles and probably all the ingenious designs that have incited exotic theories about alien messages are in our view the result of hoaxing. What we are referring to are the few very simple circles and rings which physicists and meteorologists take seriously. We believe these to be a real and natural phenomenon for four main reasons.

They have been traced through various historical records back at least 500 years. Clearly something has been producing circular impressions on fields for a long time, perhaps as long as people have been present. They are known from all over the world, as any natural phenomenon should be. At least thirty well-documented cases exist where eye-witnesses have consistently reported the formation of circles as being forged by rotating atmospheric forces. Finally, three separate university research teams have experimentally verified the proposed theory explaining their presence.

Physicist and meteorologist, Dr Terence Meaden, is the originator of the research but is actively supported by many others, such as top ball lightning investigator, Professor Yoshi-Hiko Ohtsuki from Japan. This man is involved because there could well be a direct link between the circle vortex and ball lightning. At the very least they have several things in common.

Indeed, whilst our studies in this book of the strange electrical forcefields, ball lightning and energy vortices may appear to have ranged over a diverse assortment of unrelated issues and skirted round the edge of SHC, it is very possible that they are all just reflections of the same essential force of nature. In fact they may even be one single phenomenon appearing in different guises – with SHC, just like crop circles, being an extreme and unusual consequence that occasionally results.

As for the circles themselves, those scientists who have researched it for many years contend that a rotating column of air with strong ionization properties descends to earth like a corkscrew and dissipates rapidly, creating the circular mark as it does so (see *Crop Circles: A Mystery Solved*). Usually it is invisible, except because of the effects it has on the crop, but occasionally the energies involved are so intense that air may literally turn into a glowing plasma. If so it may inevitably be misperceived by witnesses as yet another so-called UFO.

The presence of the strong electrical and ionizing radiation fields in this vortex can lead to peculiar effects sometimes reported as 'mystic' in the proximity of circles. These include tingling sensations, pounding headaches, nausea – indeed precisely the same symptoms we have met many times before in different contexts throughout the past couple of chapters.

This may indicate a direct link between circles and SHC. We are not necessarily proposing that if you stood in the middle of a field at the precise few moments when a vortex forges a crop circle that you would spontaneously combust. The chances are remote of someone being in one of those rare places where such an event occurs during the very short period when it actually manifests. Eye-witnesses so far have been outside the circles looking on – perhaps rather fortunately for them. A particularly energetic vortex could conceivably appear right on top of someone. Possibly there are circumstances under which that person might not emerge unscathed. As to whether SHC is something that could occur in particularly extreme circumstances, at this stage in the research we simply do not know.

A very interesting observation of what seems to have been one of these energy fields or ionized vortices was made by Mr R. Roberts of Kent. It occurred in July 1966 and is potentially very significant.

He was in a van on the old road from St Margarets Bay to Dover when a sheet of intense rain hit the windscreen and forced him to a halt. On his side he had a better view of an isolated field of rough grass with some derelict iron-clad buildings – he thinks probably remnants from First World War sea defences. Some cows were in the field nearby.

Suddenly a loud hissing sound began. The cows heard it and looked round at once. Expecting to see a lightning strike fell the cattle, instead Mr Roberts was to be amazed. A vertical tube of some twelve feet diameter was there as if from nowhere. It had the appearance of glass or plastic but was really only visible because of his close proximity and the weird effect it had on the downpour. This was striking the side of the tube and running down as if it were solid. No water was getting inside the created tubular zone at all!

In other words, the vortex was producing a circular forcefield and preventing the rain from intruding. He could see that inside the region the grass was pressed flat to the ground and was apparently dry. It was as if someone had placed a giant glass beaker over the landscape.

Unfortunately, Mr Roberts did not see how the thing disappeared. But the story does compare with the cases of unseen forcefield barriers which seemed so bizarre and unlikely. Possibly these mysterious incidents would have appeared rather similar to their onlookers had they been outlined by falling rain and not had a science-fiction-like invisible nature.

Bear in mind that you cannot see the electromagnetic field that is a TV signal. But turn on a television set and its effects become visible. Neither can you see the wind unless it moves some trees by its force. Similarly the forcefields we are discussing are innately invisible, unless something else interacts with their energies to show that they are there.

Yet another representative and rather frightening case was reported by researcher Peter Rendall in the *Journal of Meteorology* (December 1990). It occurred in mid to late October on the outskirts of the city of Bristol within a field of rough land beside the Downend sports centre.

Two young girls were throwing a plastic frisbee back and forth when it apparently struck 'some invisible force' and reversed its course immediately. It was like hitting a brick wall that was not there.

Following this the two girls found themselves surrounded by a 'yellow bubble' – seemingly akin to the vortex tube described by Mr Roberts in Kent. From their perspective inside the tube the girls were able to offer an account of its effects. They were hit by a force that they describe as like a mild electric shock and were thrown to the ground by its strength. They also found it rather difficult to breathe, possibly because the air was actually more rarified within the field. Fortunately they did not stay inside until the air ran out (as it may well have done in time) but rushed forward and 'broke through' the wall of the 'bubble' to escape.

There was speculation about beams from space producing this effect, but again we see how this terminology masks an intriguing natural phenomenon. In this case we have some direct evidence that the invisible forcefield barriers may be at least partly electrical in form.

We debated whether to discuss one further remarkable incident in this chapter, because we have no desire to give credence to something likely to remain unproven and seem fantastic. But we decided it had to be mentioned, on the understanding that we recognize its highly contentious nature.

In fact, to set the scene, there have been several instances where ships have reported encounters with unusual electrical and magnetic fields.

Fortean Times reported an incident found in the *Indianapolis Star* of 27 February 1910 by folklore researcher Dr Thomas Bullard. This describes the adventures of the *Trafalgar* which it said occurred on the morning of 26 February whilst it steamed past Wolf Rock, south of Cornwall. In fact, Nigel Watson and Granville Oldroyd traced earlier British reports which prove the incident must have happened before this day. They date it to the evening of 28 January 1910.

The basic facts are agreed to be as follows. There was suddenly a loud bang, the ship began to shake and a ball of fire appeared to tumble into the sea some twenty feet from the hull. It cast up a plume of water and was making a hissing noise, suggestive of ball lightning.

Coincident with its appearance the ship's mast and part of the metal superstructure began to glow with what may well have been coronal discharge. Indeed, the ship's captain, Captain Davies described it as 'a faint violet light from which millions of sparks emanated'.

One of the crew who was striking a bell at the time received a violent electric shock and after the effect faded the ship's compasses were found to be pointing in the wrong direction as if temporarily influenced by powerful electromagnetic fields. Apparently when these were taken off the ship some hours later they were all found to be working perfectly.

Crop Circles: A Mystery Solved summarizes a quite similar incident which occurred on the 23 or 30 July 1904 (the date is uncertain) when the *Mohican* was in the Delaware breakwater off Philadelphia. It encountered an odd grey cloud and again the ship began to glow with a ghostly electrified aura. The compass-needles spun wildly. Sailors' beards stuck out (a clear indication of strong electrostatic forces) and all returned to normal only when the cloud vanished. Again this case was documented in the press at the time.

We have come across several other similar incidents.

Such precedents make the alleged 'Philadelphia Experiment' (as the book by William Moore and Charles Berlitz calls it) slightly easier to accept. The difference is that this story contends that in 1943 the American destroyer escort the USS *Eldridge* was *deliberately* subjected to such forcefields through a top secret scientific experiment. This depended upon research initiated by electronics genius Nikolai Tesla and had reluctant theoretical input from a team of experts including Albert Einstein.

The intention was to perfect invisibility using controlled but very powerful electrical forcefields generated by equipment placed on the ship. The experiments supposedly had incredible side-effects. The affected area and the ship became radar invisible as expected, but also turned optically invisible. In other words the *Eldridge* disappeared from sight! Even worse the vessel was reputedly teleported across the ocean from its location off Philadelphia and briefly appeared in another place before returning to its original position in the breakwater. There were even more unbelievable alleged consequences, including – most significantly for us – reported spontaneous combustion of some of the crew members.

Of course, all of this presumes that the story is more than a myth, which many sceptics understandably presume it must be. The Moore/Berlitz book was stimulated by a tale of fairly questionable origin dating back to early 1956 when a scientist and UFO writer heard it from one of his correspondents in a series of rambling letters. This is hardly a promising start for such an incredible tale.

However, a Naval Research Department subsequently called in the author, Dr Jessup, and they discussed the matter several times. It seems they had received an annotated copy of Jessup's book – apparently sent them from the same correspondent and alleged eye-witness to the experiment. Two of the senior staff at this research facility took it seriously enough to order a limited reprint of the book complete with its annotations to circulate for discussion; although the Navy are today at pains to make clear this was an unofficial act based on the personal interest of these two officers.

The book *The Philadelphia Experiment* was published in 1979 and was a genuine report with some interesting research and speculation. It offered only limited hard evidence that the case was genuine. There was an indication that the official records of the USS *Eldridge* had been doctored. The man who first told the story to Jessup was established as being where he said he was on the dates in question. As for any sign of the project or those involved, the authors quote from an interview with one scientist they found before he died, but the case remained hard to pin down, as they admit.

None the less it has become a *cause célèbre* within the paranormal community. The tale has spawned *Thin Air*, a quite fascinating thriller novel based upon the incident and was possibly an influence on the fictional movie *The Final Countdown*, where a US nuclear-powered aircraft-carrier encounters a strange electrified vortex and is teleported forty years back through time. Here it must decide whether to engage and presumably decimate the Japanese fleet on its way to attack Pearl Harbor.

More directly the Philadelphia Experiment became a science-fiction movie named after the Moore and Berlitz book and crediting this as a source, even though its storyline shared little more than the basic premise and then took off along some sidetracks of its own.

But in September 1989 the saga of this reputedly great wartime catastrophe and its allegedly unprecedented cover-up took a dramatic turn when a man named Al Bielek came forward to claim that he was one of those who had actually been aboard the *Eldridge* durings its fateful mission.

Bielek was prepared to tell all and to answer questions about 'Project Rainbow', as he says the experiment was code-named (although this name is in fact hinted at in the Berlitz/Moore book). Jenny Randles was fortunate enough to meet Bielek at a conference in Phoenix, Arizona and can report on his quite incredible story.

He says that the first partial success with a model came as early as 1936. He joined the project in 1939 and by 1942 it was obvious it could work with a full-sized ship and crew. However, Tesla was adamant that human beings might suffer terrible harm and wanted to continue with no people on board. With the war at its zenith the pressure for results was too great. When Tesla's approach was denied he sabotaged the first trial so that it failed inexplicably, then quit. A few months later Tesla was dead. The sabotage attempt was traced and the tests continued.

Bielek says that the first real trial began on 22 July 1943 and the ship did become both radar and optically invisible (although there was a misty cloud surrounding it and the outline of the unseen hull in the water gave away its presence). The navy decided to scrap the optical invisibility function after this because they had real fears about convoys of unseen and undetectable ships ramming one another and sinking.

A hasty second experiment occurred some days later but this time there was a blinding flash and the ship totally disappeared (i.e. not even leaving an impression in the water). It was gone for several hours. There were fourteen crew on board but few knew fully what was happening, only that they were part of an electronics experiment going disastrously wrong. Bielek claims that when the ship rematerialized five of the crew were partially imbedded within the steel bulkhead. One was lucky, only his hand was so affected. The rescue team had to chop this off but he was saved. The other four had 'merged' with the metal so completely that they were dead. Others came back mentally unstable. A couple of them had appeared as a mass of flames and burnt to a crisp in seconds. Several simply vanished and never returned.

Allegedly the scientists had not calculated that by playing with such huge forcefields they would actually warp the local space-time environment and transmit the atoms of the ship and crew through time and space. By not realizing this fact, most crew arrived back slightly out of phase with their original selves when the field wore off, thus creating the range of horrific consequences. Reputedly atomic energy fields of living things can behave in unpredictable ways without very careful readjustments.

Bielek further claims he was personally transported about forty years into the future where he was greeted by project staff waiting for him. The resurrected experiment was now outlawed as far too dangerous.

He freely admits to having researched the subject for over twenty years before he became 'aware' that he had actually been a part of it himself. As he watched *The Philadelphia Experiment* movie on TV he began to 'remember' things which had been blocked from his mind.

We certainly have no intention of asking you to accept this amazing story at face value. We have opinions about it, of course, but no reason to openly dispute anybody's integrity. Yet anyone who makes such claims must be aware that most cautious readers will not accept such a tale purely on trust. We print a résumé of what Bielek said, not to endorse it or refute it, but simply because we think it worth bearing one or two points in mind.

First, strange forcefields do appear to exist in nature given the cases that we report in this book. Experiments attempting to unravel such energies are not inconceivable. That horrific unforeseen consequences might occur and be buried out of sight is not beyond the bounds of possibility.

However, if such things did happen then the claim that SHC was one terrible side-effect is obviously significant for our research. It would establish that the natural occurrence of such a phenomenon might result from interacting electrical fields imposing themselves on a human body and creating an imbalance within the atomic structure of a biological system.

Einstein's unfinished 'unified field theory' was supposedly put to the test in the Philadelphia Experiment. In his most famous equation $E = MC^2$ the physicist proved that if you do unleash the energy (E) within an atom its power is utterly incredible (equalling the sum of its very tiny mass − M − but then multiplied by the fantastically immense number C^2 − which is the speed of light squared). We see this vast eruption of energy from just a tiny seed in terrifying action during an atomic explosion. If this were to occur in another form within a human body then it is by no means unimaginable that a significant outpouring of energy could emerge from a small confined space and that this might be enough to precipitate huge levels of searing and continuing heat – in other words SHC.

All of this is pure speculation and we again make that very clear. As with most readers, no doubt, we can only suspend judgement about the claims. However, there is one rather intriguing 'coincidence' that should be mentioned.

The legend of the Philadelphia Experiment involves a ship at some unknown point just off the coast of this city and somewhere in the Delaware breakwater. It was reputedly swathed by perhaps the most powerful electrical forcefield ever artifically generated. According to Bielek (different slightly from the Moore/Berlitz book) this first occurred on 22 July 1943 and again less than three weeks later. As a result the USS *Eldridge* was covered by a cloud of misty energy and there was an intense electrostatic power present. One side-effect was to project the ship and its cloud of energy through space-time about forty years into the future.

We have no way of knowing if this happened, but suppose it did. Is time a two-way street? Should there be an equal and opposite reaction as with most physical forces known to science? If you go forty years forward might not part of the field have also been sent forty years backward?

We say this only because, as you saw before, the SS *Mohican* encountered a strange misty cloud with incredible electrical power that appeared out of nowhere above its position just off the coast of Philadelphia out into the Delaware breakwater. This was on either the 23 or 30 July 1904 – as near as not thirty-nine years to the day before the alleged Philadelphia Experiment took place at what looks to be more or less the same spot in the Atlantic Ocean.

The *Mohican* story is well documented and exists within the newspaper records of 1904, as has been clearly established. Oddly nobody discussing the Philadelphia Experiment has (to our knowledge) linked these two events and the 1904 incident formed no part of the original legend or Al Bielek's more recent story. Of course, it may be that if the experiment was invented by someone in the 1950s they based it on these relatively obscure real press reports about the SS *Mohican*. But it is odd that the link with this marine curiosity was never brought out if that were so.

Furthermore, Michael Shoemaker noted something else in his detailed study of the 1904 press accounts. In his first publication of his research, which appears to be his 1987 *Fortean Times* article, he said there was 'some extraordinary thunderstorm activity during the period' (i.e. late July/early August 1904).

In fact, the area around Philadelphia and Delaware was struck by several terrible electrical storms, causing death and destruction within a period of just a few days around the turn of the month.

Thomas Bullard also notes that there was a freak tornado, several ball lightning incidents and at least one unusual electrical discharge of more peculiar nature at the same location during this time. Evidently the atmosphere around Philadelphia and Delaware was a seething mass of energy fields at this rather appropriate moment in the year.

Perhaps this means nothing beyond coincidence. However, if there is any substance to the supposed Philadelphia Experiment this deluge of incredible electrical energy in the same area where it occurred and precisely thirty-nine years before the main tests took place takes on a new significance.

How does any of this relate to the phenomenon of SHC? Obviously we are not suggesting that people are being fried by numerous top secret experiments. However, there are those who think that powerful forcefields natural to the earth's own environment can under freak conditions reproduce a very localized 'Philadelphia' effect. These natural forces may even be what the experiment was trying to recreate.

British researcher Paul Devereux is a recognized authority on the contentious subject of 'leys' (energy pathways said to criss-cross the earth and which may generate strange phenomena at points of intersection). Devereux uses the term 'earthlights' to describe the glowing forms which float about certain geophysically active regions of the world, and he has been working with various scientists to isolate the trigger factors of electrical and magnetic fields. In books such as *Earthlights* and *Earth Memory* he also contends that ancient civilizations may have been more 'in tune' with this natural energy and perhaps even built monuments like Avebury or Stonehenge to mark out the lines of power. Interestingly in *Goddess of the Stones* Dr Terence Meaden suggests much the same for his closely related vortices of ionized plasma.

American SHC researcher Larry Arnold has a parallel concept of 'fire laynes' running across the earth. We are as yet unpersuaded by the concept simply because lines between locations of SHC incidents spread across maps are easy to draw if you try hard enough. Ley researchers have discovered that it is simple to plot lines between a few points which seemed significant at first but are merely coincidence. We have also seen how hard it is to decide which cases really are SHC (if any). As a result some of Arnold's fire laynes may be the result of well-intended if doubtful calculations.

There has been quite a strong link claimed by some UFO researchers between magnetic fault lines beneath the earth's surface and hot spots of UFO activity. Dr Michael Persinger, a Canadian specialist in the interaction between electro-magnetic fields and the human brain, extended this further to look at all unusual phenomena (including poltergeist outbreaks, mystery apparitions etc). A massive computer study of 6,000 events convinced him and colleague Gyslaine Lafreniere that they were onto something and they published their results in a 1977 book called *Space-Time Transients and Unusual Events*. Persinger has continued the investigation and provided impressive concrete data that supports Devereux's ideas. The scientist correlates luminous electrical effects in the atmosphere with earthquake activity below the earth, which he suggests sets the forcefields in motion.

Other research, such as that by Livingston Gerhart, has attempted to show a direct relationship between outbreaks of SHC and increased magnetic disturbances in the atmosphere. Whilst the idea is of interest we believe there are as yet far too few solid cases of unequivocal SHC for any meaningful conclusions to be drawn from such small numbers.

When we were testing the twenty-five alleged British SHC events in the period 1978–87 for comparison with lightning activity reported by the Meteorological Office we also looked at their data for solar radiation. There was no match between increased levels and reputed SHC. Even if there had been one the figures would be meaningless with so few pieces of data.

It should be noted that Persinger does suggest that there may be a near-symbiotic relationship between electro-magnetic disturbances in the atmosphere (e.g. as generated by solar radiation storms or sunspot maxima) and subterranean earthquake activity. 'Cosmic shock waves' may result in earth movements.

One man who has taken this to an extreme is Andrew Davie B.Sc and FGS from Alloa in Scotland. In 1991 he was invited to be a director of the International Institute of Geo-Rheology, which position seems to supplement a consultancy called Geo-Rheological Surveys Co Ltd. operated from his home for several years. Davie told us that he has developed what he terms a 'simple – although rather unusual – method of quantifying and forecasting natural geophysical phenomena'. He includes in this list all sorts of spontaneous fires, including SHC. In other words, he believes that he can mathematically predict their occurrence.

Davie told *Fire* magazine in June 1984 that he was trying to interest brigade officers in taking courses to learn 'about the predictive and analytical techniques' that he has devised. So far as we know these courses are not yet established. Nevertheless, he alleged a number of successes.

For example, Davie claims that he calculated in advance that at 15.14 hours on 18 May 1970 there was a danger of some type of spontaneous fire beginning in the Coatbridge area of Scotland. At 15.30 on that very day the local brigade were called to Marnoch Drive, Glenboig to investigate a smell of smoke in a room.

Investigation revealed a strange sight in a cupboard. A pair of wet swimming-trunks had been thrown in the closet a couple of days before after a young boy had returned from the local pool. By chance the trunks had fallen onto a bag of sugar and a spontaneous chemical combustion had followed, presumably because of the chlorine in the swimming-baths. The packet was charred and the trunks had fused with the bag. Luckily the fire was out when the brigade arrived.

We find it hard to understand how Davie could have predicted what was clearly a random event – a combination of chance circumstances. However, he says that he submitted to fire services advance information on several 'danger periods' as indicated by his calculations and cited other instances where spontaneous fires supposedly resulted. But the official report on the Glenboig fire had no reference to his predictions.

The precise details of how Davie works out his calculations have not been given, despite our requests. Of course, he may just be understandably reluctant to share his secrets with outsiders. But Davie has told us that he uses simple methods that 'any 9-year-old boy with a pocket calculator can carry out in a matter of a few minutes'.

He submitted a paper in which he describes how he allegedly predicted the nuclear explosion at the Chernobyl reactor in the Soviet Union on 26 April 1986. He claims to have isolated this location as a danger spot some two years prior to the event. The fire occurred because staff engaged in risky pursuits at a time when the geographical location was at a maximum of its predicted danger potential. This seems to us to be a proposal not unlike the scientifically disputed claim of 'biorhythms' which can be charted in advance and supposedly isolate periods of risk in one's physical or emotional life. But without further details it is hard to be sure.

Davie indicates that he bases his calculations on patterns of earthquake activity. He appears to regard earthquakes as the trigger factor which sets ripples of energy into motion. In essence, Davie says anomalous energy fields are generated by interacting natural forces and can alter the atomic structure of both organic and inorganic matter.

These forces cause disruption in the electro-magnetic fields in-

herent within all things and can generate various sudden catas-
trophes as a result.

He claims a 97% accuracy rate for forecasting that some major
disaster will occur within a predicted zone at a precisely defined
point in time (amazingly – he gives this to within a second!)
Obviously, the true test of this theory is to demonstrate that he can be
specific ahead of an SHC event. We did ask him to provide some
advance calculations on further danger areas, giving positions, dates
and times, even if he could not explain to us how he came up with
these figures. Sadly no predictions were forthcoming.

Before we went to press we phoned to ask why Mr Davie had not
backed up his claims. He seemed very sincere in his regret that he was
dependent on others and, as he put it, 'the powers that be don't want
it broadcast until they are ready'.

Instead Mr Davie offered us details of a possible incident of SHC
dating back to the year 500 BC, during the time of the 'Hoh-He
denomination' of rulers. If we understood Davie's story correctly,
this comes via a translation he and others have made of some
Japanese-like hieroglyphs that were written down in 1988 by an
Egyptian psychic whilst the mystic in question was in some form of
trance.

We thanked Mr Davie for his material, but decided it was inappro-
priate to include details secured in this way as part of our catalogue
of SHC cases compiled for this book.

17   The Kundalini Fire

In our search for answers to the mysterious combustion of human beings, we have turned our attentions in many directions, from the simple to the complex and the mundane to the esoteric. The Kundalini fire undoubtedly falls into this latter category, but must be considered if we are to examine all sincere solutions that are on offer.

According to the tantric tradition of Hinduism, an untapped reservoir of energy lies in the 'astral' body, known as 'Kundalini'. It is represented as a coiled-up serpent situated at the base of the etheric spine. For most of us, the 'serpent' remains asleep during our lifetime, but this energy can be aroused by the practice of Kundalini Yoga, with dramatic, and sometimes frightening consequences.

The astral body, where the Kundalini energy resides, is said to fit hand in glove with our physical self. In yoga, there are seven major junctures where the physical and the astral bodies meet which are called 'chakras', or 'wheels'. These are supposedly situated at the base of the spine, the root of the genitals, in the region of the navel, at the heart in the centre of the chest, the base of the throat, between the eyebrows – sometimes referred to as the 'third eye', and on the crown of the head. It is through the chakras that the Kundalini energy, once released, allegedly flows.

Kundalini Yoga has been around for between three and four thousand years. Practitioners have sought to release this energy for very good reasons. It has been estimated that only a very small percentage of our brain potential is actually realized. That means, in theory, that there is a vast source of mental and creative talent lying dormant in all of us. Kundalini is the energy that will allow this latent genius release.

The correct method of arousing Kundalini is extremely complex, and can take many years of meditation to achieve. It is also physiologically and psychologically dangerous, we have been told. Students are warned to practice arousal only under the guidance of a competent teacher.

Practice includes certain systematic physical exercises, techniques of concentration, visualization and controlled rhythmic breathing. However, there seems to be no definitive route to the release of Kundalini. When this release does occur, the effects are said to be both physiological and psychic.

Yogis have described a trembling of the body prior to the release of Kundalini, and *an explosion of heat*. During Kundalini's ascent up the 'Rod of Brahma' – analogous to the spine – various inner sounds are heard, described as resembling a waterfall, the tinkling of bells, flutes, and the humming of bees. As the Yogi visualizes geometric shapes, flames and other forms, the head feels giddy, and the mouth fills with saliva. Visions occur, as the body goes out of control, and the energy pours up through the chakras. Writer Ajit Mookerjee, describes the release of Kundalini as: 'The body's most powerful thermal current.'

A loose definition of 'Kundalini' is 'the fiery serpent within', according to Hindu authority, Benjamin Walker. He states that one of the earliest symptoms of the awakening is a sensation of warmth at the 'Muladhara' – the chakra located at the base of the spine. The temperature changes from warm to hot, followed by a sensation of burning heat throughout the whole body. Student, Brian Van de Horst, described his own awakening. 'I suddenly felt some activity at the base of my spine. A feeling like shuddering, surging energy began travelling up my back. I felt as if every nerve trunk on my spine had begun firing. I could feel vortexes of electricity around places that have been described as chakras.'

Another student, D.R. Butler, describes his initial encounter with Kundalini. 'Suddenly, surges of energy – like electrical charges – streaked up my spine. These gradually evolved into a steady current of *hot* energy flowing from the tip of my spine to the top of my head.'

Yogis warn that it is at this stage that the 'serpent-fire' must be carefully directed, or it can become a 'destructive force'. Under the direction of a tutor, the subject can control the energy through the various chakra points to bring about a transcendent state of being. But if Kundalini is not controlled, what are the consequences?

As we have already noted, the majority of students need to practise for several years before they are able to release the Kundalini energy. However, it has been found that some students require only a few weeks. More importantly, it is believed that this energy can be released spontaneously in people who have no knowledge of Kundalini Yoga. Even for those who are knowledgeable, things can go dramatically wrong.

This was graphically brought home to Gopi Krishna when

Kundalini was aroused spontaneously in him without the benefit of a guru. It happened while he was meditating, and involved much suffering. On one occasion, while lying in bed, the Kundalini serpent stirred.

> The heat grew every moment, causing such unbearable pain that I writhed and twisted while streams of cold perspiration poured down my face and limbs. But still the heat increased and soon it seemed as if innumerable red hot pins were coursing through my body, scorching and blistering the organs and tissues like flying sparks. The whole delicate system was burning, withering away completely under the fiery blast racing through its interior.

Is this 'heat' an actual dramatic rise in temperature, or merely a psychological phenomenon, perhaps a psychosomatic reaction?

To date, there has been little objective study of Kundalini, although some clinical testing has been carried out, principally by research scientist, Itzhak Bentov. He proposed that altered states of consciousness could be brought about through the effects of vibration-frequencies on physiology. This is understood by yoga meditators. However, what is significant here, is that Bentov proposes that Kundalini energy could be released in *anyone* by environmental stimuli. He cites mechanical/sonic vibration and electromagnetic waves as possible triggers.

The effects, he conjectures, have been misunderstood by the medical establishment. Far from being psychological, they are linked to actual changes in 'bodily rhythm' and 'bio-magnetic field'.

Bentov alleges he has observed these changes in meditating subjects who were wired up to a ballistocardiogram, affecting their cerebral magnetic field. He explains: 'This magnetic field – radiated by the head as an antenna – interacts with the electric and magnetic fields already in the environment. We may consider the head as simultaneously a transmitting and receiving antenna, tuned to a particular one of the several resonant frequencies of the brain.'

Bentov suggests that Kundalini might be a development of the nervous system. Can an interaction with outside electromagnetic fields give rise to the sensation of great heat, which might, conceivably, result in spontaneous human combustion?

Dr Lee Sannella, author of *The Kundalini Experience*, relates one incident involving a woman patient which seems to indicate this. 'One day she lost awareness while meditating, with her hands on the table. She awoke to find char marks on the table corresponding to her hand prints. One may look at these cases as examples of how pentup psychosomatic energy can be externalized, since heat is one of the regular manifestations of an active Kundalini.'

During our research, a Mrs Barton of Manjimup in Western Australia contacted us, and we are wondering if her condition might be attributable to an unconscious release of Kundalini energy.

My husband always says that knowing me convinces him of the reality of spontaneous human combustion. If I am relaxed and asleep, my body sometimes overheats without me being aware of it. For instance, I can be curled up in an armchair with a rug over me, or in bed.

On several occasions when I have fallen asleep in bed, and my husband has later joined me, he has found my skin unbearably hot. On awakening I have felt quite comfortable until I have moved. Then I would feel suddenly very hot and throw back the covers.

Sometimes I have woken in the night and felt quite comfortable – not hot at all, not even cosy. But as soon as I make a movement, suddenly, instantly, I am unbearably hot.

Mrs Barton wonders what would happen to her if she did not wake up and throw back the covers. As a number of SHC victims seem to be overcome by the phenomenon while in a relaxed – perhaps meditative – state, even asleep, should we consider the Kundalini option along with all the others?

But Kundalini can be realized other than in a meditative state. According to Ajit Mookerjee, music and dance can also arouse this potentially dangerous energy. This brings to mind a possible link with fire victims Phyllis Newcombe and Maybelle Andrews.

22-year-old Phyllis was an enthusiastic dancer. On 27 August 1938, she was dancing at the Shire Hall, Chelmsford, Essex. As she was leaving the dance-floor with her fiancé, Henry McAusland, in a matter of a few seconds her dress turned into a mass of flames. She was taken to the manager's office to await an ambulance, but it was over half an hour before it appeared. The poor girl died from her horrific injuries.

The dress was modelled on an old-fashioned crinoline, so the coroner speculated that a lighted cigarette had brushed against it, setting it on fire. However, her father demonstrated at the inquest that it was not possible for a cigarette to have set light to the dress. It needed a direct flame.

About twenty years later, there was an almost identical tragedy, this time in a large public room in Soho, London. 19-year-old Maybelle Andrews was dancing with her friend, Billy Clifford. Suddenly, her back, chest and shoulders burst into flames, igniting her hair. Billy and some other men tried to beat out the flames, but she died on her way to hospital. He later commented: 'I saw no one smoking on the dance-floor. There were no candles on the tables and I did not see her dress catch fire from anything. I know it sounds incredible, but it appeared to me that the flames burst outwards, as if they originated within her body.'

If SHC is the result of a psychic-inspired energy source, one must consider poltergeist incidents, and how this might tie in. Amongst a plethora of activity, objects are thrown around a room, drawers mysteriously empty onto the floor, and items disappear and reappear. This can last a few days or many months according to witnesses. Researchers have found that the phenomenon usually centres around one person. Biologist and author, Dr Lyall Watson, told us of the hundred or so poltergeist cases he has personally investigated from all over the world. No country is immune.

The popular theory is that the pent-up anxieties of a particular individual are exteriorized by an internal 'energy' in the form of violent and mischievous movements of inanimate objects. That is why usually, although not always, teenagers going through puberty are at the centre of poltergeist activity.

A feature of some cases involves the breaking out of spontaneous fires.

Cases date back many years. In 1889, the Daggy household suffered a spate of such mystery conflagrations. A statement was made based on the testimony of seventeen witnesses, which said: 'Fires have broken out spontaneously throughout the house, as many as eight occurring in one day, six being in the house and two outside; that the window curtains were burned, this happening in broad daylight whilst the family and neighbours were in the house.' The full details are given in Herbert Thurston's book, *Ghosts and Poltergeists*, published in 1953.

Six years later, the *New York Herald* reported the 'many fires' which plagued the Brooklyn house of Adam Colwell during the fourth and fifth of January, 1895. The final outbreak razed the building to the ground.

Colwell's 16-year-old step-daughter, Rhoda, was at the centre of all the fires, but witnesses demonstrated she could not have started them. Police officers witnessed the strange fires which combusted furniture, a bed and wallpaper – along with other poltergeist activity which included pictures falling off walls, the toppling over of a heavy unlit stove, and a heavy lamp which was observed falling from its hook.

Rhoda was being questioned when some of the incidents occurred. The fire marshal, and Captain Rhoads of the police, admitted that they had no explanation. However, the day after the house had burned down, the authorities stated that the girl *had* been behind all the incidents. A Mr Hope claimed that Rhoda had previously worked for him as a housemaid, and while she was in his employ, fires had broken out in the house.

It was decided that Rhoda had used her good looks to distract fire and police officers while she resorted to trickery. The teenager was put under intense pressure by the police to confess, until finally, 'confess' she did.

A modern example of spontaneous fires, linked to a young woman, actually resulted in a trial in Italy, on 12 December 1983. It involved a Scottish nanny called Carol Compton, who worked in three different houses. Poltergeist-type phenomena followed Carol around, and altogether five fires brokes out in the various households. Of the worst, one caused five thousand pounds worth of damage, and another almost brought about the injury or even death of a small child.

Carol was the only obvious common factor linking all the fires. She was arrested on arson charges and attempted murder, and waited months for her case to come to trial. When it did, she was branded a witch by some parts of the media, and put in a cage in the courtroom. She denied she had started any of the fires, and indeed she was never caught doing so, but it was too much of a coincidence for many people.

Scientific evidence seemed to indicate that the fires were not *natural*. In court, Professor Vitolo of Pisa University, said: 'In all my forty-five years of this sort of investigation I have never seen fires like this before. They were created by an intense source of heat, but not by a naked flame.'

No spent matches were found, and there was no evidence of inflammable substances. The fires burned in a pattern that could not be repeated in scientific experiments. Dr Keith Borer, a British forensics expert, conducted his own tests. Dr Borer was sceptical of the paranormal option, but admitted he was stumped.

The trial lasted five days. At the end of it the attempted murder charge was dropped, but Carol was found guilty of arson, although no proof was ever presented to the court and she continued to protest her innocence. Carol was released immediately because of the time she had already spent in prison.

Cases such as this might suggest that fiery energy may perhaps form within the human body without the person being aware of what is happening. Occasionally destructive consequences may result. But can the fire also burn within instead of finding an outlet into the open?

Does an untapped 'energy', which the Hindus call Kundalini, reside inside all of us? If it does, could this energy occasionally erupt in a fiery heat capable of incinerating everything, even bones, into ash?

Conclusions

18 Fire Patterns

So here we are. The final chapter; which might end this book, but, we are certain, will not be the closing word on spontaneous human combustion. The debate is ongoing, and we hope that the new cases, speculations and fresh expert opinion we have presented will encourage an unprecedented, objective, scientific investigation to really begin.

In truth, none of the mundane explanations have been proven. Of course if we accept that we exist in a nice orderly universe, they *make sense*. In some cases they may turn out to be the answer and the spectre of SHC will disappear like a phantom. At the end of the day this may be true of the entire phenomenon, that it was in effect an illusion derived from a multiplicity of different tragic death situations, but none of the half-cocked experiments we have witnessed to date go very far to demonstrating that.

It could be that the answer sits somewhere on the fringes of physics, in little-understood phenomena such as ball lightning, electromagnetic forcefields or electrostatic energy. Or could it lie, as Larry Arnold suggests, with a subatomic particle he calls a 'pyrotron', that vaporizes a human being by an internal subatomic chain reaction? For those who believe that we exist in a *dis*orderly universe – that everything is not known and predictable like a tube of smarties – the more esoteric theories, such as poltergeist phenomena and mind over matter death wishes, become real possibilities. Of course, such exotic solutions may not apply. The need for them might be an illusion created by evidence which at times is deceiving.

We are not saying which theory we might favour, because in truth at this stage *we do not know*. The answer could be any, or none of the above. It may be a combination or coming together of

179

several events that brings about the almost total destruction of a living human being.

Our work over many years in the contentious field of ufology has taught us a fundamental lesson. There is no single answer to what a UFO might be. 'UFO' is an umbrella term for a variety of diverse phenomena, some mundane, such as bright stars, aircraft landing-lights and atmospheric effects. Others perhaps are purely psychological, where percipients in a state of sensory deprivation are 'triggered' by a mundane light into experiencing something exotic. Other reports indicate at least the possibility that some encounters might indeed be 'alien' – in its widest possible context.

Might the term SHC similarly turn out to be a catch-all for various kinds of mysterious fire deaths, most of which have regular explanations, but which lumped together with any 'genuine' incident, merely cloud the path to any real understanding?

During our investigations several patterns emerged. Occasionally coroners were helpful (usually after great perseverance on our part). The Harpurhey case took us on an incredible switchback ride through officialdom when – had facts been provided early on – many questions could have been resolved. In the end Manchester coroner Leonard Gorodkin did agree to answer all our questions, for which we were grateful.

But most would not cooperate to a lesser or greater degree. Perhaps the reasons for this are to protect relatives from media attention, or merely out of a belief that death is a private affair. Maybe sometimes there are more sinister factors at work. Some coroners might actually be frightened of the implications suggested by just the *possibility* of spontaneous human combustion.

We know of a coroner who disallowed evidence from an inquest which might have cast doubt on a particular 'rational' theory. Others have also sometimes impeded our enquiries by refusing to release even the most innocent pieces of information, which at the time of the incident were common knowledge. One coroner appears to have repeatedly given us misinformation.

It all started when a gentleman sent us a newspaper cutting headlined: RESCUERS FOUND MAN WAS HUMAN FIREBALL. It told us three men who had spotted smoke spilling out from a pensioner's bungalow. They broke in and found an elderly man standing in the hallway, with his upper body ablaze. One of them dragged him out and put out the flames. He died of his injuries ten hours later. There was some doubt about the cause of the fire.

The cutting was dated February 1989, so in the first instance we contacted the journalist who wrote the story. She put us onto the local coroner's office. They appeared to be helpful, and said they would look up the file, but never actually did so. In the meantime we contacted the local fire brigade headquarters and said we were writing a book about inexplicable fire deaths, and wanted to know what their conclusions were on this particular case.

The officer said he was happy to look up the file, and would call us back in twenty minutes. He was true to his word. 'I have our report in front of me,' he informed us, 'but I've just been told I cannot reveal any of its contents.'

We explained that we needed to know whether it was worth pursuing the case. After all, the information he was withholding had been, or would be, presented at the inquest, where any journalist could hear it and take notes. He would tell us nothing at all. Back at the coroner's officer, they advised us to put our request to the district coroner's office, who had files on every death in the area. This was duly done, and eventually we received a call from the district coroner.

He said he had received our request for 'inquest evidence', but unfortunately the inquest had not yet been held. When we pointed out that it was two and a half *years* since the incident, he replied that they had a backlog of cases still waiting to be heard, and this was one of them. He said that he would inform us when they had a date so that we could attend.

In the meantime we had traced one of the three men who had attempted to rescue the deceased. We chatted, and the subject of the inquest came up. 'If the inquest hasn't taken place,' he said, 'then what was that I attended over two years ago, where I had to stand up and give evidence?'

Could this have been a preliminary hearing, an adjourned inquest while the incident was investigated more fully? Our witness was sure it was not. We got back to the district coroner. This time he sounded annoyed. 'Look, I've told you, the inquest has not taken place! I have the file in front of me. It contains the results of our official investigation. This evidence will be heard at the inquest, *once it is arranged.*' He repeated again that he would duly inform us of the date.

Perplexed, we let it drop for the moment, then out of the blue, a week later, we received a call from the district coroner's office. This time it was a woman. She sounded embarrassed and was very apologetic. 'I'm sorry to tell you that you've been given some wrong information about the inquest. It did in fact take place on 23 May 1989.'

When we asked how we had been misinformed by the district coroner when he claimed that he had all the information at hand, she muttered something about 'holidays', then continued, 'Look, we can't let you have the inquest evidence, but if you would like to arrange an appointment at the office, you can read the file and take notes. Would this be alright?'

We thanked her and agreed with her that it was a good compromise, and once again she apologized.

At the office we were given the file to examine under guard of an employee. We learned that 75-year-old John Dover* had been a very ill man, suffering congestion, angina, circulatory and dehydration problems and cancer of the throat. The bungalow was one of several which had a warden. According to evidence, Dover was a careless smoker.

The fire began between 1.05 p.m., when the meals-on-wheels woman left, and 1.30 p.m. when smoke was first noticed. The victim had started eating his meal at least, because his 'stomach contained a large quantity of semi-digested food'. The seat of the fire was the armchair John Dover had been eating in. It was deduced that there had been insufficient time for a fire to have developed from a carelessly discarded smouldering cigarette, so it was decided that a lighted match must have been the cause. The resultant inferno had been sufficient to burst a ceiling light bulb and destroy a plastic window-frame.

What stood out above all else in the report, was the name of the coroner who had actually presided over the inquest. It was the same man who on two occasions had told us that the inquest had not yet taken place ...

One of the questions you may ask, is how many cases of spontaneous human combustion occur? As we have seen, one senior fireman has speculated that there *could* be up to a hundred cases annually in the United Kingdom which go unreported as SHC. We contracted the Home Office, and were able to obtain their publication *Fire statistics United Kingdom 1989*, which offered some interesting information on fire casualties.

There were 901 deaths from fires in 1989. The report states: 'Over half the deaths from accidental fires in dwellings were caused by smoker's materials or matches.' As we have demonstrated, this is something of an assumption. Often smoker's materials have been cited as circumstantial evidence when all else has failed. The highest death rates occurred for the under fives and over sixty-fives. This is interesting, as we have hardly any child victims on record exhibiting the characteristics of alleged SHC. Is it because, like animals, children do not become drunkards or, of course, smoke! Death rates for males were higher than for females.

Of accidental fires in dwellings and other occupied buildings, the main causes have been put down to cookers, smoker's materials, playing with matches and electrical faults. Out of 110,159 fires, 2,589 remained 'unspecified', which means there was not even any circumstantial evidence to allocate a cause. During these 'unspecified' fires, there were ninety fatalities, and 466 non-fatalities.

Does this mean it was only a lack of facts stopping investigators from finding 'rational' or mundane explanations, or is it an indication that poltergeist-type spontaneous combustion, and even SHC itself might occur? Certainly the figure of ninety unspecified fatalities is similar to the fire-officer's suggestion of one hundred SHC victims annually.

During our search of newspaper files, we came across this little mystery in the *Manchester Evening News* of 1 February 1954.

Peter Openshaw, aged eighteen, was awoken by smoke in the family home in Grimshaw Lane, Middleton Junction. At first he thought one of the family had risen early to light a fire in these days before smokeless zones, but on going downstairs he was met by billowing clouds. The fire brigade was called by his father, and they confined the flames to the family's confectionary shop. They believed that the fire started near a showcase, in front of a fireplace. Mr Openshaw said: 'It is a mystery how the fire started. No one had been in the shop since it was cleaned on Saturday afternoon.' The fireplace had been boarded up and not used since 1939.

Roger Ide of The Forensic Science Service, commented to us, 'Clearly by no means can all fires of any type be 'solved'. Whether the seat of the fire is an article of furniture or a human body, it is not always possible to demonstrate conclusively that a particular source of ignition was involved.'

At the back of this book we have compiled the first ever catalogue of over one hundred cases which might be attributable to SHC. We are very wary of statistics, and certainly this is too small a sample to discuss with great confidence. It must be representative of a store that is very much larger.

Nevertheless, Anne C. Arnold Silk, lecturer and a researcher into the effects of seismically generated waves known as piezo-electrical energy, produced by stresses and strains in the rocks below ground, was a help to us. As a member of the Royal Society of Medicine she offered to check the U.K. cases against British Geological Survey maps. She was looking to see how many of them occurred over fault lines in the earth's rock covering where seismic movement might cause microwave energy to manifest.

Out of forty-seven cases in our sample, Anne found that thirty-one had occurred over faulted areas. The figure might have been higher had the locations of some of the historical cases been more specific. The figure, almost 75%, must however be weighed against the low sample, and the fact that many parts of Britain are heavily faulted anyway. If one chooses a sufficiently large range almost any place in the U.K. will be near a fault line. Having said that, the correlation is intriguing, and perhaps it is something which should be pursued. Anne told us:

> If oxygen is subjected to radiation of specific types, it is highly inflammable. The lungs are full of oxygen. Radio frequency energy can cause ignition of certain gases. When seismic movement occurs deep under ground, *natural* gases are vented, and also radio frequency and microwave energy. Supposing that either a lightning strike, or a seismic energy emission enters a body, it could ionize the gas in the lungs and any flatus in the stomach. This latter would be very common in the sedentary elderly, the status of many SHC victims. The result would be a conflagration.

Mrs Arnold Silk's ideas do seem to have official backing. In a Ministry of Defence publication called *Guide To The Practical Safety Aspects Of The Use Of Radio Frequency Energy*, discussion is made of human exposure to radio frequency emissions. It then says: 'RF radiation may give rise to the ignition of flammable atmospheres ... Standards aimed at avoiding these occurrences are concerned with ensuring that the energy available is less than that required to cause ignition or initiation.'

This is reminiscent of some of the speculations that emerged as we looked at various natural energy fields and their possible effects on the human body. Is this the answer? Or do we seek it on the leading edge of biochemistry, as specialist Dennis Davies explained to us?

> The biochemical reactions in our bodies are all controlled by enzymes. The result is that although high-energy chemical bonds are involved, they are made to discharge their energy in a series of steps. Normally a cycle is involved whereby compounds of lower energy are formed while at the same time doing some work for the cell, such as, say, making a muscle contract.
>
> Let's look at the most highly energetic molecule found in the cell. This is a chemical called phosphoenolpyruvic acid (PEP for short), and has a free energy change of hydrolysis of just under fifteen thousand calories per molecule. Each of these reactions is mediated by a particular enzyme. What happens normally is that the compounds that the PEP acts on build up in the cell.
>
> This switches on a particular control gene which makes another compound which switches on the whole chain of genes making enzymes, resulting in the production of PEP. When enough has been

formed to reduce the concentration of molecules to be converted, another control gene switches the system off. It sounds complicated, but it's worked for a few billion years.

But marvellous though this process is, it sometimes goes wrong. Every so often the switch off signal doesn't get through. If this happens to the signal which tells the cell to divide, it goes on dividing and we get cancer. Even here the offending cells are destroyed by the immune system. Only very rarely does the cancer cell get out of control.

The same kind of thing probably happens with cells which are producing PEP. This is normally no problem. But suppose we get the rare occasion where the 'stop making PEP dividing' signal is lost at the same times as the 'stop making PEP' signal.

What you would get then would be a cancer which was producing large amounts of the most energetic biological chemical. If this were possible, we could make certain predictions based on our knowledge of cancer.

We could say that most victims of SHC would be in the same age group as most cancer victims. We could also make a rough estimate of the rate of occurrence. The frequency, if these 'switch' defects happened as often in all cases would be about the square of the frequency of the occurrance of cancer. So if one in ten thousand people gets cancer each day, then one in a hundred million would suffer SHC.

The first step would be for spontaneous hydrolysis to take place. This would lead to acidification of the blood. Perhaps the victim would feel ill and pass out. Once the process started, the local temperature would be raised. Fever and death would probably occur quite quickly. A stage would be reached where conventional burning would take place, allowing the 'candle effect' to take over.

Dennis made it clear to us that his 'brainstorming' was just an idea, based on suppositions, but an interesting exercise, nevertheless. As indeed have been many of the possible routes towards an answer that we have met throughout the book. All need to be explored. There is material here to keep scientists from a university full of disciplines happy for a lifetime; although sadly very few are presently aware that SHC might even just conceivably occur.

Our intention was to present the cases and their controversies as objectively as we could, to debate the various arguments from all perspectives and summarize the theories for and against the existence of something as bemusing as the alleged mystery of spontaneous human combustion. These questions were being discussed in the last century and we are little further forward today. If we continue to treat this subject as fodder for sensational yarns or supernatural nonsense of no reality or merit then they may still be continuing a hundred years from now.

We hope that this will not happen, because if SHC can occur then it represents a major question awaiting resolution. It may also very possibly open up unexpected avenues of technological advance.

When Benjamin Franklin dangled a kite on a wire amidst a raging thunderstorm he was wrestling with dangerous forces and powerful energies. At the time it seemed like a minor matter of academic interest only, but it led to an understanding of electricity, which led in turn to a complete revolution in every person's life on earth.

Almost all we do today – from watching TV to saving lives through heart massage – depends upon this power that has writhed and danced around the world since time began. If SHC does happen then it may be triggered by forces that are just as puzzling for us as electricity was to Leonardo da Vinci. Yet, like electricity, it is probably a natural – not a supernatural – energy dormant in our midsts. If we can learn to tap into it, to harness its raw power and perhaps control its anger, then who knows what advantages it might bring to our children?

References

Case Abstracts: An SHC Database

We have listed below incidents which we have on record that feature some of the hallmarks associated with the alleged phenomenon of spontaneous, or preternatural, human combustion. We do not pretend that the list is exhaustive, nor do we vouch that the details are entirely accurate or that all cases *are* a proven result of SHC. This is meant as a guide only.

Patterns created by gaps or clumps of incidents may not be too important. But note the 1980 total as an example of one possible period of intense activity. Remember that these are only the *reported* incidents. There must be others which have never been made public.

Note also how in many eighteenth- and nineteenth-century accounts it seemed necessary to state that the victim was a heavy drinker – even when this was not true!

Our researches have convinced us that although SHC is a relatively rare occurrence, the cases cited below are very likely to be no more than a fraction of a larger total.

The letters in brackets refer to sources, which are explained at the end of the catalogue.

With your help we would like this database to grow. If any readers know of other possible incidents or wish to report (even in full confidence) events you may have personally witnessed, please write to us at 37 Heathbank Road, Stockport, Cheshire, England SK3 0UP.

1.   *26 June 1613   Holnehurst, Christchurch, Dorset, England*

Carpenter John Hitchen went to bed with his wife and child after a hard day's work. Mrs Hitchen's mother, Agnes Russell, sleeping in a separate bed, was awakened by a terrible blow to her cheek. There was an electric storm going on at the time. She cried out to the rest of the family to help her. Receiving no reply she got up and awoke her daughter, who was burnt down one side. Mr Hitchen and the child were dead beside her. They dragged him out into the street, but his body was burning, and they had to abandon him. He continued to burn for three days, although outwardly there was no sign of fire. Smoke issued from the carcass which was eventually reduced to ashes. (H.A.)

2.   1673 or 1692   Paris, France

An unnamed poor woman was mysteriously consumed by fire. Reputedly a strong drinker, she went to sleep on a straw pallet and burned during the night. Only her head and fingers remained. The incident was first reported by Pierre-Aime Lair. (H.A.)

3.   1717   Amsterdam, Holland

John Henry Cohausen, in a book published in the above year related: 'That a Polish gentleman, in the time of the queen Bona Storza, having drank two dishes of liquor called brandy wine, vomited flames, and was burnt by them.' (H.A.)

4.   19 February 1725   Rheims, France

Apprentice surgeon Claude-Nicolas Le Cat was involved in an SHC incident at an inn. The drunken, nagging wife of the innkeeper, Mme Millet, was discovered by her husband close to a fireplace, incinerated, at 2 a.m. Nothing else in the room was touched. Jean Millet was arrested for murder, as it was believed he was sexually attracted to one of his serving girls, and wanted to get rid of his wife. Le Cat testified on behalf of the innkeeper, at an appeal in a higher court, and it was deemed to be a case of human combustion. But Millet's health and business was ruined, and he died shortly afterwards. (H.A.)

5.   1731   Cesina, Italy

The Countess Cornelia Bandi retired after feeling unwell. The following morning her maid discovered the 62-year-old woman burnt to ashes except for part of the head and both legs from the knees downwards. The room was remarkably untouched by the fire, although there was a degree of soot and yellowish grease everywhere. This latter was probably fat from the incinerated victim. (H.A.)

6.   *9 April 1744   St Clement, Ipswich, England*

Grace Pett was discovered with the trunk of her body converted to ash. Combustible objects nearby were untouched. Other people in the house were unaware of the fire until morning, and contrary to most reports, at the inquest it was stated that she was *not* an habitual drinker. It has emerged in recent years that there was a witchcraft dimension to the case. (H.A. & C.F.)

7.   *1749   France*

A French priest called Boineau, reported the case of an 80-year-old woman reduced to a carbonized skeleton as she sat sipping brandy. (H.A.)

8.   *1749   France*

A French woman, Madame de Boiseon, aged eighty, allegedly a heavy drinker, was left by her maid seated near the fire. Not long after the maid returned to find the woman ablaze. When she tried to put the flames out with her hand, they adhered to it. Water only made the fire worse. It could not be extinguished until most of the body had been incinerated. (H.A.)

9.   *2 March 1773   Coventry, England*

52-year-old Mary Clues (or Chies) of Gosford Street, liked a drink and was found by a neighbour combusted. She had been ill for some time, suffering from, amongst other things, jaundice. Her body was largely destroyed, the bones calcined, only the skull, spine and legs surviving. She was found between the bed and the fireplace, although the feather bed was undamaged. She had previously told her neighbour that the devil had appeared in the room, and that he would return to take her away. (H.A.)

10.   *October 1776   Fenile, Italy*

Dr Battaglia related the incineration of a priest in a medical journal of the above date. Don Gio Maria Bertholi burst into flames just minutes after arriving at his brother-in-law's house. Several witnesses heard a scream, and found the priest on the floor surrounded by a 'light flame'. The man survived for four days. He told Dr Battaglia that all he remember was a blow like a cudgel to his right hand, and at the same time saw a bluish flame attack his shirt. Once again, certain items were burnt while others escaped. (H.A.)

11.   *February 1779   Aix, Provence, France*

Mary Ann Jauffret, the widow of a shoe-maker, burnt to death in her bedchamber. She was reportedly fat and susceptible to cold. A surgeon named Roccus investigated the incident and found a mass of ashes. Only a part of the skull, a hand and one foot had escaped a fire that had calcined even the bones. There was a stove nearby which contained fire, but other things, such as a supper-table, were untouched. (H.A.)

12.   *10 December 1779   Paris, France*

On this date a couple by the name of Bias were discovered burnt in their home. Their whole trunk appeared like a mass of charcoal, sending forth a disagreeable odour. The breast bone and the muscles of the abdomen appeared more affected than the rest. The head of one victim was bloated and puffed up. Out of all the furnishings in the room, only a chair and table were damaged. Neighbours declared they had heard the woman working and talking just two hours before discovery of the calcined remains. (H.A.)

13.   *1780 or 1781   Caen, Normandy, France*

Surgeon, M. Valentin told a M. Fodere that he investigated the case of an unmarried woman aged sixty. Apparently she was fond of 'strong liquors and petting animals'! Just a skull and two feet remained in a pile of ashes discovered on the floor of her apartment. These were some distance from a small fire in a grate. Crowds flocked to the house which exuded an odour of burnt fat. (H.A.)

14.   *1788   England*

A chambermaid was scrubbing a floor when her master entered the room. The man cried out, because the girl's back was a mass of flames, although she was unaware of it. She died before he could put out the fire. (H.A.)

15. Early 1800s   Dublin, Ireland

We have no date for the following, related by a Dr Apjohn, Professor of Chemistry at the Royal College of Surgeons in Ireland, except that it occurred 'between twelve and one o'clock on a Saturday night', at the beginning of the nineteenth century.

45-year-old Anne Nelis, wife of a Dublin wine and porter merchant, had a row with her husband after he returned from a party. The couple were allegedly drunk at the time. Anne stayed up while her husband went to bed. Her maid-servant discovered Mrs Nelis in an armchair, at a distance from the fire-grate. Her trunk was reduced to cinders, but her upper and lower extremities survived. Indeed, although her face was scorched, her hair was totally untouched. A penetrating and offensive odour filled the room for some days, although nothing else was touched. There was no inquest and the entire affair was hushed up. (H.A.)

16. Early 1880s   County Down, Northern Ireland

This next incident is also undated, but was investigated by the Revd Ferguson of Dublin, and conveyed to Dr Apjohn.

The victim, a woman of sixty, lived with her brother. She retired to bed one night with her daughter, both allegedly, in a drunken state. Other members of the family were awakened in the early morning by an offensive smell of smoke. They burst into the room and found that the smoke was issuing from the older woman, who was burning with 'an internal fire'. She was 'as black as coal', and although there was no flame, was very difficult to put out. Amazingly, the daughter who shared the same bed was untouched, as were the sheets and bed itself. There was no fire anywhere else in the room. (H.A.)

17. 16 March 1802   Massachusetts, USA

The body of an elderly woman 'disappeared' in the space of one-and-a-half hours. Several members of the family retired, while the old woman remained to lockup after the return of her grandson. The boy came home to discover some remains and greasy soot in the hearth and on the floor. There was an unusual smell, and the fire in the grate was only small. (H.A.)

18.   *25 or 26 December 1804   Paris, France*

M. Vigne reported the combustion of a 68-year-old woman in Paris. (H.A.)

19.   *1809   Limerick, Ireland*

This case was recorded in the above year in the pages of the *Methodist Magazine*. The body of a Mrs Peacock (or Pocock) was discovered 'burning with fire as red as copper' by the keeper of an alms-house. The body had burned through the floor and dropped into the room of a man who lodged below. There were only ashes in the grate of the victim's room, and no candles. The only fire damage was to the floor where the body had burned through it. Mrs Peacock was said to have 'indulged immoderately in intoxicating liquor'. (H.A.)

20.   *Circa 1809–10   Cavan, Ireland*

'Died by the visitation of God' was the verdict at the inquest of twice-married Mrs Stout, of Coote Hill, who met a fiery death at around the same time as the above case. She went to bed one evening in apparent good health, but was found the next morning on the floor, reduced to ashes, although, apparently, her nightdress survived. 'Vapour' was still issuing from her mouth and nostrils, but when her remains were moved they immediately crumbled. Mrs Stout was said to be 'an inveterate dram-drinker'. (H.A.)

21.   *1813   place unknown*

An elderly gentleman, allegedly drunk on a tincture of valerian and guaiacum, apparently rolled out of his bed, which was near the fire, and burned to a cinder without injuring the bed or bed sheets. (H.A.)

22.   *January 1822   Italy*

This case appears to be an example of someone on the brink of combustion but who survived. A 26-year-old farmer was seized with an intermittent fever connected with an irritation of the stomach. On the seventh day he experienced a burning heat in his throat, ascending from the stomach, as intense as red-hot coals. His breath began to smoke, and heat could be felt from the emission up to two feet away. Cold water made little difference to his thirst, which was succeeded by a voracious appetite. Finally, continued immersions in cold baths, and the drinking of iced water seems to have brought an end to the torment. (H.A.)

23.   5 January 1835   Nashville, Texas, USA

On this date, James Hamilton, Professor of Mathematics at the University of Nashville, apparently survived SHC.

Returning from a walk, he built a fire, then set about obtaining the weight and temperature of the atmosphere by examining a barometer and thermometer. This took about half an hour. Whilst outside studying his hygrometer, he experienced an intense pain in his left leg. A light flame appeared, and he cupped his hands around it, cutting off the oxygen, upon which it went out. The case was reported by his physician, Dr Overton. (H.A.)

24.   October 1836   Auney, Avalon, France

'A very fat woman, aged seventy-four, addicted to drinking brandy', met a fiery fate according to the *Medico-Chirurgical Review* of the above date. The mayor of Auney ordered the woman's house to be broken into when the neighbours had not seen her for some time. They found her partially-combusted remains near the chimney. A blue flame was playing along a trail of grease which the mayor could not put out. There were no other signs of fire. It was concluded that while trying to ignite some embers in the fireplace with her breath, the fire had communicated itself along it to the body. (H.A.)

25.   13 July 1847   Darmstadt, Germany

At eleven o'clock in the evening, the Count of Gorlitz returned home to find his wife's badly-charred body lying in her room, close to some burnt pieces of furniture. No evidence of crime could be found. Her physician, Dr Graff, concluded the woman must have died of spontaneous combustion, because had she been ignited by a candle for instance, she would have had time to call out for help to her servant, Stauff. A second physician was unsure, but a third agreed with Dr Graff.

The man-servant, known to be a thief, was at one point charged with the murder of his mistress, supposedly setting the corpse alight to cover up his crime. He was eventually absolved of murder when it was demonstrated how difficult it is to ignite human flesh, although by this time Graff had changed his mind about his original conclusion of SHC. In time Stauff made a full confession of his incendiary activities, although it is not clear in what circumstances the 'confession' was procured. (H.A. & H.)

26.   1847   USA

In an article published in *Scientific American*, of the above year, a Dr Nott reports on his first-hand experience of SHC. A 25-year-old man, an 'habitual drinker', was seen by him at 9 p.m. When he called again, two hours later, he found the man 'literally roasted, from the crown of his head to the sole of his feet'. He was discovered in a blacksmith's shop by the owner, standing erect, in the midst of a silver coloured flame. There was no fire in the premises, and according to the doctor, 'neither was there any possibility of any fire having been communicated from any external source. It was purely a case of spontaneous ignition'. (H.A.)

27.   5 February 1851   Paris, France

A house-painter, whilst drinking, bet he could eat a lighted candle. 'Scarcely had he placed it in his mouth, when he uttered a slight cry, and a bluish flame was seen upon his lips ... In half an hour the head and upper portion of the chest were entirely carbonized. The fire did not cease till bones, skin and muscles were all consumed, and nothing remained but a small heap of ashes.' (H.A.)

28.   December 1851   France

M. Devergie reported in 1852 the fate of a washerwoman called Marie Jeanne Antoinette Bally, aged fifty. She had returned to her lodgings in a state of drunkenness. At eight o'clock the following morning, her remains were discovered, along with those of the chair she had been sitting upon. From the shoulders upwards, including her hair, there were no effects at all. Neither were her legs burnt, but the trunk of her body was badly charred. There was no fire in the grate, but nearby was an earthenware pot filled with coals, used by the poor to warm their feet. (H.A.)

29.   July 1852   Darnaway Forest, England

John Anderson, aged about fifty, was carting wood from the forest of Darnaway. A herd-boy, a quarter of a mile away, saw him get down from the cart, stumble, and fall by the roadside. The boy found the body burning and extinguished the fire with water. The man was allegedly a drunkard, and his lighted pipe was found under the body. (N. & F.)

30. 1861 *Ireland*

The case was related in this year by George Lewes, citing Apjohn as the source. A 60-year-old woman, referred to as 'A.B.' retired, intoxicated, to bed with her daughter. Before daybreak, family members were alerted by smoke and discovered the woman's body smouldering, 'black as coal'. (H.A.)

31. 1866 *England*

The corpse of an Englishman was found burning in its vault, thirteen months after burial. Aged around thirty, he had died of typhoid. The day before the fire, a foul smell was noticed in the church, issuing from a crevice in the floor. The coffin had 'burst', and liquid matter was oozing from the body. Sawdust was put into the coffin. The next morning the vault was discovered burning 'with a bluish flame and most offensive smell'. It was conjectured that a workman had carelessly discarded a lighted taper after igniting a cigarette. (N. & F.)

32. 1870 *France*

Reported in the above year, a 'drunken woman' was found incinerated two hours after retiring to her room. Her husband found the door extremely hot, and the floor was smouldering. Although the remains were lying partially across the hearth, there was no fire in the grate. (N. & F.)

33. 1876 *New York, USA*

The Rev Adams of Stockcross, Newbury, England, travelled to New York, and booked into a hotel room. His combusted remains were later found there. (H.A.)

34. 24 December 1885 *Ottawa, Illinois, USA*

Patrick Rooney, his wife and their hired help, John Larson, were drinking whisky in the kitchen. Larson went to bed, and when he came downstairs the following morning, discovered Mr Rooney lying on the floor, dead. The remains of Mrs Rooney were found on the ground beneath a hole in the kitchen floor. The remains included two charred vertebrae, a piece of skull, a few foot-bones and a pile of ashes. There was greasy soot throughout the house but no other damage. Patrick had been suffocated by smoke. (H.A.)

35.   October 1885   USA

In the *St Louis Medical and Surgical Journal* of the above date, a Dr Middlekamp reported on a 66-year-old 'drunkard' who 'fired a gun at his own breast with a ramrod'. This act seemed to have started combustion of the body which melted the ramrod and a metal buckle. Apart from the legs, head and arms, the body was entirely consumed. (H.A.)

36.   19 February 1888   Aberdeen, Scotland

A Dr Booth was called out to examine the combusted remains of a 65-year-old man discovered leaning against the stone wall of a hayloft, which was supported on beams. The body was almost a 'cinder', yet hay, both loose and bundled, lying close by, had not caught fire. Dr Booth said it was obvious there had been no death struggle, and when the 'body' had been removed, it had disintegrated into ash. (H.A.)

37.   1889   Ireland

In the *Therapeutic Gazette* of the above year, a Dr Clendenin describes the incineration of an 'old Irish woman addicted to the excessive use of whiskey'. She was discovered the following day, as were the asphyxiated bodies of two old men who also lived in the house. The inner walls were covered in greasy soot, and beneath a hole burned in the kitchen floor were discovered amongst some ashes, 'the skull, the cervical, and half the dorsal vertebrae' very nearly reduced to cinders. The feet were found in shoes, one reduced to ashes, the other nearly so. The remains weighed only twelve pounds. (H.A.)

38.   12 May 1890   Ayer, Massachusetts, USA

While making a professional call, Dr B.H. Hartwell arrived at a wood, where he found a woman who had mysteriously burst into flame. Her clothing was all but consumed, and the body, raised off the ground by the rigidity of the muscles, was burning with flames twelve to fifteen inches high. The fire was put out by smothering it with soil. The leg-bones were partly calcined. Dead leaves nearby, a straw hat and the wooden handle of a spade were unburnt. (H.A.)

39. 5 January 1899   Sowerby Bridge, Halifax, Yorkshire, England

Death struck twice in the Kirby family, at two different locations, but at the same point in time. Two sisters allegedly erupted into flames. The two houses, within sight of one another across the Calder Valley, were the locations for this horrific tragedy. In each case, the coroner could not find a source of ignition, and dismissed the simultaneous burnings as a 'shocking coincidence'. (A)

40. 16 December 1904   Rosehill, Falkirk, Scotland

Well-to-do Mrs Cochcrane was found seated in a well-stuffed armchair, burned beyond recognition – yet the pillows and cushions on the chair were unburnt. There was no fire in the room. (C.F.)

41. 23 December 1904   Hull, Yorkshire, England

Pensioner Mrs Clark of the Trinity Alms-house, was found terribly burned but survived for a time. She had no explanation for her injuries, and the bed she was laying on was not even scorched. (C.F.)

42. January 1905   Binbrook, Lincolnshire, England

There were many strange goings-on in the village of Binbrook. Poltergeist activity, mystery fires, and finally perhaps, SHC. At Binbrook Farm, a farmer called White suffered the bizarre slaughter of his chickens and felt a strange pressure around the farm-house. On one occasion, White entered the kitchen and saw his servant-girl sweeping the floor – with her back on fire. She was oblivious to this, and was nowhere near the stove, which had a guard around it. He put out the flames with a sack, and the girl was taken to hospital, but she was unable to explain the fire. (C.F.)

43.   26 February 1905   Butlock's Heath, South-ampton, Hampshire, England

That morning, neighbours heard a curious scratching sound coming from the house occupied by Mr and Mrs John Kiley. The neighbours broke in and found the house in flames. Mr Kiley was on the floor, burnt to death, and his wife was in a chair nearby. Both were badly charred but recognizable. The couple were elderly. It was accepted at the inquest that an overturned oil-lamp had caused the conflagration, yet the victims had probably burned the night before. Why had the fire taken so long to start burning the house? (H)

44.   28 February 1905   Blyth, Northumberland, England

77-year-old Barbara Bell was discovered by neighbours, her body badly charred, on a sofa untouched by fire. It was speculated that she had fallen into the fire. (H)

45.   1907   Manner, Dinapore, India

Two police constables found the burned corpse of a woman in the village of Manner. There was no other sign of fire in the room. The men carried the still-smouldering corpse, in unscorched clothes, to the district magistrate's office. (C.F.)

46.   1908   Whitley Bay, Northumberland, England

One evening, Margaret Dewar, a retired school-teacher, returned to her house and found her sister burnt to death on an unscorched bed. Ms Dewar was put under tremendous pressure by the coroner, her neighbours and the press, to change her testimony. It was reasoned that a body could not burn on a bed without damaging the sheets, and therefore the coroner told her she had to be a liar. When the inquest was recalled, she changed her story, and said she had carried her injured sister to the bed. (H)

47.   December 1916   Dover, New Jersey, USA

Miss Lillian C. Green, housekeeper of a hotel seven miles from Dover, was found badly burned on the lower floor, and later died. The floor beneath the body was scorched, but nothing else in the building was touched. However, traces of fire were found on the second floor. (G)

48. *Summer 1922   Sydenham, London, England*

68-year-old widow Mrs Euphemia Johnson returned home from a shopping trip and made a pot of tea. She carried the steaming cup to a table near a double window. Mrs Johnson was later found, fallen from her chair, a pile of calcinated bones within clothes which were not even burnt. The chair showed only a bubbling of the varnish and the rubberized table-cloth was completely untouched. (H)

49. *1929   Antigua*

A young native woman called Lily White suffered the spontaneous ignition of her clothes on several occasions whilst out in the streets. On each occasion she suffered no burns to herself. (H)

50. *22 January 1930   Kerhonkson, New York, USA*

The burned body of Mrs Nora Lake, aged forty-two, was found fully clothed on her bed. Her clothing was not even scorched. It was thought that Mrs Lake had been burned to cover up a robbery. (N. & F.)

51. *January 1932   Bladenboro, North Carolina, USA*

Mrs Williamson caught fire when her cotton dress flared up, although she was not near to any source of ignition at the time. Mr Charles Williamson and their daughter tore off the blazing dress, with neither they nor the victim receiving any injury. There were many witnesses to other spontaneous fires which broke out in the household around this time. Investigators could find no logical cause for the events. (H)

52. *29 July 1938   Norfolk, England*

Mrs Mary Carepenter burst into flame for no apparent reason whilst holidaying on a cabin cruiser on the Norfolk Broads. She 'was engulphed in flames and reduced to a charred corpse'. (sic) (H)

53. *27 August 1938   Chelmsford, Essex, England*

At midnight, 22-year-old Phyllis Newcombe was leaving the dance-floor with her fiancé, Henry McAusland, at the Shire Hall, when her dress suddenly flared up in flames. Henry tried to beat out the flames and burnt his hands. Within minutes the girl was dead. The coroner thought that perhaps a lighted cigarette had started the conflagration, but it was demonstrated that a cigarette could not ignite her dress. (H)

54.   4 January 1939   London, England

11-month-old Peter Seaton was put to bed. Some time later a visitor to the house heard the child scream and rushed upstairs. When Harold Huxstep entered the room, it was like opening 'the door of a furnace'. A mass of flames shot out and flung him backwards. The boy's body was destroyed, and the London Fire Brigade could not find the cause of the conflagration. (H)

55.   13 January 1943   Deer Island, Maine, USA

Allen M. Small, aged fifty-two, was found in his home, his body burned. The carpet beneath the body was scorched, but there was no other sign of fire. In the kitchen, the stove-lids were in place, and Small's unlit pipe was resting on a shelf. (G)

56.   6 December 1943   Chichester, Sussex, England

Mrs Madge Knight died in hospital in Chichester. Whilst lying in bed at home, something unknown had set fire to her back. The doctor had to anaesthetize her before dressing the burns. Her bedclothes were not burned or even scorched. (H)

57.   December 1949   Manchester, New Hampshire, USA

Mrs Ellen K. Coutres, aged fifty-three, was found 'dead from burns' as if she had been 'a human torch'. The wooden structure of the building in which she lived was not affected. The fire in the stove had apparently been out for some time. (N. & F.)

58.   3 May 1951   Wabash, Indiana, USA

A 44-year-old man was found burning in his car by a passing motorist. There was minimal damage to the vehicle's interior although the intense heat had melted some of the metal. The man was taken to hospital but died. (H)

59.   1 July 1951   St Petersburg, Florida, USA

Plump 67-year-old Mrs Reeser was found reduced to just a few fragments of bone and a slipper on one almost undamaged foot. There was some minor fire damage to immediate surroundings but little else. This has become the most celebrated case within SHC lore. (A)

60.   18 September 1952   Gretna, Louisiana, USA

A 45-year-old man was found by firemen in a mass of flames, although nothing else in the room was burning. Speculation that he had cut his arteries then doused himself in petrol and set this on fire was raised but is problematic. No petrol or canister was found in the room. (G)

61.   1 March 1953   Greenville, South Carolina, USA

Waymon Wood was found 'crisped black' in the front seat of his closed car, parked off Bypass Route 291. Although little remained of Wood, there was half a tank of petrol which had not burned. Only the windscreen had been affected by the heat. This had bubbled and sagged. (G)

62.   May 1953   Los Angeles, California, USA

30-year-old Mrs Esther Dulin apparently fell asleep in an overstuffed armchair. Both she and the chair were virtually consumed, burned through the floor and dropped into the room below. Nothing else in the building was affected. (G)

63.   December 1956   Honolulu, Hawaii, USA

Young Sik, a 78-year-old fully disabled man was found enveloped in blue flames sitting in a chair, by his neighbour. During the fifteen minutes it took firemen to arrive, the victim and the chair were reduced to ashes. Nothing else in the room suffered. (H.A.)

64.   May 1957   West Philadelphia, Pennsylvania, USA

A widow's remains were found face down in the basement of her two-storey house. Only the torso, burned beyond recognition, remained. The legs were totally consumed leaving just the feet still in their shoes. 65-year-old Mrs Anna Martin was found in front of a coal furnace which was not lit. She was the mother of fireman Samuel Martin. (G)

65.   29 January 1958   Pimlico, London, England

Mrs Edith Middleton was ill with Parkinson's disease and high blood pressure. On the above date a Mrs Annie Law visited her, and left her sitting on her bed. Between 5–6 p.m. Mrs Law noticed an unusual amount of sparks and smoke coming out of the chimney. Mrs Middleton's charred body was found lying partly on the hearth, having also burned through the floorboards. However there was no other damage to the room, and an inquest heard she had died of a heart attack, before being incinerated. (A)

66.   Spring 1959   Rockford, Illinois, USA

4-month-old infant Ricky Pruitt was found mysteriously burned to death. His garments showed no scorch marks, neither did the bedding in the crib in which he was found. (G)

67.   13 December 1959   Michigan, USA

Billy Peterson committed suicide in his car using a hose connected to his exhaust. But what drew the attention of a passing motorist was smoke coming out of Billy's garage. His arm was badly burned, his genitals charred to a crisp, his nose, mouth and ears were burned – yet his clothes were not even scorched, even though a plastic statue mounted on the dashboard had melted in the intense heat. (A)

68.   October Late 1950s   Soho, London, England

19-year-old Maybelle Andrews was dancing with her boyfriend, Billy Clifford, when flames erupted from her back, chest and shoulders, igniting her hair. She died on the way to hospital. Her boyfriend said there were no naked flames, and the fire seemed to come from within the girl herself. (H)

69. 28 November 1960 Pike County, Kentucky, USA

Five men were discovered dead by fire along a rural lane, their bodies 'charred beyond recognition'. The front right-hand door of their vehicle was open, and blood was found nearby. The car had run over a slight embankment. Foul play was ruled out when autopsies revealed the men were breathing when the fire took hold of them. (N. & F.)

70. 2 February 1964 Clapham, London, England

A 72-year-old woman was found almost totally incinerated in a small room with some immediately surrounding damage but little else beyond that. (M)

71. May 1964 Naphill, High Wycombe, Buckinghamshire, England

A 13-year-old boy was found dead in his kitchen with serious burns. The carpet was damaged but there was no other fire in the locked room. (C. & D.)

72. July 1964 Hampton Hill, Middlesex, England

A 77-year-old man was found dead in the corner of his basement with very severe burns. It was speculated that he had doused himself in paraffin and set this alight. (C. & D.)

73. October 1964 Dallas, Texas, USA

A 75-year-old former actress, Mrs Olga Worth Stephens, was seen by passers-by blazing like a human torch in her parked car. Fire investigators found no cause for the severe burns that killed the woman. (H)

74. 5 December 1966 Coudersport, Pennsylvania, USA

92-year-old retired Doctor Bentley was found dead in his bathroom by a postman. The body was almost destroyed apart from the lower parts of his feet which were untouched. The nearby toilet-seat was undamaged. (L.A.)

75. September 1967   Birmingham, West Midlands, England

The body of a male vagrant of middle age was found in a derelict building at dawn. There was no gas or electricity in the premises. He was on the stairs and a fireman discovered flames still emerging 'like a blowlamp' from a slit in his abdomen. The autopsy failed to find a cause for the fire but noted that he died from asphyxia. He was alive when burning commenced and had inhaled the fumes. (M)

76. 7 February 1974   Oakland, California, USA

An elderly man was found dead in a chair placed in front of a stove. The top part of his body was badly burnt but the lower half was untouched. (F.T.)

77. 28 March 1974   Blacon, Chester, Cheshire, England

A 35-year-old woman was found dead in her flat, still sitting in an armchair. The fire was localized. No reason for its cause was reported. (F.T.)

78. 26 April 1974   San Francisco, California, USA

An 80-year-old man was sitting on a sofa when his wife went to the garage for a few minutes. Smelling burning she returned to find him engulfed by flames. He died without explaining what had occurred. (F.T.)

79. 12 November 1974   Savannah, Georgia, USA

Clothing salesman Jack Angel, in his fifties, fell asleep in his motor-home and awoke several days later. He experienced a pain in his chest and severe burns to one hand, his legs, groin, and to a lesser extent, his back. An electrical fault was suspected, as was some form of scalding from a heater, but neither were proven. The hand had to be amputated. (L.A.)

80.   *20 August 1976   Bath, Avon, England*

A 23-year-old woman was found badly burnt in a basement by her father who was awoken at 7 a.m. by the smell of a fire. Speculation was that her nightdress somehow ignited. (F.T.)

81.   *24 December 1976   Mayfair, London, England*

An 84-year-old woman was found burned to death inside her house. No details known as to cause. (F.T.)

82.   *29 December 1976   Isleworth, Middlesex, England*

A 32-year-old woman was found burnt in her living-room, where a small fire had occurred. No smoke or fire was detected from outside. (F.T.)

83.   *1 June 1978   Handsworth, Birmingham, West Midlands, England*

A 20-year-old woman died from the gases given off by a fire as she sat on a blazing settee. No explanation was given for the localized fire or why she did not apparently attempt to escape. (F.T.)

84.   *2 August 1978   Harpurhey, Manchester, Lancashire, England*

A 50-year-old man and a 49-year-old woman emerged from a second-floor flat described by witnesses as human fireballs, and died as a result of their injuries. Speculation about self-ignition was made but the inquest reached an open verdict. (A)

85.   *20 August 1978   Biddeford, Maine, USA*

A 54-year-old woman was found burnt to death in her apartment. No cause known. (F.T.)

86.   *22 August 1978   West Cornforth, Durham, England*

At 5 a.m. a 33-year-old woman was discovered incinerated in her basement by her 6-year-old daughter. Little of the room was damaged. A theory was suggested, but not proven, that owing to her depressed state, nervous tremors, had caused her to accidentally knock over an electric fire and set herself alight. (A)

88.   *25 January 1979   Hutton-le-Hole, North Yorkshire, England*

A postman found a 76-year-old woman in a chair by the fireside. Only her legs and a pile of bones were left. Thick smoke alerted the man, although there was no fire. It was suggested that something fell from the grate and set her alight. (F.T.)

89.   *13 December 1979   Bodfish, Bakersfield, California, USA*

A married couple awoke in their trailer having lost forty-eight hours. They were paralysed, with serious burns on their heads, heels, waists and hips. After alerting neighbours they were treated in hospital. Stories linked the case with UFOs. (L.A.)

90.   *6 January 1980   Blackwood, Ebbw Vale, Gwent, South Wales*

A 73-year-old man was found with only body extremities remaining on the floor by the fireside of his house. Damage to the remainder of the room was minimal and plastic tiles below the carpet had not melted. Vapourized skin coated the room. (A)

91.   *January 1980   Benchill, Manchester, Lancashire, England*

Whilst trying to light a cooker, a 53-year-old woman was mysteriously set on fire. Before she died, she wondered if the cooker 'blew back' flames, but this was said by experts to be impossible. (A)

92.   *February 1980   Newport, Gwent, South Wales*

A 71-year-old woman was found almost incinerated inside her house. There was speculation that she had fallen into the fire. (A)

93.   4 March 1980   Chorley, Lancashire, England

An elderly woman was found in her house, partly on the hearth and partly on the carpet. There was smoke but no fire, yet only the legs below the knees were not turned into ash. It was speculated that she died after falling into fire whilst urinating into a bowl. (M)

94.   13 May 1980   Birmingham, West Midlands, England

A 20-year-old male student awoke in a bed a mass of flames. Friends put the fire out with pillows. There was little surrounding damage, but he suffered serious burns to his neck, back, chest, abdomen, arms and legs. He could not explain the fire and died soon afterwards in hospital. (M)

95.   11 June 1980   Todmorden, West Yorkshire, England

Discovered dead from a heart attack, a 56-year-old man was found to have burns to his body from an unknown source. He was on top of a large pile of coal, but no one knew how he got there. He had vanished five days before from another Yorkshire town some miles away while going on an errand in the middle of the day. Open verdict recorded. (A)

96.   19 June 1980   Toronto, Ontario, Canada

A 31-year-old woman awoke at 2.30 a.m. with major burns on her thigh and abdomen. There was no damage to surroundings and her nightdress was untouched. She survived. (L.A.)

97.   4 August 1980   Singapore

A delivery man helped extinguish a 30-year-old mother and her 6-year-old son whom he found aflame, but both later died. The woman claimed that at 5.20 p.m. she was watching TV when she heard her son scream in his bedroom. She rushed in and found him mysteriously on fire, presumably catching light herself in attempts to save him. Open verdict. (F.T.)

98.   *November 1980   Darlington, Durham, England*

A 19-year-old woman burst into flames in the powder room of a disco, but survived despite extensive burns requiring skin grafts. Tests on her cotton dress seemed to show it was not highly inflammable as had been speculated to be the case. (F.T.)

99.   *22 November 1980   Telford, Shropshire, England*

A middle-aged man was found badly burnt in his car but there was little damage to the vehicle. Suicide was suggested but not proven. (F.T.)

100.   *4 December 1980   Lockwood, Huddersfield, Yorkshire, England*

Apart from a small hole in a rug, there was no other fire damage to the kitchen where a 78-year-old woman was found dead with serious burns to her legs but little damage to her clothing. (A)

101.   *3 May 1981   Wath on Dearne, Rotherham, Yorkshire, England*

A 37-year-old mother burst into flames whilst striking a match. There were severe burns to her body and clothing but little damage to the room. She survived, and theories about hairspray causing the flames to rapidly spread have been mooted. (A)

102.   *24 December 1984   Newton Abbot, Devon, England*

A middle-aged woman survived with serious burns after catching fire for no apparent reason whilst just sitting in the living-room. Her husband was badly burnt trying to put out the flames with water. The house was barely touched. (F.T.)

103.   *28 January 1985   Widnes, Cheshire, England*

The back of a 17-year-old girl burst into flames as she walked down a flight of stairs some minutes after a cookery class. She was in the company of several other students. Two students saw a small ball of light falling down her back. She survived for fifteen days but died in hospital. The inquest concluded that her clothing caught fire by smouldering while in contact with a cooker, and flared up in the draught from the stairwell. (A)

104.   *25 May 1985   Stepney Green, London, England*

Whilst walking along a street, a 19-year-old man caught fire from the waist up. He said it felt like he was suddenly doused in burning petrol, but no traces were found. He rolled onto the floor and moments later the flames went out, and he then staggered to hospital. (A)

105.   *5 February 1986   Preston, Lancashire, England*

Two workers alerted a neighbour and they discovered the body of a 71-year-old man. His head, part of the shoulders, the lower legs and part of one arm were all that was left beside a fire grating, partially within the disturbed fireplace. However, there was minimal fire damage to the room and a settee just inches away with loose covers was not even scorched. The man had last been seen at 4.30 p.m. and was found the following morning. The room was well ventilated. The fire investigation concluded that the wick effect must have occurred after the man had fallen into the grate. (M)

106.   *27 March 1986   Essex County, New York, USA*

A 58-year-old lean and fit retired fireman died in his bed during an intense and localized blaze that damaged the house mainly because of smoke. Matches just feet from his remains were not even ignited. All that was left were a few bones and 3½ lbs of ash. SHC was contemplated by investigating officers according to some sources. (A)

107.   *3 October 1987   Shalbourne, Wiltshire, England*

An 86-year-old man burst into flames in front of his housekeeper whilst sitting on a settee. Fire allegedly emerged first from his nose and mouth and spread to his stomach. Police reputedly could find no sign of cause of death. The body and settee were badly destroyed. (A)

108.   *28 December 1987   Folkestone, Kent, England*

A 44-year-old man was discovered in the kitchen of a flat at a baker's shop at 10.30 a.m. He was last seen the previous evening. The man was very badly burnt apart from his feet but surrounding plastic materials in the kitchen were barely damaged and there was only minimal fire damage in the proximity of the body. A kettle half-full of water was on a lighted gas-ring suggesting that death cannot have occurred more than a short time before discovery. The inquest reached an open verdict, indicating that the victim had a very high blood-alcohol level but was alive when the burning commenced as fumes from the flames had been inhaled. The medical cause of death could not be ascertained owing to the state of the body. (A)

109.   *8 January 1988   Southampton, Hampshire, England*

Neighbours smelt burning, and found an elderly man, over sixty-five years old, in his house. Only legs and feet remained but there was little surrounding damage to the room except for a hole in the floor beneath the body. (A)

110.   *20 July 1988   Wheatley Hill, Durham, England*

A 71-year-old woman caught fire when in her garden but survived. Her husband was badly burnt trying to put out the flames. The cause was unknown according to police, although media speculation about SHC reportedly angered the family. (A)

111.   *September 1990   Hurstpierpoint, Sussex, England*

A 34-year-old man was found dead in his bedroom suffering from severe burns to his arms, legs and other parts of his body. A 5-day-old bonfire was in the garden and it was speculated that this was in some way connected. (A)

SOURCES OF PRIMARY INFORMATION

A	=	Authors' own investigations
C. & D.	=	Maxwell Cade and Delphine Davis
C.F.	=	Charles Fort
F.T.	=	*Fortean Times*
G	=	Vincent Gaddis
H	=	Michael Harrison
H.A.	=	Historical archives traced and researched
L.A.	=	Larry Arnold
M	=	Tony McMunn
N. & F.	=	Joe Nickell and John Fischer

Cade and Davis, *The Taming of the Thunderbolts* (Abelard-Schuman, 1968)

Fort's books originally published in 1930–31 are available separately or as a collected work

Fortean Times magazine, bi-monthly, subscription from 20 Paul St, Frome BA11 1DX

Gaddis, *Mysterious Fires and Lights*, New York, 1967

Harrison, *Fire from Heaven* (Sidgwick & Jackson,1976)

Arnold has published many articles as referenced in *Fate, Fortean Times* and *UFO Universe*

Nickell and Fischer have published several reports in *Skeptical Inquirer* and elsewhere as referenced

Sources

PROLOGUE
Shaw, Bob, *Fire Pattern* (Gollancz, 1984)

INTRODUCTION
Hough, Peter, and Randles, Jenny, *Death By Supernatural Causes?* *(Grafton, 1988 and 1989)*

1 A HISTORY OF INCINERATION
Corliss, W.R., *Incredible Life: A Handbook Of Biological Mysteries*, USA, 1981
Dickens, Charles, *Bleak House* (Penguin, 1985)
Harrison, Michael, *Fire From Heaven* (Pan, 1976)
Hough, Peter, *Witchcraft – A Strange Conflict* (Lutterworth, 1991)
Fortean Times, No. 35 (summer 1981) 'The Grace Pett SHC: A Re-Examination' Peter Christie
Minutes Of The Royal Society (November 8 and 15 1744)
The Mirror Of Literature, Art & Amusement, Vol. 32 (1838)
Mysteries Of The Unexplained (Readers Digest Assoc, 1982)
The New Wonderful Museum & Extraordinary Magazine, London, Vol. 3 (1805)
Notes & Queries, No. 184
Philosophical Transactions Abridged, London, Vol. 11 (1744–9)

2 THE BURNINGS AT SOWERBY BRIDGE
Halifax Evening Courier (April 13 1985)
Plus personal correspondence

3 HEATED EXCHANGES
Hartlepool Mail (21 July 1988 *et seq.*)
Plus personal correspondence and interviews

4 Q.E.D.
Harrison, Michael, op. cit., 1976
Tullett, Tom, *Clues To Murder* (Bodley Head, 1986)
Plus personal correspondence and interviews

5 THE TRUTH ABOUT MARY REESER

The Fire & Arson Investigator, Vol. 34, No. 4 (June 1984), 'Spontaneous Human Combustion: The "Cinder Woman" Mystery', Joe Nickell and John F. Fischer

Letter from J.R. Reichert, Chief of Police, St Petersburg, Florida, to Chief Inspector John Kelly, Philadelphia Police Dept, June 11 1957

'Report Of The FBI Laboratory', Washington D.C. (July 31 1951)

St Petersburg Times (June 30 1991), 'Burning Death Remains A Mystery', Jacquin Sanders

The Skeptical Inquirer, Vol. 11 (summer 1987), 'Incredible Cremations: Investigating Spontaneous Combustion Deaths', Joe Nickell and John F. Fischer

'Special Police Report of R.H. Lee and R.H. Boyd', St Petersburg Police Dept (July 2, 3 and 4 1951)

True Magazine (May 1964), 'The Baffling Burning Death', Allan W. Eckert

Plus personal correspondence

6 A FIREMAN'S STORY

Personal correspondence and interviews

7 A BLAZING ROW

Manchester Evening News (3 August 1978 *et seq.*)

Plus personal correspondence and interviews

8 A RATHER UNUSUAL DEATH

Fortean Times (summer 1981), Robert Rickard

New Scientist (15 May 1986), 'Forum' column, John Heymer

New Scientist (29 May 1986), Letters Page

New Scientist (12 June 1986), Letters Page

Plus personal correspondence and interviews

9 A FIREMAN'S INVESTIGATION

Personal files, correspondence and interviews

10 WHO FLAMED ROBERTA RABBIT?

Harrison, op. cit. (Pan 1976)

Personal correspondence and interviews

11 THE SURVIVORS

Hough, Peter, and Randles, Jenny, op. cit. (Grafton 1988 and 1989)

Fate (May 1989) 'Did Jack Angel Survive Spontaneous Combustion?', Joe Nickell and John F. Fischer

Fate Vol. 35, No. 9 (September 1982), 'The Man Who Survived Spontaneous Combustion', Larry E. Arnold

The Fire & Arson Investigator, Vol. 34, No. 3 (March 1984), 'Spontaneous Human Combustion', Joe Nickell and John F. Fischer

Fortean Times, No. 39 (spring 1983) 'Jack Angel, SHC Survivor', Larry E. Arnold

Transactions Of The Medical Society Of Tennessee, 1835

Plus personal correspondence

12   CHEMICAL REACTIONS
Fortean Times, Nos. 50 and 52, 1988 and 1989
Plus personal correspondence and interviews

13   A SHOCKING SUGGESTION
London Times (5 May 1934)
Plus personal correspondence and interviews

14   BOLTS FROM THE BLUE
Journal of Meteorology, Paul Brown (September 1991)
Vehicle Interference Catalogue, BUFORA (1979)
Lee, W.R., 'Lightning injuries and death', in *Lightning*, Vol. 2, ed. R.H. Golde (Academic Press, 1977)
Plus personal correspondence and interviews.

15   BALLS OF FIRE
Various cited scientific papers from *New Scientist, Nature* and *Journal of Meteorology*
Interview by Mark Chorvinsky with Vincent Gaddis in *Strange*, 7 (1991)
Viemeister, Peter, *The Lightning Book*, (MIT Press, 1972)
Singer, S., 'Ball lightning', in *Lightning*, Vol. 1, ed. R.H. Golde (Academic Press, 1977)
Plus personal correspondence and interviews

16   MAY THE FORCE BE WITHIN YOU?
Berlitz, Charles, and Moore, Bill, *The Philadelphia Experiment* Grafton, 1979)
Devereux, Paul, *Earthlights* (Turnstone Press, 1982)
Fuller, Paul, and Randles, Jenny, *Crop Circles: A Mystery Solved* (Hale, 1990)
Lafreniere, Gyslaine, and Persinger, Michael, *Space-Time Transients and Unusual Events* (Prentice-Gall, 1977)
Meaden, Dr Terence, *Goddess of the Stones* (Souvenir Press, 1991)
Shoemaker, Michael, *Fortean Times* 48 (1987)
Watson, Dr Lyall, *Earthworks* (Hodder and Stoughton, 1986)
Plus personal correspondence and interviews

17   THE KUNDALINI FIRE
Hough, Peter, and Randles, Jenny, op. cit., (Grafton, 1988 and 1989)
Mockerjee, Ajit, *KUNDALINI – The Arousal Of The Inner Energy* (Thames & Hudson 1989)
Man Myth & Magic, Part–Work (Purnell)
Yoga Journal (September/October 1985), 'Kundalini Demystified', David T. Eastman

18   FIRE PATTERNS
Fire Statistics United Kingdom 1989 (Government Statistical Service, April 1991)
Guide To The Practical Safety Aspects Of The Use Of Radio Frequency

Energy, Issue 1, (Ministry of Defence, 9 January 1989)
Science Digest, Vol. 89, No. 9 (October 1981), 'Human Fireballs', Larry E. Arnold

ADDRESSES:
BUFORA, The Leys, 2C Leyton Road, Harpenden, Herts AL5 2TL
MUFON Journal, 103 Oldtowne Road, Seguin, Texas 78155, USA
Fate, 170 Future Way, Marion, Ohio, 43305, USA
Fortean Times, 20 Paul Street, Frome, Somerset BA11 1DX
Journal of Meteorology, 54 Frome Road, Bradford-on-Avon, Wilts BA15 1LD
Skeptical Inquirer, Box 229, Buffalo, New York, 14215, USA
Strange, PO Box 2246, Rockville, Maryland 20847, USA

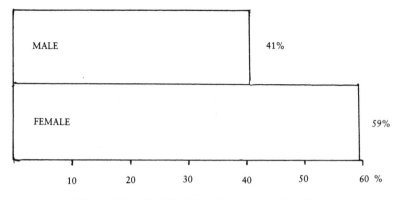

SEX OF KNOWN VICTIMS OF REPORTED SHC
[FROM OUR DATABASE OF 111 CASES]

NB: UNDENIABLY MORE WOMEN EXPERIENCE SHC THAN MEN

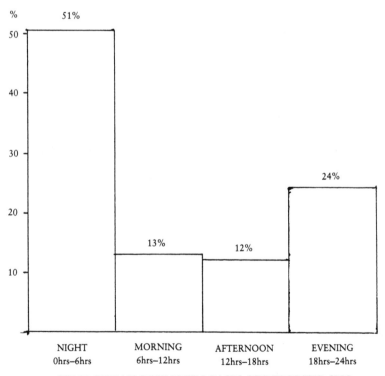

TIME OF DAY OF KNOWN CASES OF REPORTED SHC
[FROM OUR DATABASE OF 111 CASES]

NB: THREE-QUARTERS OF SHC EVENTS ARE REPORTED DURING HOURS OF
DARKNESS

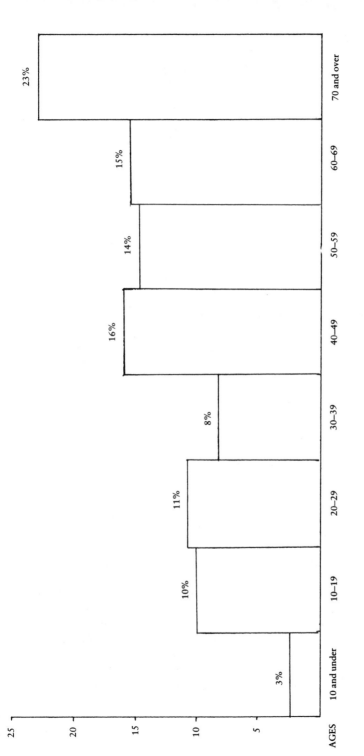

AGE OF KNOWN VICTIMS OF REPORTED SHC
[FROM OUR DATABASE OF 111 CASES]

NB: THE OLDER THE AGE GROUP THE MORE COMMON IS SHC. OVER HALF OF SHC VICTIMS ARE AGED FIFTY OR OVER

Acknowledgements

A book like this does not just happen on its own. It requires the help and cooperation of many diverse individuals and sources. Some of these are credited in the text, but many are not. Each added a tiny piece of the jigsaw to the picture we were slowly building up. We would like to thank the following in particular, and apologize if we have left anyone out:

Association for the Scientific Study of Anomalous Phenomena, British UFO Research Association, *The Burgess Hill Leader*, *The Evening Standard (London)*, *Exeter Express & Echo*, *Farmer's Weekly*, *Fate*, *Fire magazine*, *The Fire Engineers Journal*, *Fire Prevention*, The Forensic Science Society, *Fortean Times*, *Journal of the Forensic Science Society*, *Hartlepool Mail*, The Home Office, *Huddersfield Examiner*, J. Allen Hynek Center for UFO Studies, *Journal of Meteorology*, London Fire & Civil Defence Authority, *Manchester Evening News*, Meteorological Office, *Middleton and Blackley Guardian*, Mutual UFO Network, *New Scientist*, *The Scottish Farmer*, *Reading Chronicle*, *South Wales Argus*, *Spiritual Healing*, *The Times (London)*, *The Times (New York)*, *TV Quick*, Trinity College Library, West Country Studies Library, *The Western Morning News*.

Also grateful thanks to numerous services; including:

The fire departments of Cheshire, Cleveland, Derbyshire, Greater Manchester, Hampshire, New South Wales, Sussex and West Midlands and the police departments of Greater Manchester, Gwent and St Petersburg, Florida.

In addition, the following individuals:

Larry Arnold, Gary Baptiste, M. Batten, Edna Bayliss, Bernard Beeston, K.A. Beer, Geoff Blundell, Dr Thomas Bullard, S.D.T. Candler, E.D. Chambers, Diana Chardin, William Cooney, A.M. Davie, Dr Paul Davies, John Dawes, Dr Dougal Drysdale, David Edwards, Stan Farnsworth, Ross F. Firestone, A.J. Gover, Harry Godfrey, Leonard Gorodkin, G. Grundill, Lynn Harrison, John Heymer, Steve Hoselitz, Glenn E. Huffman, David C. Jolly, William Ketley, F.G. Lindsay, Andrew MacDonell, Edmond B.

McCabe, Richard K. McDonald, Ian Jon Marten, Colin Mather, Dr Terence Meaden, Raymond Millard, Dr Joyce Nelson, Kathleeen J. Nelson, Ralph Noyes, Professor Yoshi Hiko Ohtsuki, Philip Paul, Roger Penny, Mike Rowe, Sergeants Rodney and Russell (Gwent Police), George St Aude, Roy Sandbach, Paul Screeton, Sylvia Smith, Mark Stenhoff, P.D. Stocker, Edward Stott, R. Tighe, Eric Turpin, Jo Lee, Saul Pressman, Connie Watson, postman Jason Vizard, D. Waters, Sheldon Wernikoff, Arnold West and R.M. Windle. Thanks also to Bob Shaw for permission to quote from his novel *Fire Pattern* (Gollancz).

We would like to give a special thanks to Tony McMunn, who provided us with much useful background material.

Index

220